Lily leaned into him and gave in to the urge to touch him again.

She lightly ran a finger along the stern edge of his jaw. A delicious frisson of awareness shot down her spine at the contact. Nash didn't move. Did he truly feel nothing between them?

"Don't," he said in a harsh, tight voice.

"Why? You don't really believe you're cursed, do you?" Her hand crept to the back of his neck, fingers combing his smooth black hair.

Abruptly, Nash pulled her to him, his lips crushing against hers. Heat flared and liquid warmth pulsed through her body. His strength was more than the physical, unyielding planes of his mouth, chest and arms. It was an aura as primal and mysterious as anything nature could produce. Lily parted her mouth, inviting him to deepen the kiss.

Nash thrust her away. "Good night, Lily."

SIREN'S CALL

DEBBIE HERBERT

Published in Great Britain 2015
by Mills & Boon, an imprint of Harlequin (UK) Limited,
Eton House, 18-24 Paradise Road, Richmond, Surrey, TW9 1SR

© 2015 Debbie Herbert

ISBN: 978-0-263-91541-9

89-0615

Harlequin (UK) Limited's policy is to use papers that are natural, renewable and recyclable products and made from wood grown in sustainable forests. The logging and manufacturing processes conform to the legal environmental regulations of the country of origin.

Printed and bound in Spain
by CPI, Barcelona

Debbie Herbert writes paranormal romance novels reflecting her belief that love, like magic, casts its own spell of enchantment. She's always been fascinated by magic, romance and gothic stories. Married and living in Alabama, she roots for the Crimson Tide football team. Her oldest son, like many of her characters, has autism. Her youngest son is in the US Army. A past Maggie Award finalist in both young-adult and paranormal romance, she's a member of the Georgia Romance Writers of America.

First and always, for my husband, Tim, who has always believed in me. For my father, J.W. Gainey, who takes such pride in my accomplishments. And I want to mention several special friends who have helped me on my writing journey with either their support or the brainstorming of ideas, or critique of this book as it was written: Sandra Wilson Cummins, Sherrie Lea Morgan and Becky Rawnsley.

Chapter 1

"Look at her…"

Snicker. "Thinks she's somethin'…"

"Heard about her latest?"

Lily ignored the whispers and kept the corners of her lips slightly upturned as she studied the dead fish on display. Her insides churned as cold and slushy as the fishes' beds of ice.

"Miss Bosarge!" The portly seafood manager beamed behind the counter. "What can I get ya?"

She pointed to her selection and he wrapped it in white paper, all the while looking her up and down, a lecherous glimmer in his eyes. He winked. "I'll make a special deal for you."

The buzzing from behind grew louder.

"Disgusting."

"Slut."

That was going too far. Lily placed the fish in her cart and withdrew her makeup compact. She held it up and dabbed on a touch of lip gloss, checking out her latest tormentors. Yep, Twyla Fae was with a couple of friends and no doubt the ringleader. Twyla still smarted from the time her then-boyfriend-now-husband briefly dumped her to pursue Lily. You'd think the woman would be over something that happened two years ago.

Lily composed the habitual all-is-well smile as she faced Twyla. "How's J.P. doing?" she asked with double-sugar-fudge politeness. "I haven't heard from him in the *longest*. I *really* should drop by and say 'hey'."

Twyla paled beneath her tan but quickly recovered and glowered. "You stay away from J.P." She shifted the whining toddler in her arms. "We're a family now."

Lily moved her cart straight at the trio. They jumped out of the way.

"Maybe I will, maybe I won't," she threatened in honeyed tones, strolling down the aisle. *Never let them see you care*—her mantra since puberty, when her siren's voice had developed and unleashed its power over the entire male population of Bayou La Siryna.

Lily took her time filling the cart with dozens of cans of sardine and tuna and cases of bottled water. The usual fare.

An explosion of green bean tins hit the floor, but she didn't flinch. A teenaged stock boy gathered the spillage, so focused on Lily he made a worse mess and cans rolled in all directions. Almost without fail, men ran into stuff or dropped what they were doing when she walked by. She would have helped the boy, but experience proved it would make matters worse. He'd say something stupid or his girlfriend would see them and get mad, or he'd continue to bumble on or… It was always something.

The grocery store's sliding glass doors opened, bringing in a wave of humid Alabama air. A tanned stranger walked in with an aura as hot and powerful as the bayou breeze. He didn't look around the store to get his bearings, but immediately turned right and went to the produce department. He had a patrician vibe, as if he were Mr. Darcy strolling across English moors, not a local good ole boy grocery shopping at Winn-Dixie.

Lily leaned against the cart and watched as he efficiently grabbed a sack of potatoes and loaded it in his cart, paying no attention to the admiring glances of all the women. Something about the angle of his jaw and the gleam of his long, dark hair looked familiar.

Tingles of awareness prickled her arms and legs. She *had* to get closer. He drew her like a thirsty traveler to an oasis. Is this how men felt around her? The same clawing need for contact? It was a new experience, and Lily wasn't sure she liked the loss of control—no matter how exciting the sensations.

Ignoring the dirty looks from other women, she approached. Bettina, once an elementary school friend, rolled her eyes and deliberately jostled against Lily.

"Fresh meat, huh?" Bettina whispered, breath whooshing against Lily's neck like a poisonous vapor. "Can't you leave one guy for the rest of us?"

Lily refused to glance at her old friend, afraid of losing it. Bett had deserted her like all the other jealous bitches. She lifted her chin and continued toward the stranger, who was culling through vegetables. What to say? The only opening line running through her brain—*Hey, haven't we met before?*—was way tacky. But really, it didn't matter *what* she said. The mere sound of her voice would be enough.

"Hello," she purred, pulling her cart alongside Mr. Darcy-cum-Brad Pitt.

He threw some corn in his cart without looking up. "Hi," he answered in a voice so clipped he might as well have said *back off*.

Shock disconnected Lily's brain from her limbs and

she stood immobile while pounding blood made her ears ring. How odd. He acted impervious to the dulcet tones that made other men cross-eyed. Lily stiffened her spine. She'd bowl him over with more talking, would force him to look into her ocean-blue eyes. That ought to do the trick.

"Are you from around here?" she asked.

"No." He pushed away and started down the dairy aisle, his back to her.

What the hell? Lily froze again as she tried to grasp the foreign concept of being snubbed by the opposite sex. It really kind of sucked. Snickering noises from all around sent heat rushing to the back of her neck.

"About time she had a comeuppance," Bettina said with a loud snort.

Lily faced her directly. "What's your problem?" she snapped. "What have I ever done to you?"

Bettina's lips curled. "You really don't get it, do you? How about stealing Johnny Adams in junior high? And then Tommy Beckham in high school?"

It's not my fault, she wanted to scream. But they would never understand. Their dislike and mistrust ran as deep as the Gulf waters, their tears and anger as salty and bitter as the sea that encompassed the bayou. *Forget them.*

Lily shoved away in a huff, turning her attention once again to the handsome stranger's retreating figure. Her fingers gripped the cart handle until her knuckles were white as sea foam against her already pale skin. She lifted her chin. Nobody ignored her. Envied, yes. Lusted, of course. Later left humiliated and angry at her inevitable rebuff, check. But never this total lack of interest.

Lily hurried toward the mystery man. "Hey, you. Wait a minute."

He slackened his pace but didn't stop as she drew close.

"Have we met before?" She'd thought so at first, but

she must be wrong. This brutal disregard would have been memorable.

The man turned so slowly, Lily had a sense of inevitability as the seconds wound down into a series of freeze-frames. One: broad shoulders flexing under a dove-gray T-shirt. Two: a profile of a strong chin and deep facial planes. Three: a lock of obsidian hair falling across high, prominent cheekbones.

It wasn't a tan after all; his skin was the shade of light cinnamon from Native American heritage. Leaf-green eyes lit upon her, so shot through with a golden starburst they were startling in their brightness. Not a speck of recognition sparked in them, though.

But, oh, Lily knew those eyes. "Nash," she breathed. "Nashoba Bowman."

He frowned slightly. "Do I know you?"

She swallowed down the burn at the back of her throat. Not only was he immune to her siren's voice and unaffected by her physical beauty, but also he didn't even remember her. A riptide of humiliation washed over Lily. Only years of hiding her emotions kept her from betraying hurt. She licked her parched lips. "You used to spend summers here with your grandfather when you were little."

Nash stared long and hard. The brightness of his pupils deepened to a darker hue as the seconds—minutes?—sped by.

He *had* to remember. She held up her right hand and twirled her wrist. His gaze shifted to the colorful beaded bracelet he'd given her when they were children. *Friends forever*, he'd said when he'd tied it on her wrist. Lily willed him to recall those long-ago walks on the shore, the jaunts in the woods, the picnics and bike rides and… A glimmer of warmth lit his face.

"Lily?"

"Yes," she whooshed in an exhale of relief.

He gave her the once-over, a slow appraisal that left her hot and breathless. His dilated pupils and smoldering aura suggested he might not be as indifferent to her as he tried to act. Or it might be wishful thinking on her part.

Did Nash also remember that chaste, sweet kiss they'd once shared as curious twelve-year-olds?

His eyes met hers again, blazing green and gold. Yet the stoic, expressionless face more resembled Nash's inscrutable grandfather than the kid she used to know. The heat from his skin and a faint, familiar scent drew her closer, strong as the full moon's pull on the tide. The same odd compulsion to approach Nash now drove her to touch him. Lily dropped her gaze and rested her pale hand against his bronzed forearm, admiring the contrast of fair and dark. Her gaze swept lower, noting that no gold band adorned his fingers.

Nash's skin was hot as the Southern sun and his muscles rumbled and flickered under her touch, like thunder over deep waters. His jaw tightened at the brazen contact, but he didn't pull away. His fingers curled tightly on his cart. *Indifferent, my ass.* Lily closed her eyes and inhaled, using her heightened senses to identify Nash's enticing scent— a woodsy, sandalwood base with wisps of pine and cedar and perhaps a touch of oak moss. He smelled like the backwoods they used to roam together.

Bet his kiss was anything but chaste now.

"There you are!" a trilling voice bore down upon them.

She opened her eyes and watched a tall redhead grin as she lifted a couple of plastic bags. "I picked up the last of what we need for the shoot. Doughnuts and dozens of protein bars while we stalk the elusive mating habits of Alabama clapper rails."

Lily blinked and glanced at Nash as he subtly inched away from her touch. The loss of contact left her oddly disoriented. "Elusive… What did you say?" she asked the woman, feeling stupid.

"They're birds. Also known as marsh chickens or clappers." The redhead held out a hand. "I'm Opal Wallace, Nash's photographic assistant." Opal's face was sprinkled with freckles, and a faint scar marred one cheek. A bit plain overall, but her wide smile and merry eyes made up for any lack of sculptured perfection.

A flush of pleasure shot through Lily at Opal's kind greeting. It had been a long time since a female, outside of family, had bestowed a genuine smile her way. She shook the proffered hand, pathetically grateful for the friendly gesture.

Opal winked. "Figured I'd introduce myself since Nash appears speechless."

Nash cleared his throat. "You didn't give me a chance to introduce you," he answered, frowning slightly. He lifted a hand in Lily's direction. "This is Lily Bosarge, an old friend."

"Hey, ole buddy Lily." Opal waggled her eyebrows. "How close of *friends* were you two?"

"Purely platonic," Lily joked. *Well, mostly. Except for one experimental kiss.* "Can't get into too much trouble before the teen years." Nash had been long gone by the time she'd developed her siren voice. Not that it mattered; he seemed unaffected by its magic. This time, *she* was the one flushed and bewildered in the presence of the opposite sex.

And she didn't like it one little bit.

"Let's get together one evening, okay?" Opal whipped out a business card from one of the many pockets on her khaki vest and pressed it into Lily's palm. "Gotta run. There's a ton of stuff I need to set up before we get to work." She gave Nash a brisk wave. "See you on the island in a couple days, boss. I'll have the area scouted out and set up, the usual."

As suddenly as she'd intruded, Opal disappeared in a swirl of red hair and a cheerful smile.

Awkward silence descended and Lily felt an odd jolt of dismay when Nash glanced down at his watch. She didn't want to say goodbye. If he walked out now, would she ever see him again, ever discover why he acted immune to her enchantment? Besides, he was the last good friend she'd ever had, and certainly the only one in the male species. Everything had turned to shit in junior high when the guys started chasing her unmercifully. At first it had been tremendous fun—for maybe half a year. Until the girls turned as one against her like a tsunami of destruction.

Lily grasped at the first conversational thread that popped into her head. "I hear you're a famous wildlife photographer now. I remember how you used to carry around an old 35 mm camera your grandfather bought at a thrift store."

"Most of the time I didn't have enough money to actually load it with film." The taut muscles in his jaw and chin relaxed and the green eyes grew cloudy. He shook his head slightly, and the corners of his mouth twitched in a semismile.

Warmth spread inside at this glimpse of the boy she used to know.

"And you were never without your sketchpad," Nash said. "You were damn good, too. The detail of your drawings impressed me. Please tell me you still draw."

Lily returned the smile, delighted she'd drawn him into a real conversation. "I do some. Mostly, though, I paint with watercolors." She kept her tone deliberately light and casual, as if painting were a mere hobby and not a passion.

His brow furrowed. "Watercolors?"

"It's not like the kiddie paintings you make with cheap dime-store kits," she answered quickly. Too quickly, judging from his knowing expression, as if he'd guessed her art was more than a casual hobby.

"I see. Didn't mean to belittle your art."

Lily shrugged, let her facial features smooth into its familiar mask. Nash wasn't the only one who'd learned to hide emotion over the years. "I'm no artist."

"So you say."

Perceptive eyes drilled into her, as if he saw past the pretty, past the superficial shell she presented to everyone in town who only viewed her as the slutty dumb blonde who'd worked as a hairdresser until a few months ago.

It was exhilarating.

It was scary.

Lily retreated like a trembling turtle, so different from the young girl who had scouted the piney woods and shoreline with Nash. Deflection time. "I'm not surprised you photograph animals. You have some kind of…rapport… or something with all living creatures. It was downright eerie."

Nash shrugged and the warmth left his eyes. "Not really."

"Yes, you do," Lily insisted. "Anytime we were in the woods it seemed the trees would fill with birds and we'd almost always startle a deer or raccoon by getting so near them. Once we even found that den of baby foxes—"

"So what?" Nash cut in, lips set in a harsh, pinched line. "This place is so isolated even the animals are bored out of their minds. Makes them overly excited when anyone draws close."

Ouch. What kind of nerve had she hit with her innocent remark? "You used to love coming here in the summers," she reminded Nash. "Said it was an escape from the city and a chance to run free."

"I get it." His lips curled. "I'm Indian, so I must have a special communication with nature, right? Since we live so close to nature and worship Mother Earth and the Great Spirit and all. Well, that's bullshit."

Damn. Her own temper rose at the unjust accusation. "I don't deserve that. We used to be friends and I thought we still could be. Guess I was wrong. You're nothing like the guy I used to hang out with every summer."

First Twyla and Bett, and now this. Lily jerked her cart forward, eager to escape the grocery trip from hell. Sexy or not, some men weren't worth the trouble.

Warmth and weight settled on her right shoulder. Fingers curled into her flesh, halting her steps. "Hey," Nash said. "Look at me."

Lily turned. The harsh stranger melted and his face softened.

"I'm sorry."

Anger deflated in a whoosh. If Nash was anything like his grandfather or the guy she used to know, he spoke the truth. Lily nodded. "Well, okay, then. Let's start over." She took a deep breath and plunged on. "How about dinner at my place tonight or whenever you're free? Your grandfather's invited too, of course."

Nash rubbed his jaw, as if debating whether to accept the invitation. Any other man would have followed her home then and there. Any other man wouldn't have picked a fight or brushed off her advances.

But Nash wasn't like any other man she'd ever met. And Lily was more than a little intrigued.

"Sorry," he said, dropping his hand to his side. "I'm pretty busy right now. Maybe after I finish this assignment on Herb Island we can get together. Grandfather always liked you. He'd enjoy seeing you again."

The novelty of male rejection left Lily nonplussed until the sting of it burned through the haze of disbelief. "You're turning me down?" she squeaked.

Nash retreated a step. "Like I said, I'm swamped at the moment. Good running into you again, though. Take care."

Unbelievable. Lily mustered her tattered pride. "Okay, then," she said in a high falsetto, gripping the cart. "Tell your grandfather I said 'hey.'"

She hurried down the aisle, not daring to look back and risk exposing her feelings. The air pressed in around her, leaving her a bit dizzy. She scrambled through the line, paid the cashier and stumbled out of the refrigerated environment into the untamed, sizzling bayou air that always held the droning of insects and an echo of the ocean's wave. First thing when she got home, she'd go for a long, cool swim underwater, get her bearings.

Instead of heading immediately to the car, Lily strode down the boiling sidewalk to the drugstore next door. She left the cart by its front door—it would be safe for a minute. Inside the store, Lily hurried to the makeup aisle and gathered up half a dozen lipsticks in every color from baby-doll-pink to siren-red. She peeked at the mirrored glass lining behind the shelves, half expecting to see some glaring new imperfection marring her appearance. But no—same long, flaxen hair, creamy skin and large blue eyes.

So what had gone wrong with Nash? Why hadn't he been attracted to her?

Lily grabbed some blush and a tube of mascara. She'd have to try harder. She hastened over to the cashier and dumped her ammunition on the counter. *I'll go see him. Pay a visit looking my best.* She dug into her pocketbook for a credit card, but the purse lining blurred and morphed into a pool of filmy sludge.

"Are ya crying?" the elderly lady behind the counter asked.

"I'm not—" Lily paused, hands touching her damp cheeks. "Guess so," she admitted in surprise.

The lady handed over an opened box of tissue. "Yer a pretty little thing. Some man ain't treating ya right, get you another."

"Right," Lily sniffed, swiping her cheeks. She had to get out, get herself together before she ran into anyone she knew. Twyla Fae and Bettina would find the tears a hoot. "Um, thanks. I'll take the tissue, too." She paid, retrieved her grocery cart and got to the car. Another five minutes and she could be alone with her thoughts and cry as much as her heart desired. Lily carelessly shoved in the bottled water, bags of seafood and tuna cans. Almost home free.

She corralled the cart and returned to her car, not noticing anything amiss until she almost stepped on it.

A dead, bloody rat lay directly outside the driver's door. The entrails were fresh, and blood was seeping into the shelled pavement. Its skin was precisely cut down the tender underbelly.

Lily pressed a hand to her mouth as bile threatened to creep up her throat. *It's only a rat. No big deal. Just an accident.*

She clutched her purse tightly against her side and glanced around the parking lot. The few people around paid her no attention, yet the tingles shooting along her spine alerted Lily that someone was indeed watching.

Watching and enjoying her fear.

She turned back to the car and noticed the long key scratch that started from the front left tire all the way down to the fender. Anger outweighed fear as she read the large, childlike scrawl etched on the car door.

D-i-e S-l-u-t.

Chapter 2

The whir of electric grinder against metal grated on Lily's ears. She whistled and waved her arms to get her sister's attention.

Jet frowned and switched off the grinder. "What?"

"Are you almost done? You've been at it long enough I'm surprised you haven't sanded a hole through my car."

They stared at the long, narrow patch of bare metal on the red Audi S4. Lily ran a finger over the warmed surface, perfectly manicured nails and graceful fingers a stark contrast against the ugly gash. She tried to joke. "Sure can't see those words now."

Jet scowled, not amused. "'Bout time I had a word with Twyla Fae and her posse of bitches."

"Don't. You'll make it worse."

"Can it get much worse? They're crossing the line into criminal territory with this latest harassment." Jet gripped the sander so tight in her right arm, her biceps bulged and a network of veins popped against taut flesh.

Her sister was strong enough to best any man in a fist fight, courtesy of the supernatural strength from her paternal Blue Clan merblood. But against the verbal warfare of scorned women, Lily considered her own reserved veil of indifference a superior tactical maneuver. "Ignore them like I do."

"Don't see your plan working," Jet grumbled. The fierce glow in her dark eyes contrasted with the large, womanly bump at her waist. Lily shook her head in bemusement. On the surface, their beauty and temperament appeared leagues apart. If she was the ethereal one—silver sparkles drifting on moon-drenched water, soft and shifting and subtle—Jet was more like the oft-admired coral undersea—brittle, bedazzling, with razor-sharp edges that wounded the unwary.

Down deep, they could each be deadly in their own way.

Lily placed a hand on Jet's belly bulge. "Don't get worked up and disturb the baby."

"And don't you try distracting me." Yet Jet's harsh features softened. "Seriously, how about we get Landry and Tillman involved? File a formal complaint."

"I'll think about it." She had no intention of seeking help from her cop brothers-in-law. Lily sensed their wariness of her, their suspicions about her morals.

Jet returned the grinder to a shelf. "Translation—you're too proud to seek help." She dug into her baggy, denim jeans and produced a set of keys. "Drive this until the body shop in Mobile repairs the damage. I'll rent something in the meantime." Jet tossed the keys.

"Or you could buy a soccer-mom van." Lily caught the keys and cast a sly smile. No way Jet would forego her clinker of a truck. They could afford anything, thanks to a tidy trust fund built from pawned sea treasure sold by generations of Bosarge mermaids. Why Jet chose to drive the monstrosity was a mystery. Lily's own aesthetic sensibilities ran along a selective, pricey line. She'd drive something even flashier, but the bayou brine rusted everything eventually.

Besides, Lily drew enough attention from her voice. No need to give the locals more fodder. They'd be convinced she had a rich sugar daddy in hiding.

"Maybe I will." Jet grinned. "But it won't be as funny as you driving my truck."

"Got me there," Lily conceded. She started the truck, wincing at the beater's clickety-clackety rumbling. She fumbled with the clutch and, with a loud screech, backed out of the driveway, nearly sideswiping the mailbox. Jet's smirk faded and her brows knitted.

The beater's ornery procession out of town matched Lily's fitful mood. She'd had a restless night. Not even a long swim beneath the slithering roots of sea grass last night had calmed her restless spirit. The twin mysteries of Nash's indifference and the anonymous etching on her car both tossed and swirled in her mind like a lingering storm.

Today, she would confront both issues directly. If Twyla wanted to get nastier, she had to up her own game. As far as Nash went…perhaps there *had* been some flicker of interest in her siren charm, but like her, he'd learned to hide emotion. At least that theory made a little sense.

Houses grew sparser and paved town roads ceded to red-packed clay lanes as she headed out of town. Live oaks and palmetto shrubs spilled over from the side and encroached until only one vehicle could pass at a time on the narrow lane. She hadn't traveled this way in years and didn't recall it being so forsaken. A curlicue of claustrophobia flickered at the edges of her mind as the choking foliage strangled the open air. It was as if the bayou's wilderness soul were slowly clamping down and reclaiming its territory from human invasion.

Good thing she'd driven the truck after all. Lily's jaw

clamped at the jarring scrape of branches against metal. The high-pitched squall set her nerves pulsing and she cursed the siren nature that made her so sensitive to sound vibration. Although excellent for detecting predators at sea, it was hell on land with certain tones and pitches.

A log cabin came into view. In spite of its rustic nature, Lily appreciated the way it seamlessly blended into the landscape. The scene would make a cool picture.

She got out of the truck and lifted her cell phone for a photo, eyeing the detail of the log pine's myriad grooves and knots. This piece wouldn't be a watercolor like her ocean scenes. Only a detailed pen-and-ink composition would do it justice.

Disappointed, she noted that there was no other vehicle in the driveway. Nash had mentioned he wouldn't start the job on Herb Island for a couple of days. Maybe he and his grandfather were in town and would return shortly. Lily scanned the backyard and found the small opening for an old trail she and Nash had hiked often. She'd take a little walk, and with luck, Nash would be back when she finished. Lily ditched her silk scarf and switched from designer sandals to a pair of old Keds that Jet kept on the back floorboard. They were a size too large but doable.

Lily hiked the narrow trail, the ground as familiar as when they'd explored the area as children. Pine needles cushioned the sandy soil and released bracing wisps of fragrance as her feet crushed them, a smell she'd forever associate with Nash.

At the clearing, Lily leaned against a large oak and listened to bird calls—the distant screech of seagulls, thrush and coots. He'd taught her so much, passed on everything his grandfather had taught him, including Choctaw animal folklore and legends.

How she'd longed to share her undersea world in return, show him their sea vegetable garden and swim past the salt marshes and explore a different, equally fascinating new world. But her family's vow of secrecy was absolute. If one mermaid was exposed, their entire race was in danger.

Her eyes swept the clearing, then doubled back to the far edge of the tree line.

A coyote fixed its gaze on her, unmoving, eyes gleaming with intelligence and feral hunger. Lily didn't move either and didn't break eye contact. *Coyote is a trickster*, she remembered, *a sign of an ending and a new beginning*. She wasn't alarmed, but aware. Nash used to say that was the most important thing—to stay aware. He'd even admitted once that he could sense what animals were thinking. Become one with them or some such thing.

The coyote lowered its head and took a step closer, still staring. Its copper eyes held a feral sheen that made Lily quiver from her scalp to the soles of her borrowed sneakers.

To hell with spiritual communication.

Lily turned and ran back down the trail. Twilight had deepened and the trees cast long shadows. Spanish moss hung from live oaks, fluttering in the breeze like ghosts. The cushioned, pine-needled ground gave way to a labyrinth of twisted, jutting tree roots. Lily stumbled but stayed on her feet. *I'm being ridiculous. It isn't after me.*

Yet she ran on. The sound of blood roared in her ears as if she were swimming undersea against a powerful current. Lily wanted to peek over her shoulder but didn't dare divert her attention from avoiding the tree roots, which now appeared as black and deadly as the moccasins that slithered through the swamps.

She ran and ran and ran until the accelerated beat of her heart matched the panicked cadence of her thoughts. *Coyote is the end. Coyote is the end.*

The end, the end, the end.

* * *

A violent cracking of twigs, the rustle of leaves and snapping branches, a vibration under his bare feet—Nash stilled and searched the woods. Something was spooked and running toward the cabin. He focused on the dark edge of the tree line and felt to his right for the shotgun. Smooth metal cooled his fingers. *Found it.*

He soundlessly exited the porch, shotgun at the ready. Unlikely it was a chased animal—he hadn't sensed that faint odor of musk and sweat or picked up the panicked energy of an animal hell-bent on escape.

An apparition of white burst into the clearing, like flood waters over a dam. A ghost? Grandfather told tales of the kwanokasha, or Kowi Anukasha—the tiny, fairy people of the forest. But this was no pygmy-sized being. His eyes narrowed, and like a camera lens focusing on a subject, the wall of white morphed into detail: a tall woman with waist-length, pale hair lifted in every direction by the sea breeze.

"Lily?" he called out, his voice sharp and biting. It was as if his own brooding melancholy had summoned her from the forest's darkness. He scanned her white shorts and T-shirt and the scratches decorating her arms and legs like tattoos.

But no blood; she was unharmed. His relief quickly gave way to anger. Was someone after her? Nash's right index finger curled on the shotgun trigger and he searched behind Lily for the danger.

Nothing was there.

He hurried forward. "What happened? Is someone chasing you?"

Lily looked back. "I don't know." She turned to him with a sheepish half smile on her paler-than-usual face. She drew a jagged, uneven breath. "It may not have even followed me."

"It?"

She rubbed her arms, stomach heaving with labored breath. "A coyote."

He raised a brow. "I've never known coyote to chase humans. It's probably more afraid of you than you of it."

"Not this coyote." She shook her head. "The way it looked at me…" She bit her lip. "As if he were sizing me up for dinner. Instead of running off, it lowered its head and stepped toward me. I didn't hang around to see if it chased me or not."

He'd accuse Lily of making a ploy for attention, but she didn't know he'd returned to the cabin and he could see her fear was real. "Go up on the porch and I'll take a look around."

"Why?"

"If a coyote really chased you, it must be eat-up with rabies. It's not normal behavior. If it's got rabies, the kindest thing would be to put it out of its misery. And it sure as hell doesn't need to infect other animals and cause an epidemic."

"Be careful," she said in a trembling, faint voice.

Lily's vulnerability left him flushed with an overwhelming desire to protect her from all danger. And he didn't like the feeling a bit, didn't like the peculiar pull she had on his senses. He stalked toward the woods and tried to concentrate on the immediate problem. If the animal was sick or deadly, he'd pick up on it easily. He'd been near infected, diseased creatures before. Rabies had a metallic smell of pus combined with sweaty musk from an animal's scrambling terror over its changed condition.

Nash entered the tangle of trees and shrubs, into a world he was uniquely attuned and equipped to master. A world where sound was amplified and the energy of every living thing—animal, mineral and insect—vibrated inside him at a cellular level. Even the energy of trees, moss and stone whispered its presence. The rustling of the wind in branches and leaves was nature's murmur and sigh.

He used to struggle more against this odd communion, creeped out by the immersion of his senses. He'd even tried staying indoors most of the time, only emerging to go places in the city surrounded by people and the noisy clutter of civilization. But it was no use. The abstinence made him restless and edgy. Midway through college he changed from a business degree to photography, determined to put his skills to use as a wildlife photographer.

But it was an uneasy compromise. Yes, he worked outdoors. But he erected strict mental barriers to keep from being entirely sucked in by his senses. Lily disturbed this equilibrium. Something about her was too different...too intense. She drew him to her like a force of nature.

Nash inhaled deeply and slipped into the woods' living essence. Beneath the pervasive undercurrent of sea brine nestled the scent of pine and leaf mold. He paused, listening. A faint crackle of dry leaves, a bit of rustling of branches from above, a squirrel several yards away scrambling up an oak. He went farther up the trail, which he well-remembered traversing with Lily. What had she been doing out here? Was the woman determined to hound him? He'd come home to escape that kind of attention.

There. Faint, but detectable, was the smell of sickness. A rabid animal had indeed run along the trail. But the scent was so subtle, he knew it was no longer in the area. He'd have to be on the lookout for the coyote and alert a wildlife management officer of the potential danger.

Nash trudged back down to the cabin where Lily waited on the steps, eyes troubled.

"Did you see it? I didn't hear a shot."

"It was long gone." Nash walked past her and put the shotgun away. "I did pick up a trace of something, though."

"How do you do that?"

He shrugged. "You get a feel for it when you're in the woods for long stretches all your life." Nobody's business about his freakish talent.

"Hmm," Lily said, cocking her head, as if assessing something left unsaid between them.

Nash crossed his arms, daring her to challenge his answer.

"So you say," she drawled.

He stared into mesmerizing blue eyes that he was sure had enticed many a man. The world narrowed until every detail of Lily enveloped his senses. He felt the rise and fall of her chest as she breathed, found his own breath synchronizing to hers.

No. This won't do. If you get involved, you'll only hurt her in the end. Just like all the others. Nash's fingers curled into his palm. Lily was too alluring for her own damn good. He suspected no one had ever rebuffed her advances or broken her heart.

Lily spoke, breaking the spell. "Your grandfather used to say the coyote was a clever trickster. It probably made me more afraid than it should have."

"You can't be too careful when you're alone in the woods." He regarded her sternly. "Especially when you're alone and unarmed."

Lily laughed, not intimidated. "Didn't think I'd run into anything more ominous than the fairy forest dwellers."

Grandfather and his wild, crazy stories. "His old Choctaw tales did a number on you, huh?"

"They're fascinating. Where is he, by the way?" She stood on her tiptoes and peered around his right shoulder.

"He works at the animal shelter on Fridays. I expect him home for supper any minute."

Damn. He shouldn't have said that. Now the woman would stick around and try to wrangle an invitation. He narrowed his eyes. "What were you doing on our property?"

She didn't flush or look away. "Don't see any harm in it. I've walked here over the years and your grandfather's never complained."

Nash opened the screen door and went into the house, Lily close on his heels. He snatched his car keys from the kitchen table.

"Where are you going?" she asked quizzically.

"I've got errands to run." He lowered his chin and stared at her without smiling. "I really don't have time for your friendship. Sorry to be so abrupt, but I'm busy." And the last thing he needed was a gorgeous woman hitting on him—again.

"Who doesn't have time for friends?" She tilted her face to the side and studied him.

Damn, he felt like a jerk. But she was far too beautiful. What if it became more than friendship? He couldn't let anything happen to her. Two women were already dead because of him.

"Look, you're better off forgetting you ever knew me. I'm poison. Okay?"

Her eyes widened. "What are you talking about?"

Nash ran a hand through his long hair. "Drop it."

"No way. I can't believe you'd say something like that. What's happened to you over the years?"

"Life happened," he said past the raw burning at the back of his throat.

"More like a woman is what I'd guess." She arched one perfectly groomed eyebrow. "Someone break your heart?"

Other way around. An image of Rebecca, broken and bleeding, the steel frame of her car bent in two, flashed in his mind, immediately followed by an image of Connie, ashen-skinned and lifeless, a bottle of pills by her side.

"Maybe I don't have a heart to break," he rasped. Nash

rubbed his forehead, as if by doing so he could erase the deathly images. "Besides, I'm not the only one who's changed."

Lily's impossibly large eyes widened a fraction more. "How have I changed?" She swept a hand down her body. "Other than the obvious physical development, I mean. I was a flat-chested twelve-year-old girl last time we were together."

He considered. "You used to be…more open. Easier to read. Now it's hard to tell what you're thinking. Except for the obvious fear on your face when you hightailed it out of the woods just now."

She gave a snort that contrasted with her pristine, angelic features. "*I'm* hard to figure out?"

His lips twitched involuntarily. Even as a child, his nature was to retreat to silence when disturbed. And Lily would bug him until she unearthed the problem. "Guess you're as outspoken now as when you were a kid. Always pestering me about things I didn't want to talk about."

"And you used to answer all my questions. How come you stopped coming every summer? I asked your grandfather, but he only said it was a family matter."

The woman was relentless. And shameless. Better to answer what he could and get her off his back. "My parents divorced and Mom got custody. She wasn't too hip about me spending so much time away from her, much less with my paternal grandfather." He continued walking to the front of the house, Lily close in tow. Parents were a safe topic. Events of the past four years overshadowed painful childhood memories.

"Your mom ever remarry?"

"Nope. Don't see that happening. She's not the marrying sort." After his father's numerous affairs, his mother had soured on marriage.

They reached the front door, and Nash opened it, beckoning her out with a grand sweep of one arm. She slowly, reluctantly stepped outside.

Another twenty yards and he'd be rid of her and her questions. She made him uncomfortable and want things he had no right to want anymore. Time to turn Twenty Questions on her. "Did your mother ever remarry?"

"No. She's not interested in marriage, just like your mom."

Lily's reply was quick enough, but he'd always sensed there was much left unsaid, even when they were young. She'd been an open book about most everything except her family. When they weren't outside, they were at the cabin listening to his grandfather's stories.

But he had met her family a few times. Lily had grown into her mother's beauty. He remembered going into their house was like stepping into fairyland. Their huge home had an old-world, rich vibe with carelessly cluttered gold coins, heirloom pottery and solid pieces of antique furniture.

A pair of elliptical beams pierced the twilight. Nash wanted to groan. He was only a few feet away from escaping in his truck. But his grandfather would disapprove at the lack of hospitality. The old man was bound to invite Lily for dinner.

"Your grandfather," Lily squealed. "I haven't seen him in ages."

Sam Bowman exited his truck and approached, eyes focused on Lily. "We have a guest tonight," his baritone boomed, half statement, half question. "Hope you're staying for dinner."

"She was leaving. Maybe next—"

"Why yes, that would be lovely," Lily interrupted, cutting mischievous eyes at him.

Nash stifled a groan. The more he was around Lily, the

more she seemed determined to snag him. And the greater his temptation to let her.

His grandfather raised an eyebrow. "You're the little Lily that used to run around here in pigtails with my grandson?"

"The one and only."

"Please, come inside," he invited. Even dressed in worn khakis and an old University of Alabama T-shirt proclaiming national championship number 12, Samuel Bowman garnered respect.

As a kid, he might have sassed his parents all day long, but when his grandfather laid down the law, he unquestioningly obeyed. Not from threat of punishment, but because of his grandfather's unfailing politeness and show of respect to everyone, including smartass kids.

"This will be like old times." She had a hop in her step that took Nash by surprise. Such a contrast to her guarded nature at the grocery store this morning when he'd asked about her paintings. There was something mystical about her, like she was fae or one of Grandfather's mystical creatures come to life. For the first time he noticed her voice held a musical quality—as if several voices were harmonized into one melody. A bell tone of fairies singing in the woods, beckoning small children and the unwary to enter their realm.

Nash shook his head at the fanciful images. He wanted no part of anything that smacked of otherworldly. He had enough weirdness on his own without adding more to the mix.

If he wasn't careful, Lily Bosarge could be trouble.

Chapter 3

Ugly.
Hideous.
Monstrous.

Opal scrubbed the wet washcloth against her right cheek, leaving a skid of pigmented foundation on the yellow terrycloth. With the tip of her left index finger, she traced the white scar that ran from under her right ear to the corner of her mouth. Three plastic surgeries had smoothed the ridge of keloid tissue, yet the white pigmentation of dead skin would always remain.

Scarred for life. If she could only get the last of it gone… But the doctors assured her this was as good as it would get.

She threw the washcloth against the shower wall. The abomination was a curse. A person as perfect as Nash deserved so much more. Opal pictured his smooth, unmarred olive skin and grimaced at her reflection.

It's okay, love, Nash whispered in her mind, the way

he did every night. *Soon I can declare my love for you in person.*

The moist heat from the shower was like his hot breath caressing her skin with endearments. *You're all I ever wanted, Opal. The others meant nothing to me. It was always you I secretly wanted. Always you.*

Opal's fury evaporated, the scent of soap morphed to Nash's scent of sandalwood and musk. He was here, caressing her. Opal cupped her breasts and moaned. Yes. Yes! One hand sank lower and the wet heat between her thighs was as scalding as the hot water pounding her skin.

Nash wanted her as much as she wanted him. Her hands were his hands, touching the soft folds of her womanhood. A finger slipped inside and she clenched as it went in and out. Harder, faster. An orgasm violently racked her body and she slid down the shower stall, weak and sated. Only he could do this, make her crazy in dreams.

Dreams that would soon be reality. He spoke to her like this, and more frequently since she'd taken care of Rebecca and Connie. He hadn't been with a woman in almost a year now.

Now it was her turn. Her time to show Nash that she was his one true love. He'd open his eyes. The veil would lift. *Oh, Opal. How could I not see it? How you must have suffered. No more, my darling. From now on, you are mine. I'll adore you forever.*

Opal rose unsteadily and shut off the water. The signs all pointed to this island assignment as the right time to make her move. And when she did, Nash would remember every conversation, every murmur of endearment he'd been whispering in her brain for the past five years.

He'd never loved those other women, or so he claimed. But she didn't believe Nash and couldn't stand the thought of another woman in his arms. So she'd done them both a favor getting rid of Rebecca and Connie. No one could love him as much as she did. She alone knew his secret, had watched him meld into nature and mesmerize wild beasts with a whisper. Nash was extraordinary, otherworldly, and she wanted him to tame the wild storms of her internal landscape. No other man could understand the violent, explosive yearnings in her soul. No one else could save her from this crushing isolation. Only one other man had ever come close.

And he was dead.

Opal dried off, caught another glimpse of herself in the mirror and drew in a sharp breath. That slightly overweight woman—with muddy-red hair plastered like rotten seaweed around her head and neck and that hideous scar—wasn't the real Opal. The real Opal, the one Nash would see, was impeccable. Like…that Lily woman.

She scowled in the mirror—making her image that much more repulsive. The ghost of an old nursery rhyme skittered through her brain.

Mirror, mirror on the wall, who's the fairest of them all?

Lily. The slut bitch.

She was the most beautiful woman Opal had ever seen. That hair, with its pastel strands and silver-blond shine; creamy skin unmarred by any scar; and lush body all combined into an irresistible package. Worse, something about Lily's voice was almost…magical.

It wasn't fair.

And the looks that had passed between her and Nash. You could feel a sensual alchemy brewing between them. Plus, they were old childhood friends—which meant they had a history together, an old bond to explore.

This was supposed to be *her* time. He should be here at the island cabin with her instead of spending so much time in the bayou with his grandfather. She'd taken care of Nash's old girlfriends, had undergone all that plastic surgery, arranged and finagled assignments so they worked alone together on a beautiful, practically deserted island, and then this Lily had come along, upsetting her careful plans.

Opal tried to resist, but the compulsive need to again scrub the facial scar festered in her fingers. They twitched and tingled until she caved, soaping up yet another washcloth and scrubbing at the old wound. If only she could get rid of it, her problems would be solved. But no, the damn thing would haunt her forever. Opal flung the washcloth against the mirror and soapy water dripped down, distorting her scar into a mélange of distorted pixels.

Bet Lily had been brought up like a little adorable princess while she'd been shuffled around in foster care. Just when she'd gotten used to one place, she'd be uprooted. The only childhood constant was the fantasy Norman Rockwell world in her mind. A safe retreat.

At least she'd had a little luck today. What a coup to catch that woman keying the car with the "Lily" vanity tag. How convenient that Lily already had an enemy. If it became necessary to kill the blond whore, a suspect was ready for framing. Opal hoped it didn't come to that, hoped that Nash would have no time or inclination for a dalliance. She'd gotten away with two eliminations; a third might be pushing it.

Still, sluts needed to be warned and punished. As the woman and her brat-in-arms tore it out of the parking lot, Opal had dashed over and carved "Die Slut" alongside the gash the other woman had made. In a burst of inspiration, she'd run into the nearby pet store, bought a rat and disemboweled it by Lily's car.

A cache of stainless-steel razor blades were always stashed in her purse.

Cutting open the rat's tender flesh had relieved some of the tension and anxiety from seeing Nash and Lily together. Just like cutting her arms and wrists eased pain in those moments when memories clamored and gnawed.

She'd have to find out more about this Lily. This time, unlike the others, there wouldn't be weeks of warnings and warfare. Time was precious. This assignment was only for a month or so and Nash would be hers by the time it was through. Nobody would stand in her way.

Earlier, she'd driven by Nash's grandfather's home, saw the light from the curtain-less window, saw the cozy bunch at the table eating. Stabs of jealousy prickled her skin all over like leprosy. She was in the dark, on the outside looking in. Her childhood repeated. The ugly redheaded foster kid no one wanted.

Lily bit into the hot, buttered corn bread and forced the crumbly mixture down her throat. "Delicious," she lied, chasing it down with a sip of sweet tea. *More like wet sawdust.* Determined not to offend her hosts, Lily swirled a mound of pinto beans around the plate and lifted a forkful to her mouth. This tangy rotten mush was worse than the tasteless corn bread. *Human food—bleh.* Soon as she got home she'd eat a real meal—a bowl of seaweed salad and a barely blanched lobster. Still, she enjoyed sitting in their cozy kitchen with its rustic pine cabinets and table. This place had been a second home for her growing up.

"Nash says you volunteer at the animal shelter," she said, diverting attention from the uneaten, rearranged food on her plate.

Sam nodded. "Every Friday."

"What do you do there?"

He chewed a piece of venison and put down his fork and knife. He always spoke carefully, as if mindful of the power of words. "Clean cages, bathe them, take them for walks."

"That's admirable." She didn't care for animals all that

much. She loathed cats and the way they licked their chops around her, as if she were a delectable morsel they wanted to devour. "Jet has a dog that's around a lot. Ugliest thing you ever saw."

Neither man responded. Lily wanted to stamp her foot in frustration, but instead she surreptitiously studied the two.

They were similar: tall and large-boned with prominent cheekbones and the same aura of strength. Both had long black hair, although Sam's was streaked with silver. Each had olive-colored skin, Sam's a shade darker. Nash was a younger, more virile version of his grandfather. The only other striking difference between them was the green eyes Nash had inherited from his mother.

Those eyes that avoided her own at every opportunity. How could he resist her siren's voice? The more he retreated, the more determined she became to get answers.

Lily took another stab at starting a dinner conversation. "The dog's name is Rebel, and he's supposedly a Chinese crested, but I say he's a mutt. Got the ugliest yellow teeth and mangiest fur ever."

Sam lifted an eyebrow. "You aren't fond of animals?"

Rats. They would find that odd. Nash worked photographing wildlife and Sam was devoted to all kinds of animals, even nursing wild ones back to health. She remembered an orphaned squirrel he'd fed from a dropper bottle that had hung around their backyard for years before disappearing.

Lily lied for the second time. "They're okay."

A corner of Nash's mouth turned up, as if realizing she wasn't being truthful.

"I have a saltwater aquarium," she said in defense. "It's like an undersea rainbow of colors. I've got violet dottybacks, blue damselfish, spotted dragonets and orange pipefish—" Lily broke off, aware she was rambling.

Nash nodded at his grandfather. "She still fits the name

you gave her long ago." He fixed his gaze on her. "Chattering Magpie."

"I am *not*—" Lily closed her mouth abruptly. Defending herself with more words was a trap. She smiled sweetly at Nash's smirk. "Perhaps a bit." She didn't often have much opportunity for conversation. Truth was, she didn't often have anyone to talk *to*. No girlfriends. And Mom gallivanted at sea most of the time. Jet and Shelly, her cousin, had their own lives now, complete with adoring husbands. Jet had a baby on the way and Shelly helped her husband care for his teenage brother, who had autism.

Damn, so much had changed the past two years, and not all of it in a good way. She'd always been the special one of the family, the youngest and fairest and most beloved. Now she felt alone and outcast, taking refuge in her painting. Why the hell didn't she leave Bayou La Siryna? Undersea with the merfolk, her siren's ability made her special—admired by male and female alike—not despised, like in this place.

"He teases you," Sam said. "Your voice is most engaging. This old cabin's been too quiet for too long."

A flicker of something—guilt or annoyance?—crossed Nash's face, and she sensed the tension between them.

"I've invited you to go on assignments with me," Nash said to his grandfather, a muscle working above his jawline. "Get away from the bayou. It wouldn't kill you to take a trip once a decade."

"I can't leave."

"You don't *want* to leave. Big difference."

"My home is here," Sam insisted with a trace of stubbornness.

"Home can be anywhere you want."

"I have no need for traveling the world, nor the time. I provide healings for our tribe. And I have my shelter work and my fishing."

"You can fish and work with animals anywhere," Nash countered.

"This is my place. Bowmans have lived here since the Choctaw first claimed this land as theirs. It means something to me to walk the land of my ancestors."

Was that a veiled jab at his grandson's wanderlust? Sam must be lonely living so far from town. A nicer person, like Shelly, would have been thoughtful enough to visit occasionally. Lily bit her lip. It had never occurred to her. Lily took advantage of their absorption in each other to rise from the table and scrape out her almost-uneaten meal in the garbage can.

She spotted a pie on the counter. "Who's ready for dessert?" she asked brightly. "Smells heavenly." The third lie at dinner. She was on a roll. Lily set the pie between the men. "Is this pumpkin or sweet potato?" she asked.

"Sweet potato. Nash's favorite."

The tension eased at Sam's olive branch of peace.

"Thank you, Grandfather." Nash cut a slice. "I haven't eaten this in…" He paused. "I guess it's been decades."

Lily cut a piece for Sam.

"Aren't you having a slice?" Nash asked.

"I'm stuffed," she said, waving a hand to dismiss his comment. She beamed at Sam. "Dinner was wonderful."

His deep wrinkles settled into a frown as he folded his arms and nodded at the scratches on her arms and legs. "What happened?"

"Got them walking on that trail behind the cabin." She sipped more tea, reluctant to tell more.

Neither man said anything but their unblinking stares meant they were waiting for her to elaborate. Lily flushed and twirled a tendril of pale pink hair near her neck. "I got spooked by a coyote," she admitted.

Sam glanced at Nash.

He nodded. "I checked it out. We may have a rabies outbreak."

Sam turned back to her. "Why did it spook you?"

"It…it stared at me weird. After a few seconds—or maybe minutes—I don't know—it lowered its head and started toward me. I took off. Was I wrong to be scared?"

Sam frowned. "Normally a coyote is more afraid of you than the other way around. But rabies can make animals do strange things."

"That's what Nash said, too."

Sam pushed away from the table. "Think I'll sit on the back porch a spell. I'm sure the two of you have lots of catching up to do."

Nash rose immediately. "Actually, I'm retiring early. Got to get up before dawn to catch the first ferry to Herb Island."

Lily sighed inwardly. No gracious way to stay longer and probe for clues to explain Nash's strange indifference to her voice and his cryptic remarks about poison. She stood also. "I'll clean up in here and head on out."

"You are an honored guest." Sam held up a hand. "I'll take care of the kitchen later." He nodded at Nash. "You should walk Lily to her car. Just to be safe."

"Of course," Nash said stiffly, in a way that meant he'd rather not.

Too bad. She lifted her chin and forced a smile at Sam. "Thanks for the delicious dinner."

"You are most welcome."

She edged past Nash, brushing against his right arm and shoulder. Heated energy danced between them. On her end, anyway. His face was as rigid and inscrutable as ever.

"Wait," Sam called out. "I must warn you. Although it could be aberrant behavior from rabies, consider another possibility. If a coyote singles you out in the woods. It is a sign."

Nash gave a low growl.

Lily frowned at Nash's rudeness. "What kind of sign?" she asked. "I remembered you once said the coyote was a mischievous, sly trickster and that it could mark an ending or beginning."

"In this case, I would say your coyote sighting was meant as a warning."

Her throat went dry. "Warning?"

Sam's brown eyes held the wisdom of experience and secret knowledge. "You are being deceived."

Chills crept up her spine as she pictured the precisely vivisected rat by her car, the *Die Slut* etching. Not hard to figure out the enemy. "I know who it is."

"You do?" Nash narrowed his eyes.

"There's this petty woman in town who hates me over something that happened years ago."

"Why would anyone hate you?" Nash asked.

If Nash stayed around the bayou all summer, he was bound to hear the rumors of her loose morals. But she'd rather he learned it later, after he knew her better. That way, perhaps he wouldn't judge her too quickly or unfairly. Lily shrugged, watching Sam rummage through a kitchen drawer. She hoped Sam's isolation had kept him from hearing talk of her in town.

"There's one," he muttered, returning with a smudge stick in his hand. "This is for protection."

Nash rolled his eyes.

"White sage?" Lily guessed.

"Smudge your car and your home every day. It may help keep away trouble."

"Thank you." And she meant it. It might not even hurt to pay Tia Henrietta a visit and get some backup voodoo protection; if nothing else, the woman was entertaining. She hadn't seen the crusty old hag in ages.

Impulsively, Lily gave Sam a quick hug for his kindness.

When she'd first met him as a child, she'd found the man intimidating with his stern features and the Native American symbols tattooed on both sides of his neck and forearms. But she'd quickly come to realize his gentle heart.

She and Nash slipped out into the humid soup that marked bayou summers. A fine coat of perspiration popped all over her body, making the scratches on her arms and leg itch.

They said nothing until she reached Jet's truck.

"I don't like all this talk of danger and deception," Nash said, leaning sideways against the Chevy truck. "Grandfather's superstitious, but you believe you really have an enemy. Who is this woman you mentioned?"

Lily sighed. Should have known Nash wouldn't let it go. "Her name's Twyla Fae." Warmth flamed her face and she was thankful for the cover of darkness. "She thinks I'm after her husband, J.P."

A beat passed. "Are you?"

"No! I have no interest in married men."

"Then why does she think you want her husband?"

"Because J.P. dumped her for a few weeks and dated me. This was *before* they got married," she hastened to explain.

"Sounds like you were the injured party."

"No. I realized we weren't suited before they got back together." It had started out like all the others. She began each new relationship with hope that it would lead to love. The men groveled and proclaimed undying love—but only because of her voice and looks. No one saw *her*. It was always kindest to say goodbye sooner rather than later. A fact that no man appreciated and that had lead to her name turning into the town joke. Lily was *that* girl in the bayou. The one men were sure was an easy lay and the one women condemned as guilty.

"I don't understand why this Twyla is still angry."

"J.P. broke off with me when she told him she was pregnant with his child. Guess Twyla suspects he married her out of a sense of obligation."

"That behavior's juvenile. What's the woman done to you?" he demanded.

"Usually she and her friends settle for whispering behind my back or giving me the cold shoulder. But yesterday morning was different. One of them called me a slut and when I went outside they'd left me a nasty surprise." She quickly filled him in on the details.

"That's beyond petty. She needs to be prosecuted." His green eyes darkened to the color of an Amazon rain forest at midnight.

"You sound like my sister," she said lightly.

"Maybe I should talk to this Twyla."

Lily's heart lightened at his defense. He had to care about her—at least a little bit. "No, I can handle this," she said hastily. If Nash talked to Twyla, the woman would cast her in the worst possible light. "I was going to confront her today, but it's too late tonight. When I do, I'll carry the sage your grandfather gave me—as a precaution."

Nash snorted. "The old man must be the last Choctaw who takes all the old stories and ways as truth."

"And you don't?" His attitude surprised her. They used to sit around for hours listening to Sam's stories. Back then, Nash was proud of his tribe and its traditions.

"Let's say he takes it too far. Besides, we were talking about you and your problem."

Lily leaned into him and gave in to the urge to touch him again. She lightly ran a finger along the stern edge of his jaw. A delicious frisson of awareness shot down her spine at the contact. Nash didn't move. Did he truly feel *nothing* between them?

"Don't," he said in a harsh, tight voice.

"Why? You don't really believe you're cursed, do you?" And he accused Sam of being superstitious? Her hand crept to the back of his neck, fingers combing his black, smooth hair.

Abruptly, Nash pulled her to him, lips crushing against hers. Heat flared and liquid warmth pulsed through her body. His strength was more than the physical, unyielding planes of his mouth, chest and arms. It was an aura as primal and mysterious as nature's spring fever erupting in every creature and living organism to mate and bring forth new life. Lily parted her mouth, inviting him to deepen the kiss.

Nash thrust her away. "Goodnight, Lily."

Shock doused her like a blanket of snow. "Wh—Why did you stop?"

He didn't answer or look at her, but walked back to the porch, hands thrust in his jeans pockets.

"Of all the rude, inconsiderate..." Lily sputtered, at a loss. She was the one who walked away from men, not the other way around. She folded her arms and smiled grimly at his fading figure.

You can run, Nashoba Bowman, but we aren't done. I'll find out all your secrets. And in the end, I'll be the one to decide when it's over.

Chapter 4

Nash crept closer, honing in on the low, slow snorting. *Bup-bup-bup.* Definitely not the high-pitched clattering of the common *Rallus longirostris*. Ever so carefully, he raised his binoculars. There… This bird was the size of a chicken, rusty-feathered, long-beaked. It lifted its head, revealing chestnut-hued cheeks instead of the gray of its close relative, the common clapper. He'd found the species he'd come to photograph.

Camera replaced binoculars. Nash focused the telescopic lens and started snapping away. Good enough shots, but he wanted something spectacular, more worthy of the Nashoba Bowman standard he'd developed over the years. He crept ahead on all fours, the razor-sharp sea grass edges cutting his fingers and palms. It didn't matter.

His heart fluttered faster, like that of the bird. For every yard forward, Nash halted five seconds, until he drew so close the bird lifted its beak and black, wary eyes focused on him.

Not here to hurt. I'm admiring you. Nothing to fear.
Nash pushed the thoughts toward the Clapper Rail before raising his camera again and taking one incredible close-up.

A haunting melody sounded through the brackish bayou island, disrupting their connection. Startled, the clapper opened its beak. *Bup-bup-bup-bup.* In a bustle of feathers and churned water, the bird half flew, half swam in a mad scramble for safety.

Damn. He'd been so close to connecting with the bird, so close to slipping into its essence and establishing trust.

The singing grew louder, sounding like a chorus of perfectly blended tones. Did Opal have a hidden talent for singing? He'd never heard her sing before. But she knew better than to interrupt a shot. Besides, she was supposed to be on the other side of the island photographing another species.

Lily emerged from a clump of cypress trees. Only this time when she came out of the woods she was smiling, not running from a demented coyote. She wore a wide-brimmed straw hat and grinned and waved, holding up a wicker picnic basket.

"Hello," she sang out.

Nash frowned. He should have guessed it was Lily. Looking as damn beautiful in the summer sun as she had last night under the moonlight. "What are you doing here?" he asked gruffly, tamping down the memory of that scorching kiss.

Her smile faltered. "Didn't you hear me sing?"

What a strange response; the woman made no sense. "Of course I heard. You were so loud you scared off the bird I was stalking."

"Loud?" Lily's eyes widened. "That's all you have to say about my voice?"

He cocked a brow. She sounded mildly outraged when

he was the injured party here. Although to be fair, Lily might not have realized she was interrupting. "It was... uh...nice, I suppose."

"Nice?"

"Are you going to keep repeating everything I say? 'Cause I've got lots of work to do."

Blue eyes blinked and she breathed deeply, as if to regain her composure. "You are an unusual man, Nashoba."

She didn't know the half of it. Only Opal might have an inkling that he'd gained fame as a wildlife photographer because of his unnatural ability to sense animals' thoughts and calm them with his own form of mental telepathy—or whatever the hell it was that gained their trust for the few nanoseconds it took to get the perfect picture.

Lily held up the basket. "Figured working outside would make you hungry, so I brought us a lunch."

She assumed too much from that short kiss. It meant nothing. Nash pointed to the sketchpad in her other hand. "What's that for?"

"I come out to the island often and sketch. We'll probably run into each other lots while you're here."

Nash stifled a groan. "I was—" he held up a thumb and index finger an inch apart "—this close to getting some incredible shots. You scared off my bird."

"Ah." Lily muttered a sound of sympathy but kept smiling. "It'll come back." She gave him a coy sideways glance. "You sure you didn't think my singing was more than *nice*? I've been told my voice is quite...enchanting."

"I noticed my shoot was ruined."

She tapped a finger on the edge of her cupid's-bow lips. "Hmm... Sorry, I suppose."

An unexpected chuckle rumbled in his throat, like a motor sputtering to life after months of neglect. "You don't have any self-confidence issues, do you?"

"Not until you started giving me a complex."

"If people say your voice is enchanting, maybe you should have taken up the opera instead of painting." He imagined Lily onstage—the limelight highlighting that mass of blond hair and white skin.

"I could have become a prima donna, but it didn't seem fair."

Again, Lily threw him off with an odd answer. The woman was either incredibly conceited or mentally defective. Perhaps both.

Fair. Was it unfair of him to compete in his field? He'd always thought he'd made a brilliant career choice. Now Lily made him wonder if he exploited his natural gifts.

"Really, your ego—" He stopped abruptly and bit back his annoyance. Lily was an old friend. He could let it go. A few weeks and he'd be on the road somewhere again. "Never mind," he said with a casual flick of his wrist. "Who am I to shake your wonderful self-esteem? More power to you."

"Power, indeed," she mumbled, so faintly he wondered if he'd heard correctly.

She beckoned him with a crook of his finger. "This way."

Nash hesitated, scowling. No harm in taking a short break, though. Now that his prey had scattered anyway. He fell in step behind Lily, his gaze involuntarily dropping to the womanly curves of her hips and luscious ass. Now *that* was impressive. *That* was power and a temptation he didn't know if he could resist. It had been too long... His breath hitched like that of a hormonally charged adolescent. *Stop it. Old friends make complicated lovers.* Next assignment he'd have to do something about his self-imposed celibacy. Find some uncomplicated part-time lover with no expectations of commitment.

Lily spread out a blanket beneath a gigantic oak and began unpacking plastic containers.

He hadn't realized until now he was hungry. And thirsty. "Got some water in there?"

"Even better. Sweet tea." She handed him a sealed mason jar with ice cubes floating like crystals in an amber ambrosia.

Nash removed the canning lid and downed half of it in one swallow. "That's good," he admitted. "I'd forgotten how hot it is down here. How do you stand the heat and humidity?"

"You'll acclimate to it again. I would think you'd be used to all kind of conditions in your line of work."

"Nothing like Southern humidity." He took off his shirt and used it to wipe sweat from his face and eyes.

He glimpsed Lily getting an eyeful of his chest and abs. The lady was definitely interested. Nash groaned inwardly. But what did he expect? He'd been a fool to kiss her last night. Of course she thought he was interested in her. Especially since— Well, he didn't want to think of the last two women he'd dated. Guilt rose in his throat like bile.

"What you got?" he asked as she opened containers.

"Fried chicken, pimento cheese sandwiches, pecan pie, shrimp cocktail and lobster salad."

He picked up a chicken wing. "I'm going to gain twenty pounds this summer," he predicted. Nash bit into the buttermilk-soaked and flour-coated goodness and sighed. "But I'll enjoy every damn minute along the way."

Lily laughed and ate a spoonful of lobster salad. "Live in the moment, I always say."

Ocean-blue eyes fixated on him and Nash couldn't move, couldn't do anything but stare into those eyes. Energy crackled between them, every bit as scalding as the noon sun.

This wouldn't do. "Show me your drawings," he commanded, opening her sketchpad without waiting for permission.

Lily's hand rested on his forearm and his skin tingled at the light touch.

"Just so you know, I'm mostly self-taught. I'm still learning and hoping to find a professional tutor at some point. If I can find one that deems me worthy of his time."

So the lady's armor of self-confidence had a chink. "Understood." A self-taught amateur? He braced himself for convoluted drawings of fruit still lifes, paint-by-number ocean scenes or Victorian-looking flowers and hearts.

"Let me see what you got there," he said huskily, conscious of her fingers over his knuckles working magic on his libido.

Lily released her hand and the tingling ceased. Nash opened the sketchpad and gave a low whistle at the detailed pen-and-ink drawings of birds, sea grass, fish and trees. This was more than mere talent. It was…seeing the bayou through Lily's eyes. Each composition was vibrant and unique as a thumbprint.

"What do you think?" Her voice was high and reedy, anxious. She gave a self-deprecating laugh. "If you don't like them, it's okay. Like I said, I'm—"

"I don't like them." He paused at a watercolor depicting swirls of light in dark liquid. "I love them." He studied it closer—saw an outline of individual fishes swimming in a school spiraling upward, their bodies incandescent in an inky darkness, like a lamp lit undersea. At the bottom of the painting was a large chunk of coral, the top alit in a violet haze and underneath gray shadows bottomed out to black. He flipped the painting toward Lily. "What kind of fish are these?"

"Myctophids, also known as lantern fish. They're as common under the sea as squirrels in a cove of oaks."

"Amazing." As much as Nash's soul longed to traverse the world, seeing new landscapes and animals, so it now also longed to be undersea, to capture the ocean's deep magic—an unexplored galaxy. Again, he had the oddest tingling that something about Lily was different. Too perfect. Too powerful. He looked up from the sketchpad and caught her twirling the ends of her hair—a nervous gesture she'd had when they were kids. Underneath her confident exterior was a sensitive artist. He returned his gaze to the sketchpad and examined the drawings.

In the midst of shades of gray pencil drawings, he came upon another watercolor popping with vibrancy. Striated bands of blue and green progressed from deep to lighter hues as if Lily's perspective originated on the ocean floor, looking toward the sky as the sun's reflection filtered down. The perspective was unusual.

"How did you capture this image?" He opened the book to the watercolor and laid it open between them. "Do you visualize the scenes in your mind or do you paint from photos?"

Lily took a long swallow of tea, canting her long neck upward, exposing the vulnerable hollow of her throat. Damn. He'd never before admired a woman's neck, for Pete's sake.

Her head tilted forward and she delicately patted her upper lip before speaking. "That one was inspired by a picture Jet took swimming one day. Have you done underwater shoots?"

"No. But I'd love to." Would he be any good? His talent came from an unnatural connection to the earth and its creatures. But fish? Undersea life? He didn't have a clue.

"I stopped by and saw your grandfather this morning," she said, turning the conversation. "He showed me a collection of your work. Very impressive."

Nash shrugged, but his gut warmed that his grandfather was so proud of him. "Did he give you any more sinister warnings?"

"No." A shuttered look crossed her face and she glanced

sideways, as if expecting another coyote to leap from behind a tree.

"Old man got to you, huh? Used to scare me as a kid sometimes with his tales of the supernatural."

Lily giggled. "Every rustle I hear in the woods, I look for the Little People sneaking up on me."

"Ah, the Kowi Anukasha," he nodded. "They're mischievous and like scaring humans, but they aren't evil. Not like the Nalusa Falaya."

Lily's smile dropped. "The Soul Eater."

"Our Choctaw version of the bogeyman." Nash scooped up a couple of shrimp and popped them into his mouth. "Grandfather has plenty of tall tales."

"Who's to say they aren't true?" She set down her plate and gave him another of her unnerving stares.

Nash shifted, uncomfortable with the question. He didn't want to believe. Life was tough enough without looking for monsters in the shadows. And despite his gift, he'd never seen anything to support the old Native American legends. "You can't be serious."

"Oh, but I am. The bayou's full of magic and mystery." Lily leaned into him, so close her breath flamed his jaw and neck. "Can't you feel it?" she whispered.

He felt something, all right—a fierce longing to meld into her essence. The need was even stronger than it had been last night. Nash closed his eyes, let the inevitable happen. Lily's lips brushed his. *Talk about magic.* His body thrummed at the contact.

"How do I wrangle an invitation to this picnic?" a cheery voice called out.

Nash winced at Opal's abrupt appearance. Normally, he heard others approach from great distances. It was a real testament to how Lily engrossed his senses. He squelched a renewed flush of irritation—this time because he wanted to be alone with Lily, wanted to explore her curves and secret places. He shouldn't feel this way. He should welcome the interruption.

Opal plopped onto the blanket between them so that the three formed a triangle.

"Thought you were miles away," he said, relieved Opal didn't mention seeing them kiss.

"Started that way this morning, but steadily edged closer here, following a blue heron." Her smile was toothy and catching. "And then I heard this…angelic singing."

Lily waved a hand. No blush stained her face and her manner gave no indication of embarrassment at being caught kissing. "Sorry I interrupted everyone's work. I come here occasionally to draw," she told Opal.

Opal leaned his way and glanced at the open sketchpad.

"Wow. You can paint *and* sing *and* look like a goddess. It's so not fair." Her smile stayed intact and the words didn't seem malicious. That's what he liked about Opal—she was an open book and was never catty.

"Your job must be fun. Bet there's not many women who can do what you do," Lily said.

"There's a few." Opal lifted her face to the sun and raised both arms by her sides. "I love working outdoors. The more primitive, the better."

"Can I see the pictures you took this morning?" Lily asked.

"Sure." Opal shifted her weight toward Lily and unhooked the camera cord from her neck. She tapped a button on the digital screen, revealing a dozen close-ups of a blue-gray crane.

Lily scanned the photos. "These are beautiful."

Opal grinned at him. "Hear that, boss? Remember that at my next performance evaluation." She turned back to Lily. "Nash takes the superhard shots, though, catching wildlife at intimate or rare moments hardly ever witnessed by humans."

Lily handed the container of chicken wings to Opal. "His grandfather showed me his work this morning, and I was impressed."

Nash finished another chicken wing and polished off a few more shrimp while the two exchanged pleasantries. It allowed him time to cool off and regain his composure. If a mere kiss made him fevered, what would it be like to make love to Lily? *Don't even think about it.* He scrambled to his feet.

"You can't be going back to work already." Lily pointed to the pie. "You haven't had dessert yet."

A few more minutes alone and *she* would have been dessert. Nash studied the slight upturn at the corners of Lily's mouth but couldn't decide if her remark was a deliberate sexual innuendo. "Been fun, ladies, but time for me to go hunt that clapper rail again." He took off his bandana and swiped the sweat from his face again.

"Why don't we take a quick swim and cool off?" Opal suggested. "The heat's brutal."

Lily shook her head. "I can't swim."

Opal gaped at her. "You practically live on an island and can't swim?"

"I had a bad experience as a child. Went to swim before a storm and an undertow almost swept me away. Been afraid of the water ever since."

He'd forgotten that. When they were young, Lily had gamely kept up with him on the hiking and biking but refused to ever get in the water. "Yet you paint it so much—one as if you were actually undersea," he mused aloud.

Lily set aside her plate of lobster salad. "Our fears become our obsessions."

"But couldn't you go in the water up to your knees and splash yourself if we stand with you?" Opal pleaded. "It would be fun."

"'Fraid not."

"Later, ladies." He pulled back on his T-shirt, slung the camera carrier around his neck and took several steps before remembering his manners. He turned around and waved. "Oh, and thanks for lunch, Lily."

Nash sucked in a breath of hot air laced with a bracing, salty tang. Good thing Opal had come along when she had. He'd taken this assignment not only to visit Grandfather, but also to escape from women constantly chasing him and from the memory of his last two disastrous relationships.

From here on, Lily was off-limits.

Lily touched her lips and sighed as he walked away. That kiss had been pure magic.

Opal gave a little laugh. "Enjoying the view? I totally see why the ladies all go for him. He's a hunk, all right."

Lily gazed at her curiously, wondering if Opal had feelings for Nash. "What about you?"

"Nah, I've got someone in my life. And it's never a good idea to date anyone you work with, especially your boss."

Lily prodded for more details. "So women swoon over him?"

"Breaks hearts everywhere he goes. Women constantly fall at his feet."

And I'm behaving like every other woman. "He have anyone serious in his life?" She put lids on some of the containers and returned them to the basket.

"Not anymore. Not since—" Opal broke off, staring out at sea.

"Not since what?"

"Not since his last girlfriend, Connie, died." Opal dug into the lobster salad. "Mmm...de-lish."

Lily gasped and stopped packing up food. "That's awful. What happened?"

"Suicide. Connie was found dead one morning, an empty

bottle of pills on her nightstand." Opal downed a long swig of tea. "Sad, huh?"

Poor Nash. No wonder he's bitter. "Tragic," Lily quietly agreed. "Did she leave a note?"

Opal nibbled on a chicken wing and delicately wiped her mouth before answering. "None was ever found. But he'd broken up with her a couple days before."

"How long ago did she...did this happen?"

"About a year ago. It wouldn't have been so bad, except..." Her voice trailed off.

Lily didn't see how the story could get any worse. "Except what?"

"I really shouldn't say anything. It kind of slipped out, ya know?"

"C'mon. Don't leave me hanging."

Opal spooned up more salad and chewed, as if mulling over the answer. "Thing is," she said at last, setting down the plate, "two years earlier, another of his girlfriends died. Rebecca."

The knot of dread in Lily's stomach grew. "How?" she whispered.

"They had an argument—probably over his lack of commitment—and she drove home. Hours later, apparently drunk, she got back in her car but lost control of it, ran off into a ditch and hit a tree."

Goose bumps pricked Lily's arms and legs and a chill set in that no blistering Southern sun could warm. *I'm poison.* Nash's clipped words echoed round her brain like gunshots in a canyon. No wonder the guy was aloof. She'd be bitter, too.

"That's—that's horrible," Lily said, putting her face in her hands. How the hell did someone cope with that much pain? One death was bad enough. But two? She shuddered.

"Sure." Opal sighed. "The doctors said Rebecca died instantly. So there's that."

Lily didn't want to hear any more details. It was too much to take in all at once. She wanted to be alone and deal with the knowledge of all Nash had suffered, was still suffering. Lily abruptly gathered up food containers and stuffed them in the picnic basket; even the smell of it nauseated her. "Don't say anything else." Lily shut the picnic basket with a snap. "Nash will tell me when he's ready."

"Sorry to spoil your lunch." Opal eyed the pie. "Mind if I keep a piece for later this afternoon?"

Lily wrapped the whole thing in aluminum foil, her movements jerky with haste. She thrust it at Opal. "Take it."

"Thanks. I'll share it with Nash."

They both rose unsteadily to their feet.

Opal frowned. "Look, I hope I didn't scare you off Nash. He's a great guy who's had a bit of bad luck lately."

"A bit of bad luck?" Lily snorted. "I'd say it's more serious than that."

Opal flushed. "Absolutely. You're right. It's— I like you, Lily. I don't want to see anything bad happen to *you*."

"No need for the warning. Nothing is going to happen to me," she said curtly, wanting to end the conversation.

"Of course not." Opal squeezed Lily's shoulder and dropped her hand to her side. "Just thought you should know. I'd hate to see him break your heart."

"Some would say I have no heart to break," Lily muttered.

"Why would they say that?"

"Not important."

Opal's face crumbled. "You don't trust me to keep my mouth shut. Which I can totally understand, given how I blabbed Nash's history during lunch."

"It's not that." Lily's fingers rubbed an itchy scratch on her leg leftover from the run in the woods. She supposed this was what girlfriends did, exchanged secrets and confided in one another. Maybe Opal had done her a favor in revealing Nash's painful past. At least now she knew the problem and could be mentally prepared when Nash brought up the news himself.

And it would be wonderful to have a real friend because Jet and Shelly were busy now with their own lives. She drew a deep breath. "Okay, you'll probably hear this anyway if you meet people in town, but I don't have a great reputation."

"Why's that?"

"I went through a bit of a wild stage years ago and no one will let me forget it. That's a small town for you. You're doomed to never live down your past. Although, in my defense, rumors of my promiscuity are greatly exaggerated."

Opal patted her shoulder. "Poor Lily. Don't worry—I won't say anything to Nash."

Lily shifted uncomfortably. Opal made her feel... beholden. Guilty. As if they shared something dirty. "Doesn't matter. He's bound to hear the talk, too."

"Maybe not. He and his grandfather live pretty isolated. And Nash has been reclusive the past couple of years. He doesn't get out much." Opal winked. "So you see, probably nothing to worry about."

Again, a prickly unease settled over Lily. She smiled uncertainly. "If you say so," she agreed. Her family had grown up secluded from the townsfolk, making it easier to keep their shape-shifting abilities a secret.

Secrecy was a habit she'd have to let slip if she wanted a girlfriend.

Chapter 5

Sunset through the pines cast coral and mauve spears of light across land and sea. Nash had returned to the cabin on the evening ferry, bent on a mission. Now he trudged through mosquito-infested lowland, shotgun at his side. Diseased or not, the coyote was clever at eluding him. In spite of pain and fear, the will to live was strong in the animal. Nash respected that.

The wind shifted, hot air rippling across his sweaty skin. The fresh scent of pine needles had an underlying taint. Nash followed it, back on the coyote's track. Another fifty yards ahead, the smell of sickness grew thicker and obliterated the pine odor.

Black energy seeped inward as he drew near. Most likely the unfortunate coyote had been ousted from his pack, a threat to the group's survival. Cold fingers of loneliness fidgeted along his spine as he sensed the animal's toxic miasma. Nash picked up a faint, rumbling groan. Not the growl of an aggressive animal, but the mewling of one suffering.

Nash emitted a calming message. *Your time has come. Let's end the pain.*

An answering whine came from behind a dense clump of saw palmetto trees not a dozen yards to his right. The coyote emerged, trembling, its amber eyes dull and flat. Mottled gray fur encased an emaciated body. Telltale foam bubbled along its tapered muzzle. Rabies had rendered the animal unable to swallow its own saliva.

Nash ever so slowly raised the shotgun, not wanting to provoke the animal. *I'm sorry. This will be quick, I promise you.* His right index finger crooked onto the metal trigger.

The coyote leapt, snarling and baring sharp teeth, amber eyes alit in a last-shot bid to escape death. Fur, fear and fury hurled toward Nash and he pulled the trigger.

An explosive boom rang out. The reverberation from the shot was still echoing as the dead coyote's body hit the ground with a thump. Nash closed his eyes and drank in the silence until peace washed through the woods.

It was done.

He took out the garbage bag and latex gloves he'd tucked into the waistband of his jeans. To prevent spread of the rabies virus, it was necessary to bag the coyote and put it in a protected place until he could return in the morning with a shovel and bury the dead body.

Quickly, he attended to the last rites. *You were brave. A fighter to the end. May you join a ghostly pack in happy hunting grounds.* Satisfied with the work, he retraced his path. The air was a shade darker than when he'd first set out. At a fork on the dirt trail he hesitated. Better check on the old man. Grandfather had missed dinner and the thought of his eighty-two-year-old grandfather being unaccounted for left Nash uneasy. Instead of continuing home, Nash set off for the marsh. Sam often fished all day out there.

Sure enough, he found his grandfather sitting in a chair,

fishing pole in hand. The tip of his cigar glowed in the gathering twilight. Nash walked up behind him.

Without turning around, Sam spoke. "Heard the shot. You get that coyote?"

"I did." Nash settled on the ground close by after making sure he was clear of fire-ant mounds. Their sting was like being poked by flaming hypodermic needles. "Sorry I haven't been to see you in a couple days."

"You're busy. Besides, I went years without seeing you. Two days is nothing."

Guilt made him defensive. "You were always welcome to visit *me*. Why do you stay here all the time? There's a big, wide world outside this backwoods."

Sam stared ahead at the black water. "True. But there's also a whole world here you're missing."

"Hardly. I've hiked every inch of this area over the years."

"Ah, but you haven't swam all over it."

Nash gave him a sideways glance. "And if I did, what would it matter? I've swam in all the seven seas."

The tip of Sam's cigar glowed brighter as he took a draw.

"Should you really be smoking with your heart trouble?"

"I'm not forsaking my little pleasures. I've lived over eight decades, you know."

"Yeah, but if you want to make another decade, you need to give up those things." He pointed to the cigar with a jab of his finger.

Sam tipped his head back and exhaled a smoke ring within a smoke ring.

"When do you go back for another doctor's visit? I want to go with you." Guilt lashed him; months ago when Sam had undergone a triple bypass operation, Nash had been on an African safari assignment. His grandfather had recouped alone until he'd finagled an assignment nearby. Nash had sent a paid home health care assistant, but his grandfather had dismissed her before two weeks were up, claiming he could take care of himself.

"At least think about giving up frying everything in bacon grease," Nash urged.

Sam didn't respond and Nash frowned at the grey tinge that underlaid Sam's olive skin. The fishing pole trembled slightly in his grandfather's unsteady hand.

A rush of nostalgia overcame Nash. As a child, his grandfather's cabin had been a haven of peace from his parents' tumultuous marriage. He'd missed the summer visits after Mom had whisked him away to her home state of Massachusetts. His grandfather could have visited them, but he refused to leave the bayou. Nash doubted he'd ever been north of the Mason-Dixon line his entire life.

The pole jerked and Sam smiled, face crinkling. He detached a good-sized brim and placed it in a rolling ice chest with several others. "Fried fish dinner tonight."

Nash shook his head. He'd suggest baking the fish but knew his grandfather wouldn't go for the healthier option. "Ready to get home and eat? It's getting dark."

"I can see well enough, plus I have my flashlight."

A knowing look passed between them. They could each sense their way in darkness. His grandfather had some of the same supernatural senses that he did, although not as strong. By agreement, they seldom spoke of it.

Sam closed the lid of the small cooler. "Let's sit a spell afore we go. Have I ever told you the story—"

Nash almost groaned. Not another story.

"—of the Okwa Nahollo?"

"No," he said, surprised. He thought he'd heard every Choctaw tale a thousand times, but this was new. "Does that translate to 'pale water people'?"

"White people of the water," Sam corrected. "Extremely white."

An image of Lily's soft-hued face flashed through him.

He hated admitting it, but he'd missed her the past two days he'd stayed on the island.

"With skin the color of trout because they lived undersea," his grandfather continued.

Talk about a tall fish tale. Nash refrained from grinning. "Like mermaids?"

Sam shook his head. "No. They aren't half fish and half human. They have human form except their legs are almost twice as long as ours. Their fingers and toes are webbed and their eyes glow like some deep-sea fishes do."

"Of course, so they can see better in dark water."

Sam narrowed his eyes, as if suspicious Nash was amused. "Exactly."

Nash wrapped his arms around his bent knees and stared out over the marsh. "Go on."

"Whenever you find patches of light-colored water in the bayou, that is where they live. If you swim near them or fish near them, they'll grab your ankles and pull you under."

The theme from *Jaws* played in his mind. "So don't worry about sharks. People should fear capture by mermaids." *Death by mermaid.*

Not even a ghost of amusement lit Sam's eyes. "Yes. Except, like I said, they aren't exactly mermaids, although they must be closely related."

"C'mon. I'm not a kid anymore. You don't really expect me to believe that tale. Surely you don't either, do you?"

"It's passed down from our ancestors." Sam's eyes flashed and his spine stiffened. "Every word is true."

Nash kept his face blank and his tone neutral. "I mean no disrespect."

"Of course you do. You think I am a foolish old man." Sam eased up out of the chair and stood, looking out to sea.

Nash reached up his hand and touched his grandfather's knee. He might be a skeptic and occasionally amused at his grandfather's ways, but he would never think him foolish. "Not foolish. Please sit."

Sam stayed rooted, as if debating. Finally, he sat. "I'm an old man. I've kept in shape by walking these woods for years, but my time's short. So while you're here I need to explain more of your heritage."

"I'm listening." He felt chastened like a small child. "I respect my people and their ways. Nothing will ever change that."

"I know it makes you uncomfortable when I speak of the spirit world. But it's there. It's real. Just as you are sensitive to nature and its creatures, my gift is seeing the spirits around people. They can be human, animal or plant spirits, sometimes all three."

"Father said you chose my name because you saw a wolf spirit near me."

Sam nodded. His serious, deeply lined face rearranged to an unexpected, wistful smile. "When you were born, I fasted three days and went on long walks, seeking guidance. The first time I held you in my arms I heard a wolf howl. I envisioned a pack of wolves celebrating your birth, tails wagging, the males wrestling one another in a show of affection."

"So you named me Nashoba—Choctaw for *wolf*." He'd heard this before, remembered Mom rolling her eyes at Dad's insistence on naming their children with traditional names. "So how did you end up with a name like Sam?"

"My parents did it to honor a gentleman named Samuel who was good to them. He hired my father as a laborer and paid him a decent wage for the times. But my middle name is Chula."

"*Chula* means *fox*," Nash said, combing through his memory of their native language.

Sam fixed his gaze back to the water's expanse with an absorbed look Nash remembered from childhood. He would stay in this same spot for hours in deep contemplation, the fishing pole loose in his hand like an afterthought.

"Do you think about grandmother out here?"

She'd died decades ago from a boating accident. The one memory of his grandmother was of her shucking corn in the kitchen. The room was cozy and warm, smelling of fried goodness, fresh vegetables and herbs. When he'd entered, her dark eyes sparkled in greeting. She'd dropped to a knee and held out her arms and he'd run into them. The safest, most loving, secure spot in the universe. And it was but a thirty-second memory.

"Yes. And all the others that have passed before and since."

It was a shame he'd never remarried. Nash struggled for words to convey sympathy while not sounding like a condescending jerk. "I wish you would leave this place. At least for a few vacations. You should see new things, meet new people."

"I can't leave."

More like don't want to leave. Sam was old and stubborn as barnacles clinging to a ship hull. No changing him at this late date.

The silence stretched between them as the sun had completed its day's journey and disappeared. All that remained was the water's memory of it in coral-and-purple sheens that rippled in the Gulf breeze. Grandfather turned to him. "The spirits say it is time."

"Time for what?" So that's what he did alone out here— communed with spirits. He should have guessed.

"One last story."

Alarm brushed the back of his neck like a nest of crawling spiders. He half rose. "Do you have chest pains? Should I call a doctor?"

"It's not my time tonight. Although it draws near."

"Don't say that. There must be something the doctors

can do." A suspicion gurgled up. "Are you taking your medicine? You can't depend only on the spirits and herbs for healing."

"There's more to tell you of the Okwa Nahollo," Sam continued, ignoring Nash's question. He fixed him with sharp, dark eyes. "You are a descendant."

"Of the mermaids?" Nash scoffed. Really, Grandfather had gone too far this time.

Sam's jaw clenched and his mouth set in a determined line. "It is in your blood."

"I want purple or pink highlights. Something striking." Opal fingered a lock of lavender in Lily's hair. "Something deeper than this."

No point mentioning the subtle pastels in her hair were entirely natural. Fortunately, Lily kept a rainbow of hair-dye colors stocked because so many requested some version of her unusual hair hues. The beauty shop, Mermaid's Lair, was officially closed, but Lily did the odd job for customers who begged for her service. Plus, it was convenient for Jet and Shelly to come in for weekly hair-and-nail maintenance—important because both grew at three times the normal human rate.

Jet winked at Lily from behind the desk where she sat running the numbers for their various family businesses: a maritime and antiquities shop, aquatic therapy and the small income from the beauty shop that kept the rent and utilities paid.

"You made a grand total of fifty dollars in profit last quarter," Jet said, frowning.

Lily laughed, expertly assembling mixing bowls and chemicals. "Ah, but it was double that amount if you included tips."

"I'll tip handsomely," Opal promised, an earnest look on her face.

Probably thought she was broke. As if. Lily styled hair because she enjoyed it and was good at it. "This is on me."

"Maybe you should reopen full-time," Jet persisted. "It would give you something to do."

Hell, no. She'd had enough of the town women's snotty, superior behavior and the men ogling her breasts as she stood close by to trim their hair. Besides, shop hours would interfere with her painting.

"Don't need to." They were stinking rich.

"But you're home alone. What do you do all day?"

Lily shrugged. "Paint."

"She's really good," Opal cut in. "I saw her sketchbook."

"Sure, I know that." Jet waved a hand around the room. "She did this, after all."

Opal surveyed the varying shades of coral, rose and ivory on the walls. Lily had painted pearly tones that gave the effect of being enveloped in the shelter of a giant conch shell.

"Remarkable," Opal said in a hushed tone.

Lily felt a tiny glow of satisfaction at the praise. She'd spent lots of time with Opal the past couple of days, enjoying the novelty of shopping with a girlfriend and showing her around the bayou.

"But I don't see art as a career path."

Jet's acerbic observation squashed the flicker of warmth. Her sis was in a lousy mood today. Must be some hormonal pregnancy thing.

Lily absentmindedly brushed Opal's red hair. She'd been thinking of entering the prestigious Garrison Hendricks art contest. All finalists would be invited to showcase their work at a premiere gallery in New York City. The chances of placing were slim, but the rewards could launch her fledgling dreams.

The click of Jet's fingers on the adding machine resumed.

"How's Nash's work going?" Lily asked Opal casually.

"It's been a challenge, but he enjoys it. Doesn't he talk to you about it?"

"I haven't talked to him in a couple days. Maybe I'll run out there tomorrow."

Opal winked. "Bet he'd love to see you. You two can pick up with the passionate kiss I interrupted at the picnic."

The clicking stopped. "Passionate kiss? I thought you were seeing Gary Ludlow," Jet said.

"I cut him loose last week." Lily sharpened her scissors, ignoring Jet's exasperated sigh.

"One day you're going to run out of men to date around here," her sister warned.

Lily placed chunks of Opal's hair between her left index finger and thumb and made the first cut. She didn't defend herself against Jet's remark. It wasn't that she deliberately set out to hurt anyone. When she saw it couldn't work, she ended it quickly, figuring that was the kindest thing in the end.

A ping sent Opal scurrying through her purse. "Gotta take this," she apologized, scooting out of the chair. "Is there somewhere I can talk privately?"

Lily pointed to the break room in back.

"Be back in a minute." Opal hurried away, the black vinyl cape flapping behind her like a bat.

Jet arched a dark eyebrow. "Kind of secretive, isn't she?"

"A little." She wondered if Opal's boyfriend might be married.

Jet sipped from her water bottle, then set it down slowly and deliberately. Her gaze drifted to the shop window. "I went for a swim last night and the current brought interesting news."

"Let me guess. Mom's coming."

Jet nodded. "Judging from the sound-wave strength and pattern, I'd say to expect her in about two days."

Mother was the last person Lily wanted to see right now.

"Maybe she wants to check on you. Make sure everything's okay with the pregnancy," Lily said hopefully.

"Nah. It's you she's concerned with."

Lily swept up snippets of Opal's hair on the floor, aware of Jet's scrutiny. Damn, she didn't want maternal pressure to leave the bayou for good and "resume her rightful position as the best siren of the sea"—words her mother eschewed with increasing regularity. Mom had gone from baffled to miffed to frustrated over the past few visits.

A few minutes of silence descended before Jet spoke up. "You okay?"

"Nothing I can't handle. She'll just pester me to take my rightful place with other merfolk."

Jet regarded her, eyes direct, brows knitted and chin down. A fierce look that Lily knew masked concern. "Not such a bad idea. Especially with this Twyla business."

"Twyla still bothering you?"

Lily jumped at Opal's voice and cast a furtive look at Jet, wondering how much Opal had overheard. She patted the seat for Opal to sit down. "Maybe."

She stirred the color and developer together and brushed streaks of color on Opal's hair. The bright colors should perk up the rather plain face with its scattering of freckles and a slight scar that spread across one cheek. "This is a temporary dye," she explained. "You can try out the effect and see how you like it."

Jet persisted with her questioning. "What does *maybe* mean? Either she is or isn't bugging you."

"I got several hang-up calls last night. They never spoke. After the third one, I turned off my ringer." The scissors trembled slightly in Lily's hands as she trimmed a few uneven locks of Opal's hair. "When I checked this morning there were seven missed calls and no voice-mail messages."

"Ouch!" Opal swiped the side of her neck and stared at a blood splash on her fingers.

"I am *so* sorry." Lily grabbed a towel and wiped the nick. "That's never happened before." Geez, how embarrassing.

"No problem, I'll live," Opal assured her.

Jet cut in, still focused on the phone calls. "Did you call back the number on the screen?"

"Of course. But I got a recording saying the number was no longer in service. Must have used a throwaway phone."

Opal circled her index finger around her right temple. "Somebody's cra-*zee*."

"Say the word and I'll have Landry talk to Twyla," Jet said.

"No need to drag him into it." Lily didn't want her brother-in-law knowing her business.

A collective mewling of cats turned their attention to the shop front. More than half a dozen felines in various colors and sizes perched along the window ledge, motionless and unblinking except for licking their mouths. As if they observed a delectable treat fit for a feast.

Jet frowned. "We ought to bring Rebel to chase them away."

"Dog's so ugly he wouldn't even have to bite or bark to scare them," Lily said drily, returning to the familiar routine of coloring and styling hair.

The three settled into a comfortable silence as Jet continued crunching numbers and Opal observed Lily at work.

A loud rap on the front window scared off their cat stalkers. A husky guy wearing a camouflage shirt waved and motioned for someone to open the locked door.

"Who's that?" Opal asked.

Lily unfastened her apron with a sigh. "Gary."

"Thought you broke it off with him," Jet said.

"I did."

Jet scowled at Gary and motioned him to go away.

Gary rapped harder on the glass. "Open up," he yelled. "I need to talk to you, Lily."

People passing by on the street stopped and stared.

"He's making a scene," Opal noted, tapping her lips.

Jet stalked to the front door in brisk strides. "I'll get rid of him."

"No. Let him in before he breaks the glass," Lily said. She picked up a pink chiffon scarf from the counter and knotted it at her throat, hiding the faint line of scars where gill slits aligned both sides of her neck. She didn't bother with it around Nash because he'd seen the marks when they were children and she'd made up a story about an accident. And she hadn't bother to cover it up around Opal. Seeing as she had her own scar to deal with, they figured she wouldn't ask prying questions.

"You sure?" Jet hesitated, hand on the doorknob.

Lily touched her scarf in a silent reminder.

Jet turned up her collar, covering the gills that were also three inches in length on either side of the neck, extending from the top of the collarbone to her windpipe.

At Lily's nod, Jet unlocked the door. The smell of whiskey preceded Gary as he staggered straight to Lily.

"Whatever I done wrong before, Lily, I'm sorry." His eyes were weepy and red-rimmed, yet also held an odd glimmer of hope.

"You didn't do anything wrong," Lily said, sweeping up her station. "I wasn't feeling it anymore."

"But why? I must have done something."

She almost winced at the pleading note in his voice. Best to cut him off quickly.

"I promise whatever it was, it'll never happen again." He stumbled closer and drew his face next to hers, trying to kiss her cheek.

Lily stepped back, eyes watering from the whiskey fumes on his breath. She hated these kinds of scenes.

He straightened, took off his baseball cap and began twisting it between his hands. "I couldn't believe it when I got your message. Thanks for giving me a second chance."

"Message? I didn't send you any message." Her sympathy vanished. Stupid drunk. What a lame pretext to make a play at her again. "For the last time, Gary, I'm not interested anymore. Let's leave it at that."

He flushed. "I can't believe this. I thought you wanted to get back together but you're so..." he waved a hand in the air "...so cold-acting."

Lily shrugged. "Move on. I have."

Gary rocked unsteadily on his heels, as if she had struck him. "But...I broke up with Wanda to see you."

Jet stepped in front of him. "You heard her. Time to move on." She laid a hand on his arm and pulled him forward.

"I'm not going anywhere." Gary jerked his arm back and glared at Lily. "Not until she explains why she's playing games."

Lily crossed her arms. "I'm not playing and I don't like *your* game." Despite the show of bravado, Lily's stomach fluttered. Had someone—Twyla—set this up to cause trouble?

Opal stood and placed a hand on Gary's arm, trying to ease the confrontation. "This is obviously not working out. Maybe you and Wanda can get back together."

"But I want Lily," he insisted like a two-year-old denied his favorite toy. He advanced toward the object of his desire.

"Oh, no, you don't." Jet clamped an arm on him and yanked. "Time to go."

"No, I don't want— Hey, you're strong."

Lily almost laughed at his stunned expression. Jet, with her rare blue mer-clan bloodline, had the strength of two men. Too bad they didn't share a paternal parentage. The physicality could come in handy.

Jet pushed him out the door hard enough that he fell on his ass. Gary shook his head as if to clear his mind, obviously stunned he'd been manhandled by a woman. Jet locked the door behind him and pulled down the shades.

"Wow." Opal pressed her fingers into Jet's biceps. "You've got muscles."

"Um…yeah. I work out a lot." Jet went back to the desk and resumed working, head bent over the figures.

"Do you get that a lot from old boyfriends?" Opal asked. "Must be scary."

"Sometimes. He was more forceful than most."

Opal clutched the plastic cape closer to her body. "Twyla might have done it to piss you off."

"Maybe. You think so?"

"Sure. Could be a warning for you to cool it with the men awhile."

Lily studied Opal's blue eyes. They were shot through with alarm. Nice to have someone outside of family actually give a damn.

"You could be right." Lily lifted her chin. "But my interest isn't with a local man right now. That should keep me safe."

"Really? I wouldn't be so sure." Opal absently ran an index finger over the scar on her cheek. "If I were you, I wouldn't see anyone for a few weeks. Let everything cool down a bit."

Lily lifted her chin. "No way. Nash will be gone by then."

"Okay, ignore the warning signs. I just don't want to see you get hurt." She crossed her legs and folded her hands in her lap. "Your decision."

Chapter 6

The red moon of August lay low and full, as if scorched and swollen from summer's heat. Lily's step skipped in time to the rhythm of her rapid pulse. It seemed like it'd been three weeks instead of three days since she'd seen Nash. She grinned at the sight of his truck and the light in the cabin. Even better, Sam Bowman's vehicle was gone. She rapped at the door, feeling like the wolf descending on the innocent Little Red Riding Hood.

The door flung open and she was eye level to Nash's bare chest. She looked up and stared into verdant green. He registered no surprise at finding her on his doorstep. Casually, he leaned an arm against the doorframe.

"You again," he said, voice tinged with smoke and velvet.

The low, deep timbre of sound vibration made her gut clench. Is that what her voice did to men? It was wonderfully disturbing.

"What kind of welcome is that?" she purred, reaching up and laying a hand on the curve of his jaw.

Nash stepped away from the heat of their touch and waved her inside. He shut the door behind her, and Lily was struck by the fact they were alone and sheltered from the world. A cozy company of two. Without a word, Nash walked into the den, snatched a T-shirt from the back of a chair and pulled it over his head.

Darn it.

"Why are you here, Lily?" he asked, plopping down on the sofa.

She sat across from him and crossed her legs demurely. "To see you, of course."

"What do you want from me? I get the feeling it's not to resume a childhood friendship."

She leaned into him, resting her hands on his bare knees. "Don't you find me attractive?" Her lips curled upward, certain of his answer.

"You'll do, I suppose," he said drily.

Lily straightened. "Why are you so hostile? I thought after our kiss we were on more…friendly terms."

He frowned. "You know I'll be leaving in a few weeks. I'm not the settling-down type."

But that's because you haven't known me. "So you say."

He crossed his arms, studying her. "I'm not in the market for a permanent relationship."

"Don't flatter yourself, Nashoba Bowman. You haven't heard me say I want anything of the kind."

"Then that leads back to my original question. What do you want?"

You. I want you. "While you're here, let's see what happens," she answered carefully. After what had happened with his past two girlfriends, she didn't want to push too hard and scare him away. "Look, you used to be my best friend. Can't we at least be friends now and explore if something else is there for however long you're here?"

His mouth twisted. "Friends with benefits?"

"Ouch. Sounds crude when you put it like that." That hurt, although given her reputation, most would doubt she'd be insulted by such an offer.

"Do you think so little of yourself you're willing to do that?"

Lily jumped up. "According to you, my problem is that I think too highly of myself, not too little. Maybe the problem here is that you're a coward. You think because of what happened in the past—"

"What do you know of my past?" He rose and glared down at her, body crackling with tension.

Oops. Best to let him tell it in his own way and in his own time. "I'm assuming something traumatic happened because of the way you act." She paused expectantly. There—she'd provided him the perfect opening.

He said nothing.

"And also because you once told me you were poison."

"The past is dead and buried."

Lily shook her head. "No, it's not. It haunts you like a ghost. Might as well have a white veil over your eyes. It clouds everything you see—and don't see."

Nash walked to the back window and looked outside. "The things I don't see," he muttered, stuffing his hands into his pockets. "Ghosts, huh?" He rubbed his chin. "Ghosts and mermaids."

Lily's stomach flopped like a fish at the conversation switch. "Mermaids?"

"According to my grandfather, there's an old Choctaw legend that people live undersea in the bayou swamps. He believes it, of course."

"Why?" Her voice was so faint, Nash didn't hear. Lily cleared her throat and spoke louder. "Has he ever seen one?"

Nash snorted and strolled back toward her, most of the former tension gone. "I can do you one better than that.

He claims I *am* one. A distant relative of the undersea white people."

Lily gripped the sofa arm. All went dark and her peripheral vision narrowed. The only light in the opaque pitch was the green rim of Nash's eyes; otherwise she was immersed in the black hole of his pupils. The leaf-green grew darker and all that remained was an awareness of being anchored by a sudden, strong grasp on both sides of her waist.

"Lily?"

The sound echoed around her brain, as if it came from some deep-sea abyss.

"Come back to me."

Oxygen and lightness whooshed back into her body, as if diving upward to the sun, breeching the surface with the speed of a dolphin.

Nash held her. Lily laid her head against his chest, closed her eyes and breathed in his scent of clean earth. The steady, strong pound of his heart hammered like a sonic boom against her ear. *Thump thump. Thump thump. I am here. I am here.*

Lily's arms folded to his back, palms pressed into the ridge of his spinal column. Sanctuary. Haven. Home.

Time warped to snail speed like an alternate dimension or a dream where every motion, every inhalation slowed enough that every detail heightened. The warmth of his skin through the cotton fabric, the scent of musk and sandalwood, the ridge of one of his nipples against her cheek. She wanted to feel the fire of his lips, explore his mouth and lick the salty taste of his skin. Lily lifted her head, half opened her eyes, then swiftly closed them again as his head bent toward her.

His lips kissed her forehead. Even with that chaste contact, his mouth imprinted heat.

Nash inched away and moved his arms from her waist

to her elbows. "What happened to you there? I was afraid you would fall off the couch before I reached you."

For once, a quick lie didn't present itself to Lily. "I'm not sure."

"How long since you've eaten anything?"

She scrunched her forehead. "I skipped lunch today, so it's been hours."

"I'd offer you something here, but I'm a lousy cook. Traveling like I do means eating out most meals. So let's go grab a bite somewhere. If you're up to it."

"What about your grandfather? Shouldn't we invite him?"

"He's in Mobile at a pow-wow. Goes at least four times a year and meets up with his old cronies."

Lily smiled as her strength returned. "So just the two of us. Like a real date?"

"You never give up, woman." His tone was mock-severe, lips twitching at the corners.

"Not when I see something I want," she agreed, dead serious.

The concern and camaraderie in his eyes shuttered. "Friends," he said harshly. "That's all I have to offer."

"It's a start. I'll take it."

Thirty minutes later, they were seated at a local diner. On the way over, she'd dropped her car off at home and continued to the restaurant with Nash. Lily ordered her usual shrimp cocktail and delicately nibbled on it as he cut into a huge porterhouse steak. She'd tried her best to coax Nash into going to Mobile for dinner, but he'd insisted she needed food in her system fast.

Lily glanced uneasily at a pack of men at the bar. Gary was there, slinging back whiskey with his buds. Her ex kept looking over and muttering something to his friends. They all stared at her, smirking. And, damn, looked like most were former boyfriends.

Between the guys at the bar and every woman making eyes at Nash, it felt as if a giant spotlight shone on the two of them. Too late, she wished they'd made do with a sandwich at the cabin.

Lily pretended not to notice the attention. "Tell me more about the Okwa Nahollo," she said, determined to learn more about the Choctaw legend. She'd have to ask Mom if she'd ever heard of it, too.

"Not that much more to tell. Grandfather said if you swam near their home, they'd grab you by the ankles and pull you under. If you stayed underwater with them more than three days, you could never return to land."

Fascinating. "So you would become one of the undersea people?"

"He didn't say. I suspect the story was told to keep children from swimming too far from home, unsupervised by their elders."

"Maybe." Lily hesitated on how to proceed, recalling how touchy Nash had become in the grocery store when she'd mentioned his unusual affinity with animals. But curiosity won out. If she wanted to know more about Nash and pursue his ability to resist her siren's call, this could be important. "Don't get hypersensitive on me, but I wonder if you're discounting the story too easily. There are plenty of unexplainable things in the world. We both know you have some kind of unearthly connection to animals."

Nash set down his fork and knife. "I don't know what you're talking about."

"Sure you do," Lily said brightly, ignoring his denial. "When we were young, you could summon birds and foxes and raccoons."

"I never told you I could do that."

"You didn't have to. I saw it for myself. Whenever we walked together, you'd tell me some Choctaw lore about an animal and within minutes one would appear. And they didn't display the normal wariness of a wild creature. They were as tame and domesticated as a dog."

"Coincidence."

"No."

His eyes were malachite-dark and hard as the stone, but Lily steeled her own sea-blue eyes and didn't back down.

Nash took a swallow of whiskey and Coke and set it down so sharply the liquid precariously sloshed near the rim, like a tidal wave about to engulf a beach. "What is it about this bayou? Do you all believe there's something supernatural happening here? That it's perfectly acceptable?"

"Yes," she answered immediately.

Nash picked up the knife and fork and resumed cutting his steak. "Okay, tell me some local legends."

Lily twisted a lock of hair, frustrated at his refusal to open up. Maybe later, in a not-so-public place, she could coax some revelations. For now, she'd play along with his conversational detour. "Well, there's your usual assortment of haints and—"

"Haints?"

"Ghosts. I can't believe you haven't heard that word before. Anyway, there's also the requisite voodoo priestess, or witch, named Tia Henrietta. People seek her all the time to read their fortune, concoct a love potion—stuff like that." She really should make time to visit Henrietta and tell her about the coyote and the phone calls.

Nash grinned. "Have you had this witch make you a love potion?"

Lily bit back a snort. "Never needed it." She waited a heartbeat. "Until now."

Nash ignored the jibe. "What about mermaids? Are there other tales about them down here?"

If you only knew. "Oh, there are plenty of legends. The town was even named after them. Bayou La Siryna— *Siryna* meaning *siren*."

"I assumed *Siryna* was a woman's name."

Lily considered her words. Should she tell him more? Give credence to the Choctaw lore? Shelly and Jet had both found human males who accepted their mer-nature. Maybe Nash could as well one day. And if there was a possibility, she could prepare the way now.

"I wouldn't say mermaids don't exist," she began. "Earth is ninety-five percent covered in water and humans have yet to explore its deepest depths. Who are we to say what lives in its depths? Our ancestors used to believe in them—as much as modern people speculate on UFOs and alien life from other planets."

Nash wasn't buying it. "I'm more prone to believe in aliens than mermaids myself."

"Mermaids are as plausible as other things, like the Choctaw legends of little people or shamans who see spirits," she argued.

He drummed his fingers along the tabletop and regarded her thoughtfully. "Grandfather is a shaman."

"He is? I never knew." Lily's respect for Sam Bowman rose even higher.

"He mostly keeps it to himself. But there were several occasions when I saw others come to the cabin for a cure."

"How does it work?" Lily made a mental note to mention this to Jet in case there was any trouble with her pregnancy or childbirth. "What does he do exactly?"

"He asks the spirits to restore a person's spiritual power for healing. He merely serves as a link between the seen and the unseen."

"That's so cool. Do the spirits always help?"

"As far as I know. He says every person is surrounded by animated human, plant and animal spirits. But some are easier to contact than others. If he's having difficulty connecting, he'll drum and chant. Sometimes the cure is instant, and sometimes it takes days—but I've never known him to fail."

"You've seen him do it?"

"Many times." He gave a sheepish grin. "He's even used it with me. Anytime I came down with a cold or virus, grandfather would zap it right out of me."

She tried to imagine what that would feel like. "Does it hurt, or is it an immediate kind of relief?"

Nash shrugged. "It doesn't hurt. But immediate relief? I'm not sure. Grandfather always did it at night, right before bedtime. The process relaxed me so much I'd fall asleep almost at once. When I woke up the next day, I wouldn't be sick."

"There you go," Lily said triumphantly. "With a grandfather like that, you should keep an open mind about *everything*."

"I try to. But some things are too preposterous." He shook his head and dug into his steak.

"Doesn't make it any less real." Lily set aside what remained of the shrimp cocktail. "How can you draw a line once you've admitted there are spirits and circumstances beyond what the rational mind can see?"

He took another slug of his drink. "You're probably right. I was disrespectful when he told me of the Okwa Naholло. I'm arrogant at times, but not so arrogant as to think I know everything."

Lily took heart at his words. "Keep an open mind," she urged. Despite all his warnings about not being in the bayou long, Lily couldn't help feeling encouraged that he might one day accept her shape-shifting. Besides, there was mystery about him as well. "Can't help noticing you neatly sidestepped the issue of your own powers. That stuff must run in your family."

Nash said nothing and ate his steak in silence. She'd pushed him enough for one night. Once he got to know her better, maybe she'd gain his trust and he'd open up about his gifts and his past.

"By the way, I buried that coyote. It did have rabies."

Lily shuddered, remembering the yellow-brown predatory eyes. If besieged undersea, she had the advantage of speed over most other creatures, except dolphins, which were friends anyway. But with human legs, the coyote could have easily overtaken her. "That reminds me of Sam's warning. Since your grandfather sees things, should I be worried someone's deceiving me?"

"Maybe. You had any more trouble with Twyla?"

She debated telling him about the hang-up calls, reluctant to sound like an alarmist. But if she hoped to gain his trust, she'd have to be a little more forthright herself.

"For several days I've had a string of phone calls where the person hangs up as soon as I answer."

Knife and fork slipped from his hands and clattered on the plate. "Harassing calls," he said slowly. His lips pursed to a fine line.

Lily wondered at his extreme reaction. "Could be kids making prank calls." Out of the corner of her eye, she saw Gary teetering off the bar stool. His posse stared straight at her, smirking.

"Coincidence," Nash muttered. "Has to be."

All her attention was on Gary. A trickle of sweat ran down her cleavage. Holy smokes, the guy was going to make another scene. Lily licked her dry lips. Should she make a mad dash to the ladies' room?

Fight or flight. Sink or swim.

She felt trapped like a caged rabbit. Gary headed over to where they were sitting. Nash scowled, deep in his own thoughts, unaware of the oncoming disaster.

No way to avoid trouble. Lily desperately sought a way to minimize the damage. Too late—or early, as it were—to call the waitress for their ticket and make a quick exit. Only one thing left to do. Lily lurched to her feet, hoping to head Gary off at the pass. She'd put her hand on his arm and talk sweet nothings to calm him until she and Nash could exit the restaurant. She'd even beg, promise Gary a date later to prevent him from ruining everything with Nash.

"Hey there, Lily-Gily girl," he slurred. "Who you with this time?" He stopped at their table and sniggered at Nash. "Well, hello there, Chief."

Lily gasped at the insult.

Nash rose slowly. "Go away," he said in a low, calm voice.

Knowing it was too late to stop the inevitable, Lily sat.

Gary pointed at Nash's whiskey glass. "Shouldn't be drinking that there firewater, Chief. Will make you a Heap Big Drunk."

Much snickering erupted from his friends at the bar and Lily glared their way. She'd expected to be the one insulted, not Nash.

Nash raised an eyebrow at Gary. "I can handle my liquor. Unlike you and your friends." He raised his glass and took a long swallow with a steady hand.

Gary switched tactics. "Got me there, Chief. Word to the wise, though, about your *date*." He spit out the word as if he'd swallowed tainted moonshine. "She's used goods. Probably every guy in this town has had Lily. And I do mean in the biblical sense."

Nash rose slowly to his feet and spoke in a low, deep voice. "Please go."

Gary opened and closed his mouth as if to speak again, but thought better of it. Something in Nash's eyes and still posture must have penetrated his beer-sodden brain. He held up both hands. "No problem, Chief." With an exaggerated swagger, Gary made his way back to the bar.

Lily stiffened in her chair and snuck a peak at the other restaurant patrons. Most were busy eating, but she caught a glimpse of Twyla at a back table. Her arm rested on the shoulder of her toddler and J.P. was by her side. Twyla stared at her intently. Lily had expected a smirk, but Twyla's face was tight and her eyes sharp with pity.

But that couldn't be right. To hell with anyone's pity. She was Lily Bosarge, the great siren of the seas.

Nash sat down and she studied his stoic face.

"Sorry about that," she mumbled, fiddling with her napkin.

"No need to apologize. You've done nothing wrong." Nash calmly picked up his knife and fork and resumed eating his steak.

Respect and gratitude swept through Lily like a wave. Nash's dignity had been a powerful weapon against Gary's mean stupidity. She wanted to signal the waitress and escape, but she followed his lead. No sense giving Gary or anyone else the satisfaction of believing such lowness had disturbed their date. Lily took a bite of shrimp, digging in with gusto.

They spoke little, as if by mutual pact. At long last, they finished and exited the diner with a deliberate grace. The ride home was also quiet and Lily's stomach churned, wondering what he thought of her in light of Gary's insults.

He pulled into her driveway and turned off the motor. The ping of the heated engine clattered in the dark night.

"Gary's an asshole," she blurted out. "I have *not* been with every man in the bayou."

Nash shrugged. "Wouldn't matter to me if you had. I've had more than my share of women. Way more."

An unexpected tightening in her chest surprised Lily. So this was how jealousy felt. Best not to let Nash see it mattered.

"Rumors of my promiscuity are greatly exaggerated," she continued. "I don't want you to get the wrong idea about me.'

"Like I said, it doesn't matter."

Lily cleared her dry throat. "Okay, then. Want to come in for a drink?"

Nash strummed his fingers on the dashboard, as if debating. "Why not?" he answered in a rush. "Been some kind of evening."

They walked to the darkened house. Strange, she usually kept the porch light on because returning to an empty, dark home was depressing. She missed Jet and Shelly more than she'd ever anticipated. Lily fished out her keys and opened the door. In the entry, she flicked on the light switch and frowned.

"Something wrong?" Nash asked.

"I'm not sure." Nothing appeared out of place, but the energy in the house felt...altered. That brush Shelly had had with a serial killer last year was making her paranoid, that's all. And that coyote stalking hadn't helped her peace of mind either. *Nothing's wrong.*

Yet Lily couldn't shake off the feeling someone had been in the house. She turned on the kitchen chandelier. Everything was as she'd left it earlier this afternoon. Lily hugged her chilled arms.

Nash pulled her to him. "What is it?"

She shook her head. "Nothing." Telling the truth would make him think she was nuts. Bad enough Gary had planted the notion in his head she was slutty. "How about a glass of Moscato? Or would you prefer a beer?"

"Whatever you're drinking is fine."

Lily pointed to the den. "Go have a seat and I'll bring it to you."

She found the wine bottle in the refrigerator and poured some into two antique crystal glasses as she admired the dancing of light in the pale citrine liquid. The fruity aroma tantalized, and she took a sip and closed her eyes, savoring the shot of jeweled ambrosia as it warmed her stomach. Another sip and the unease evaporated like fog in daylight. Nash waited in the den and she intended to get to know him better—in every way.

"It's as I remembered," Nash commented as she entered the den. He stood before an opened curio cabinet, running his fingers along a rare pottery vase. "Enough collectibles here to fill a small museum. As a kid, I imagined this place as a pirate's secret cache for his stash of treasures."

A fitting description. "Is that so?"

Nash closed the cabinet door and moved to the mantel, festooned with marine astrolabes positioned below a collection of antique swords. "Very cool." He examined one of the brass instruments and set it back on the mantel. "Your home's a stark contrast to my grandfather's cabin."

"But his is charming in its own way. Minimalistic without being stark." She hadn't considered the differences before. The ornate style of the Bosarge Victorian home, with its plethora of plundered goodies, jasmine scent and overall feminine vibe, was a counterpoint to the Bowman utilitarian aesthetic. The cabin was woodsy, everything in it had a purpose, and it held the faint, unique smell of burnt sage from smudging rituals to ward off sickness and negative energy.

Yin and yang.

Lily held out the wineglass. Their fingers touched against the delicate stemware as he took the drink, sending Lily longing for more intimacy.

Nash raised his glass for a toast. "To friendship." Green eyes bore into her, his expression intense but unfathomable.

"I want…" Her voice trailed off, afraid to give voice to her wish only to have it rebuffed once more. She took a deep breath. "I want more."

"More of what? This?" He leaned into her and kissed her, his lips hot and pressing, full of passion and promise.

Anxiety fisted through desire and Lily pulled away.

"Did you reconsider seeing me because of what Gary said tonight?"

Nash cocked his head to the side. "I'm not following you."

Geez, he was going to make her say it. "You figured I would be...you know, easy. Easy to have and easy to leave." Not that her bold overtures to Nash contradicted anything Gary had said, but her former boyfriend's words made everything appear cheap and ugly.

With Nash it will be special, she vowed.

"Hell, no. I don't think you're easy," he growled. "I can't believe you'd say that." His face softened. "C'mon, Lily. You were the first girl I ever kissed, my childhood friend. I would never think badly of you."

The tight tangle of her heart loosened. "Really?" she whispered.

"Really." Very deliberately, Nash took the wineglass out of her hand and set his and hers both down on the coffee table. Time thickened, grew heavy, as if the weight of air pressed down, making every movement languid and deliberate. Nash faced her and pulled her body alongside his own. His eyes lowered to her mouth and he cupped her cheeks with calloused hands. Ever so slowly, he leaned down to join their lips.

The kiss was sensuous and steamy with a touch of gentle wonder. Lily twined her arms around his neck, reveling in his closeness. Nash's mouth opened and she tasted a combination of citrus, peach and apricots from the Moscato. Her body felt as liquid and weightless as if she were afloat at sea. His arms wrapped around the small of her back, pressing—an anchor in the maelstrom of desire.

Nash withdrew and leaned his forehead against hers. Their deep breaths mingled and merged as one. Passion ebbed, replaced by an undertow of tenderness, like an unspoken prayer.

She'd never come close to a kiss such as this, although with each new man she'd been searching, always hopeful.

Nash straightened. "I should go."

Lily opened her mouth to tell him to stay, but thought better of it. He liked and respected her—why ruin it tonight with sex? The timing was wrong. It might reinforce Gary's accusations, despite Nash's claim to the contrary. She wanted his respect, wanted his opinion of her to be different from everyone else's in the bayou.

She squeezed his hand. "Yes. It might be for the best." They strolled to the entrance, holding hands. If Nash was disappointed at her quick agreement, he didn't show it.

At the door, he placed a quick kiss on her mouth.

"Soon," he whispered, his tone as hot and dusty as the bayou breeze.

Oh, I hope so.

He stepped into the night, olive skin and black hair blending to near invisibility. Lily hugged her arms and shivered, bereft with loneliness. The empty house mocked with a sullen silence. She craved the sea and its teeming life, from the smallest plankton to the great white whale; it afforded a measure of companionship. As a remedy for the loneliness and thwarted physical release, Lily had an even better coping strategy than a cold shower.

Time for a swim.

Chapter 7

Water swaddled Lily's body like liquid silk, a lush weight of peaceful suspension to douse the fevered need of desire Nash left behind. More than physical, the aching need inside sought communion with him on every plane, a complete opening, an illuminating light on all her secrets. A plunge together through a dark labyrinth where she hid unvoiced wishes and insecurities in secret passageways.

The idea of such intimacy both terrified and excited.

Lily navigated through an undersea field of sea-grass roots whose long tendrils swirled like locks of curly hair in the wind. The roots stroked her body in a passing caress, unbidden but welcome. She swam deeper, eyes accommodating to the velvet darkness. Nictating membranes, that useless pink clump in the corner of human eyes, spread over Lily's delicate exposed eye tissue. What was merely an unused, evolutionary holdover in humans served as protection against salt and debris while undersea.

She flipped and rolled in the water—mermaid dancing—

a spontaneous celebration after shape-shifting from land to sea. Hope kicked in, an unexpected guest in Lily's heart. She could fall in love with Nash. Really, *really* give herself over to another person. If Shelly and Jet could do it, why not her?

Love happened. Even for mermaids.

She hadn't known how lonely she was. Solitary swims, days and nights at a time with nothing but canvas and acrylics for company.

She hadn't known her childhood friend would return in a grown-man version that would quicken her heart with hope.

She hadn't known what it felt like to have no control of her emotions with a man. She'd always been the one that set the parameters in every affair.

Until Nash.

Bubbling joy could no longer be contained and her lungs opened. Lily sang. Glorious, magical notes that carried for miles in the currents. The reverberating vibrations of harmony attracted swarms of silver fish that encircled her body like a living metal gyroscope. Lily reveled in the kinship. She'd devoted so much time lately to painting that undersea time had suffered. So she danced, tail fin glittering like emeralds and diamonds and sapphires afire. And she kept singing—deeply, freely, uninhibited.

Tired at length, Lily relaxed and let the undertow pull her where it willed. Half-awake, half-asleep, she drifted like flotsam atop a wave. Healing salt water swished an eternal echo in her ears like a lullaby.

A disturbance in vibrational pattern put Lily on alert and she cupped a hand to an ear. Something large would be in range momentarily. A curious dolphin, or hungry shark? Friend or foe?

Faint humming notes wavered through sea static. Was it— Could it be? Yes, she recognized the sound pattern.

Lily began singing an old haunting melody that was one of her mother's favorites.

Adriana Bosarge cut in at once. "Lily! Over here," she called.

Lily homed in on the location and swam toward her mother, tail fin swishing eagerly. Mom was a pain at times, but she still loved her. Thanks to Jet's heads-up on the impending visit, she'd mentally prepared herself as much as possible. Through a series of hums and whistles mixed with her bio-sonar ability, Lily altered her course in a mermaid version of Marco Polo.

At last she caught site of her swimming alongside a school of speckled trout. Mom's multicolored hair streamed behind her like a paler version of her sparkling tail fin. Lily had inherited similar coloring, but Adriana was bolder, more striking. Where Lily was ethereal and angelic with delicate facial features, Adriana's cheekbones were prominent, displaying a larger nose and a more squared jawline that hinted at her formidable personality. A kind of beauty most often described as "handsome" or "arresting."

Lily mentally catalogued the image of her mom for a future painting. Of course, that particular piece would forever remain in her own private collection. But art wasn't always about public selling or trading; it was about private satisfaction and creative expression.

Adriana swam closer and rubbed her tail fin against Lily's in an affectionate mer-greeting. "You look bewitching as usual," she stated in a prideful tone, as if taking credit for the fact. "And that bewitching siren voice is absolutely wasted out here in the bayou."

A new record. Less than thirty seconds, and Mom had delivered the first jab in her ongoing campaign for Lily's return to sea.

"Not wasted. I've snagged my fair share of men."

Adriana snorted, sending a bubbling stream upward.

"Human men. You need to mate with your own kind. Do your duty."

Annoyance, along with a smidgeon of guilt, rippled through Lily. Their race was dwindling, in no small part because of past inbreeding with humans. Increasingly, the merfolk frowned on mating with humans, and those who did were partially ostracized for not procreating the mer population. Shelly and Jet had both experienced that alienation.

"Mom, please. Can you give it a rest? At least for one day?"

"Humph." Adriana swept past her, chin lifted.

Lily sighed and darted ahead. "C'mon, Mom. I'm not ready to have children and stay at sea forever."

"You're almost thirty."

"Give me some more time."

"You say that every visit."

"It's different now." Lily laid a hand on her arm. "I've met someone special."

"Heard that before, too."

Lily winced. "I mean it this time. It's Nashoba Bowman. You remember him, don't you?"

Adriana tapped her lips. "Ah, yes, the little Indian boy."

"Native American." Lily barely refrained an eye roll. At her mom's questioning look, she added, "We don't say *Indian* these days. And Nash is no longer a little boy." She couldn't hide a smile, recalling the taste of his kiss and the heat of his body pressed against hers.

Adriana resumed swimming, and Lily fell in beside her. Why couldn't her mother understand her longing for true love? True, her boyfriend track record was lousy, but she wasn't ready to give up on human males and settle for the male mermen with their wanderlust and a limited interest in monogamy.

They passed a rock outcropping, a familiar landmark

signaling they were close to home. She glanced at her mom's face but couldn't judge her mood. "You always liked Nash when we were children," Lily ventured. She'd rather hash this out now, and talking undersea was easier—freer somehow.

"That doesn't mean he's suitable for pair-bonding. You'll tire of him like you have all the other human males."

"Not this time. He doesn't care for my singing and he hasn't stumbled all over his land-legger feet to date me. I've been the one chasing him."

Adriana stopped swimming and her long locks of silver-blond hair floated around her torso like a cluster of glowing stars. "Impossible."

"It's true. I can't figure it out. Do you have any ideas?"

"The degree of a human male's response to your voice varies depending on how much merblood runs through his veins. The more distant, the greater the attraction."

"His grandfather claims they're related to the undersea pale people. Have you ever met Sam Bowman?"

"I don't think so." She tilted her head to the side. "I was aware the Choctaws had a legend about our kind. Although that's hardly surprising. Most countries and cultures do."

"But how much merblood could be in Nash? If his parents or grandparents were mer, we'd have surely seen or heard them undersea."

Adriana tapped a forefinger on her chin, musing. "There's only one explanation for a human male not being entranced by your singing. I've only heard tell of this happening once before to a siren." She looked into the distance, silent and absorbed.

"Come on, tell me," Lily urged.

"Nash doesn't just have merblood. He's a descendent of a male siren. As such, he's immune to the siren's lure himself."

Lily's nictating membrane blinked for several heartbeats. She recalled all the women vying for his attention wherever they went, Opal's hints that Nash had tossed aside many lovers, the deep timbre of his voice. Of course. "And he doesn't even know what he is," she murmured.

"No reason he should ever suspect," Adriana said. She eyed Lily sharply. "Forget him. Mate with a pure merman and spawn me grandchildren." She resumed swimming, signaling she was done with the subject.

Grandchildren. Is that what this was really about? Lily swam alongside her. "Jet's about to have a baby. Shelly plans on having children, too, eventually. You'll have plenty of grandchildren."

"And not a pure-blooded one will be among them."

Lily's tail twitched. "Kinda harsh, Mom."

"I don't mean to be. You know I love Jet and Shelly. But *you're* my only biological daughter, and the pure merblood numbers drop every year."

"You're becoming a zealot in your old age." Lily said it with a smile that contrasted with her stiff spine and fisted hands. No sense bumping tail fins tonight. Maybe when her mother met Nash again she'd mellow on the issue and yield to allow her daughter happiness.

Adriana fiddled with her pearl bracelets, which Lily recognized as a sure sign of her annoyance. "You've spent so much time in Bayou La Siryna you forget how rigid mer society has become on interspecies mating."

Ugh, interspecies mating. Her Mom made it sound vulgar and clinical at the same time. Lily's smile strained at the edges. "How long are you planning on staying?"

"Oh, I don't know. Perhaps until Jet's baby arrives."

Holy Neptune, this was going to be a long visit.

Nash's senses opened in a way they never had before. He felt summer down deep in his bones. So deep, the marrow tingled and pulsated with heat and light, a contrast

from the winter's dead darkness. It had never been this
intense before. Each day in the bayou he drew closer to
the land and wildlife.

Today was well-earned time off from work at the island
and he'd invited Lily to his grandfather's cabin for a hike.
The three days he hadn't seen Lily seemed like forever.

Nash held back a low branch for Lily. Desire as rabid as
a stag in heat fevered his skin where she brushed against
his forearm. They had hiked this trail hundreds of times
as kids, but this heightened awareness between them was
an entirely different sensation.

Each time he saw Lily, she appeared more beautiful,
more irresistible. He feared she would end up hurt when
this assignment was over and he left, but being apart was
unbearable. The island lodge was lonely and too quiet,
especially now that Opal had left for another assignment.

Lily caught his gaze, eyes widening at the desire that
must be written all over his face. They leaned in for the
day's first kiss.

Caw, caw, kow-caw. The sudden shrill bark of a crow,
accompanied by the flapping of feathers, swooped overhead.

Lily laughed. "It's as if he disapproves. I feel chided,
like I was caught pulling down my pants in town square."

The image of her naked had Nash pulling her roughly
against his body. He planted a hard, quick kiss against
Lily's lips, a promise of more to come. They continued
onward until they came to a clearing. In the center was
"their" place from old times—the base of a felled oak
whose surface provided enough space for them to both sit
on it cross-legged.

He used to bring Lily here and retell his grandfather's
wilder stories—tales of the tiny forest dwellers and the
dark spirit of Nalusa Falaya, which crept into a person's

soul, causing misery or even death. Lily had been a good
audience, wide-eyed and just younger enough that she regarded him in higher esteem than warranted. She rarely
had stories of her own. Instead, she would sing silly songs
and old-fashioned ballads that he'd found dull. Twelve-
year-old boys cared little for nonsense love songs.

Nash sat first and offered a hand, a gallantry that had
never occurred to him as a boy. Lily placed her hand in
his and he drew her to him as easily as pulling a minnow
out of water.

Caw-caw. A sweep of metallic violet swooshed within
a few feet of their bodies. The crow perched on a nearby
oak branch and cocked his head to the side, studying them.
It raised its bill and cried again, louder.

Caw, caw, caw. You again. You're back.

The crow's words sprouted in the pith of Nash's core;
he could feel the language resonate in his solar plexus like
the echo of a pealing bell. Or as if a long-dormant seed
sprouted in a burst of DNA fusion, a blade of green energy
emerging beneath the soil.

Nash stared into the dark brown eyes of the old crow.
"Yes, I'm back."

"Um, yes. I'm glad you're back." Lily cocked her head
in much the same manner of a bird, studying him with a
quizzical gleam in her eyes.

A rush of flapping erupted from across the field and a
murder of crows flew in, landing on the branches beside
the lone crow.

Caw caw. Long and short chirrups erupted in a cacophony. Nash picked up on the gist of their conversation—*he's
back, the girl with him.*

This was new territory. He'd always sensed things,
guessed at what creatures thought, but this was downright eerie.

Stay in the bayou. Bayou stay, they each shrilled in a thunder of sound.

Could they understand his speech as well? "I'm only here for a visit," he said aloud.

Lily sighed. "I know, I know. You've made that clear. As soon as your latest project is finished, you'll be jet-setting to some other corner of the world." She settled gracefully on the oak stump, tucking her long, pale legs beneath her. "How are the bird photos going?"

Nash eyed the crows warily. "Fine. I'm homing in on their secret mating and nesting sites. Those clappers are surprisingly cagey."

"Can't blame them for seeking privacy. If I were them—" She raised a hand over her forehead, squinting. "What are those crows squawking about?"

"How should I know?" Nash snapped. "Sorry," he said at the startled hurt in her eyes.

Lily's hair billowed in the breeze and he brushed back a stray lock from her face. The midday sun emphasized subtle highlights of pink and lavender blended among the blond waves. Nash caressed a handful, admiring the softness against his calloused palms. "It's like cotton candy."

She laughed. "Are you saying it's dried out?"

"No. I'm talking about the colors."

"Oh, that's the miracle of hair dye."

The crows kicked up again. *Caw—ca-caw. She's not of us. Not of us.*

Nash looked up at the tree. "What do you mean?"

Lily tugged his shirt. "What's wrong with you today? You're acting strange."

"Just distracted." If she only knew. He could hardly believe it himself. What would happen if he stayed in the bayou more than a couple of months? How much more attuned to nature could he become? Nash forced himself to ignore the crows' clatter.

"A man's attention has never been a problem for me before." The petulant words were delivered with a grin and held no rancor. She laid a warm hand on his bare knee and beads from her bracelet rubbed his skin.

The bracelet jolted a memory. "I can't believe you wear that old thing." He ran a finger along the beads that had faded over the years. A few of them were missing. The frayed fringe ties were knotted at her slender wrist. It was out of place next to her jeweled, expensive rings and thin gold bangles.

A rose glow lit her face. "It's special, a memory of our last summer."

"I remember." They'd been here, at this very spot. Grandfather had helped him string the beads, although the workmanship on his part was still clumsy.

"You said we'd be friends forever," Lily whispered. She touched the beads. "Sad to say, you're the only true friend I've ever had. Outside of family."

"Oh, come on. That can't be true." Their fingers entwined above the bracelet.

"It is true. You've seen the way women act around me. And the men…" Her voice trailed off in an unhappy sigh.

"Jealous bitches, every last one," he said quickly. "As far as the men, well, understandable that you make them a little crazy." He shifted uncomfortably, guilt arrowing him in the gut. He was as bad as the rest of them. Over the years, he'd been careless and selfish in his affections. Until the deaths of Rebecca and Connie had filled him with shame and regret.

Nash looked up at the crows that stared back with dark, otherworldly eyes. Silent at last, he imagined they judged him for past sins.

"I don't mean to make the men crazy," Lily said. "It… just happens."

One crow flew closer and perched on a nearby limb. Its eyes were blue, indicating youth. *Caw-caw-caw-caw. She is not like us. She is of two spirits.*

Nash leapt to his feet and waved his arms. "Get out of here!"

The crow flapped its wings. *Caw. Ask her.*

"I said get out. Now."

The crow dipped its head, revealing faint blue speckles on its crown. Suddenly, it took flight, the rest of the murder following in its lead.

Two spirits. Not of us, they cawed.

"Weird," Lily said. "It was as if that crow was trying to tell you something."

He turned slowly to face her. What would she think if…

"Was it?"

"Was it what?" he repeated stupidly.

"That crow. It spoke to you. When you were little, you seemed to sense an animal's feelings. Appears it might even go beyond sensing now, like your telepathy with them has grown."

His mind whirled, as if taking flight with the crows and circling from above. She'd guessed correctly. Did this telepathy expand as he matured, or was it something weird about this bayou? Could be a combination of both.

Lily rose slowly and stepped close, one hand cradling the right side of his neck. "Never mind. You don't have to tell me anything you aren't comfortable sharing. I'll understand."

Nash wavered; the need to talk about his gift was strong, but doing so would be another bond with Lily and she would be hurt even more when he left. Rebecca's and Connie's faces appeared in his mind. He was toxic to women. It never ended well. He couldn't, wouldn't contaminate her with a lengthy relationship. She might already be infected.

Nash removed her hand. "Have you gotten any more harassing phone calls?"

"No. What made you think of that?"

"I need to tell you about the last two women I was involved with."

"Okay." No surprise registered on her face.

"Something tells me you already know the whole story."

"I did hear some talk," she admitted.

So word of his past had followed him even here. "From Opal?" he guessed.

Lily kept silent.

He took a deep breath. "Rebecca and I saw each other whenever I returned from a trip. It was pretty casual on my part, and I thought it was on hers, too. But when she asked for a commitment I balked. She left that night, angry and hurt. The next morning I found out that she'd returned to her apartment and started drinking. A lot." He swallowed. "Then Rebecca got back in her car, drove off the road and hit a tree. Doctors pronounced her DOA."

Lily's lips tightened. "Not your fault. Damn it, Nash, don't you dare blame yourself for her death. It was a tragedy—"

"And then, a year later, there was Connie." Now that he was actually talking about it, he couldn't stop the flow of words. "We'd been dating a few months and I mistakenly thought I'd found a woman who could accept my long trips. But she wanted more and I didn't. Connie ended her own life." His throat felt dry, parched. "Overdose of pills," he ground out past the lump in his throat.

"Oh, Nash. I am so, so sorry." She circled her arms around his waist.

Her body felt smooth, cool, a balm to the burning hurt. But he stood stiffly, fists clenched at his sides. He didn't deserve comfort. If he'd been a better man, more selfless, more cued into another's feelings... But no. His career had always come first and there'd been some part of him that held back, that couldn't see another's needs.

"Don't," Lily whispered fiercely into his chest. "You can't accept responsibility for others' mistakes."

Couldn't he, though? Shouldn't he? He stepped back and held Lily at arm's length. "About those phone calls," he said sternly. "Are you in some kind of danger?"

"Not that I'm aware of. And if someone was upset with me, you can hardly think it has anything to do with you."

"There's more. Before Rebecca died, she had a few hang-up calls. And Connie once said that she felt like someone was following her, although she never saw anyone or had evidence."

"Coincidence," Lily insisted. "Prank calls are common and everyone thinks they've been followed at one time or another." Her tone gentled. "You can't scare me away, Nash. I'm a strong woman."

He wanted to believe Lily. The past few years had been a lonely, hard existence. An affair, however brief, would be a welcome return to some normalcy. Lily seemed lonely herself, a bit of an outcast. But the shrill cry of the crows replayed like an echo of a dream. *Not of us. Two spirits.* What was that about?

Lily made him uneasy. He wanted a nice, normal woman who didn't probe too deep or demand too much.

Nash focused on the problem at hand. First hint of danger and he would leave, whether or not the assignment was finished. To linger might place her in jeopardy. But maybe this time would be safe, a kind of healing for both of them. "You'll tell me if anything weird happens, right? And I mean immediately."

"You'll be the first to know." Lily smiled and took his hand, and Nash clasped it tightly—as if they were taking a high dive off a rocky cliff together.

Another crow flew close by. It didn't utter a sound, but

the flapping of its wings and the glisten of its coal-black eyes were like a warning. Abruptly, Nash dropped Lily's hand. "I'm not ready for this. Something's…not right."

Chapter 8

The warped voice crackled over a phone line so full of static Lily had trouble deciphering the words.

"Stay away from Nash," came the disembodied voice again. It sounded like a recording, the voice so robotic she couldn't determine if it belonged to a male or female.

"How did you get my cell phone number?"

The connection terminated and a buzzing noise filled her ears. Lily sank onto the couch and frowned. She'd had her share of such calls from irate girls while in high school, and even some more sophisticated versions of the same message later in life, but none had rattled her like this.

Nash's former women… What if they hadn't died by accident? Her skin crawled imagining a psycho, an unknown enemy intent on destroying Nash's happiness. *But why?*

"Stay away." Ha! Just as they were so close, about to take their attraction to the next level, Nash had been spooked by a bunch of birds. Birds, damn it. And how was he resisting her siren's voice? She was no closer now than when she'd first seen him at the grocery store. He drove her crazy—why not the other way around?

Lily drummed her long, pointed fingernails on the end table, the sharp clicks a loud staccato in the old Victorian house. For the first time, she wished her mother had stayed here instead of with Jet. Adriana was still in a bit of a snit over her refusal to return to sea and was giving her the old silent treatment.

She remembered how odd the house had felt a few nights ago—as if a lingering smell had been left behind by a stranger. But she'd never found anything out of place and had dismissed the feeling. Now she wasn't so sure. Lily debated how to proceed.

She had two brothers-in-law, one a sheriff and the other a deputy sheriff, but she hated the idea of getting them involved. They'd make a big stink over it and question Nash. And if there was one thing she knew, it was that Nash couldn't know the phone calls were back. He'd leave Bayou La Siryna and she'd never hear from him again.

Which left only one option.

Lily grabbed her purse and, twenty minutes later, arrived at the ramshackle cottage of Tia Henrietta. It was still decrepit but much neater than she remembered from her last visit a couple of years ago. A fresh coat of salmon-pink paint had been slapped on the exterior, complemented with vibrant turquoise shutters at the windows. Bright colored bottles hung from every low-lying branch near the house. A maze of large knickknacks remained at the entrance—conch shells, bowling balls, plastic pink flamingos—but there were less of them and they were arranged with a certain precision that suggested loving care and not random neglect.

She got out of the car, determined to tie Tia down to specifics on who was behind the calls. The woman liked to play it loose and cagey if you let her get away with it.

The screen door creaked open and Tia waved her inside, as if she'd been expecting her visit.

"Got everything already set up for yer questions." Tia's face was solemn and set. No hint of her usual mischievous smile, as if she knew a great secret but couldn't share it.

White candles flickered throughout the small den and old framed pictures of Jesus and various saints aligned the walls, shelves and tables. Dark scents of nutmeg, cloves and cedar wood permeated the air instead of the green herbal smell she remembered from long ago. A card table and two chairs were set up.

"Sit," Tia said, folding her purple sarong underneath as she sat down and shuffled the tarot cards. Bold rings and wooden bangle bracelets clinked as she manipulated the deck. Instead of her usual turban, Tia's hair was covered with a scarf. Deep lines in her face and neck were highlighted by the striated candle glow.

Did the old woman really know why she'd come? Tia had helped her decide to go for her painting dream last time she'd visited, had intuited or pulled out the artistic dreams. She'd even guessed at Lily's hurt over the way people of Bayou La Siryna treated her.

"How did you know to expect me today?" Lily asked, secretly impressed.

Tia frowned, never responding or looking up from the cards. "This time be serious," she said in her accent, a strange mixture that Lily couldn't decide if it was Creole or Gullah or something else all together. She handed the cards to Lily. "Cut the deck."

Lily moved a stack of the colorful cards from the top to the bottom and Tia asked her to select cards as she felt drawn. Lily selected a few and Tia spread them in a Celtic cross design. She flipped the cards over one by one, not commenting.

A humming sounded on the porch, a familiar, soothing rift, followed by the creak of the screen door. A dark waif of a girl slipped into the room with a wicker basket of herbs. She scurried past them singing softly, beguilingly, from the kitchen:

"Sweet little darling, adrift undersea

Float with the current, mamma's with thee

Listen to the echo of the waves

Sleepy, sleepy, all is saved"

A jolt of recognition stirred Lily's memory, turning her skin prickly with surprise. It was a song every mermaid learned at her mother's tail fin. She joined in the mermaid lullaby:

"And when the moon shines way down deep

Baby should sigh and dream, not weep."

The girl stuck her head into the den, mouth agape. "You have the voice of an angel," she said in awe.

Lily stood. "Who are you? How do you know this song?"

The girl paled underneath her olive skin and quickly scurried to the kitchen.

"Don't be so dang bashful, Annie," Tia called out. "Mind yer manners and come back and say hello to company."

Annie entered with slow steps, head down, her long black hair a veil.

"This is my granddaughter, Annie. She's come to stay with me a spell, helpin' with chores and studyin' the ways. Annie, this is Miss Lily Bosarge."

So that explained the spruced-up exterior.

"Hello," Annie mumbled in a soft voice, face still hidden beneath her hair.

"Git you a chair from the kitchen and join us. You need to be learnin' the tarot." Tia leaned toward Lily. "She'll be takin' my place one day. Gotta get her trained."

Clever old lady. Lily sat back down on the metal folding chair. "Don't try to distract me. Tell me how Annie knows that song."

Tia stared back with rheumy eyes; a mysterious smile tugged the edges of her lips.

"Of course," Lily said, snapping her fingers. Those cloudy eyes were from a descending nictating membrane, a common occurrence with elderly merfolk. "You and your granddaughter are one of us. Maybe fifth or sixth generation removed."

Tia didn't ask what she meant by "one of us." "All people, all creatures are the Good Lord's doing. Each of us goes back to the Garden of Eden."

Lily was familiar with the myth that merfolk were cast-off angels that had fallen into the sea during Lucifer's revolt from heaven. But if Tia didn't openly admit or say the word *mermaid*, then she refused to be the first to say the word aloud.

Annie dragged a chair across the wooden floor and primly crossed her ankles and folded her hands in her lap. She kept her eyes on the floor.

"I'm not cross with you," Lily said. "You just surprised me singing that song."

Annie took a quick peek from behind her long wave of hair and Lily was taken aback by her exotic beauty. Annie had dark brown eyes shot through with orange rays that made her irises appear a unique cinnamon color. They weren't the innocent eyes of a child, either. Lily noticed the ample breasts and the slight curve of her hips, whereas before she'd only caught the impression of a short, thin body.

"I can't help singing," the girl mumbled. "The songs play in my head and I have to sing."

Lily turned questioning eyes to Tia.

"It's true. An unusual gift my Annie's received from the spirit world. Never heard of no one else pick up music from a person's aura."

And the girl sang so beautifully, not as well as herself, but the notes were pure, haunting even. Lily shook her head to clear it. Fascinating, but not why she'd come. "Let's return to business. I need information."

Tia didn't respond. The only sound in the room was the slight jangle of her arm bangles as she flipped cards.

"Well?" Lily broke in, impatient with the silence.

"Not good." Tia shook her head. "Danger surrounds you on two sides."

"What danger?" Lily asked, not volunteering any information.

"There are two people who wish you harm. One is much more evil than the other. One is motivated by money, the other love."

Two? Her scalp prickled. "I need names."

Tia clucked in disapproval, as if she were a recalcitrant student. "The spirits are never that open."

"Can you at least give me some clues?"

Tia's brow wrinkled and her words dribbled out slow as honey. "It's a different person than who's troubled you in the past."

"Maybe Twyla Fae. I confronted her yesterday but she swore she's not behind my current problem." Surprisingly, Lily had believed her. Twyla had appeared tired and anxious, fretting over her sickly child. She'd even expressed sympathy for the way Gary had created a scene at the restaurant and apologized for the way she'd acted in the grocery store. A minor miracle.

Tia shook her head. "It's not Twyla."

"If you can't give me names, can you at least tell me *why* these people want to hurt me?"

Tia scooped up the cards with a deft hand and reshuffled. She laid out two more cards. "The one motivated by greed and revenge is a male. His anger is directed more at your family, but you could be hurt in the cross fire." She took a deep breath, nostrils crinkling. "I'm picking up the scent of fresh-cut wood. Like wood chips."

Carl Dismukes. Her brother-in-law's ex-deputy who'd once blackmailed Jet over her illegal maritime excavations. His image arose, sitting at the sheriff's headquarters whittling one of his many wood carvings.

"Tillman fired him months ago. He's still angry? Why can't that old man just enjoy retirement?" He'd served so many years on the force that he'd been allowed to collect his pension. "Dismukes I can handle. What about the other person?"

Tia tapped her finger on the Tower card. "This one is murkier. The Tower represents death and destruction." She frowned, as if peering into a shadowed realm.

Lily found herself holding her breath, afraid to break Tia's concentration by even the tiniest of movements.

"This person has murdered two persons, yet harbors no guilt."

Lily's heart thundered like a herd of wild stallions. Rebecca and Connie?

Tia looked up, regarding her with anthracite-black eyes. "You may be next."

The air pressed around her, thick and dense. "What should I do?" she whispered.

"Talk to your family. Report the phone calls."

An electric tingle buzzed through her body. No! Nothing would send Nash packing as quickly as believing his presence put her in danger. "There's got to be another way. Can't you tell me anything else to pinpoint who it is?"

Tia closed her eyes and laid large wrinkled hands on the table. Lily was surprised how vulnerable and frail the hands appeared. Tia was well-known in the bayou as a combination voodoo priestess/witch or gypsy fortune-teller/hustler—depending on who you asked. The woman had always seemed large and powerful and more than a little scary when Lily was younger. Lily had been afraid she'd direct those black eyes on her and pronounce her some kind of swamp monster.

Now she knew better. Tia was one of her own kind—however distant. And she was an old lady who needed her granddaughter to get by.

Tia threw her head back and began a guttural hum that sounded almost inhuman. Her chin snapped forward and the humming ceased. The rolling white of her eyeballs flickered before the black irises descended. "That's one of the most evil spirits I've ever encountered."

"What can you tell me?"

"It's a female."

Well, that cut the field by half. Lily restrained from rolling her own eyes. "What else?"

"The more evil the spirit, the more darkness surrounds 'em. Makes it hard to identify. Night and shadows stick to 'em like fly paper 'cause they don't want to be seen for what they truly are. They cower behind fog and veils and any trickery they can nab."

A loud, dissonant humming erupted. Lily jumped and stared at Annie. The girl's eyes were wide and their cinnamon rays glowed like jack-o-lanterns around the black pupils. Her lips moved as if she had no control over the jerky rhythm and nonsense words coming out. Tia placed an arm over her granddaughter's shoulder and the wildly pitched chanting slowed, giving way to a mournful parody of a children's song.

"Ring around the rosie
Pocket full of posies
Ashes, ashes
We all fall down."

Ice spurted through Lily's veins. The happy, nonsensical ditty had morphed to a low, funereal dirge like a devil's hymn, sinister as a baroque fugue.

"Ring around the rosie

Darkness befalls thee
Ashes, ashes
They all must drown."

Annie's mouth clamped shut and in the abrupt silence, the candle flames sizzled, their thin columns of fire doubling in height liked an amped-up Bunsen burner. Tia snuffed them with a brass candle snifter and they hissed like an angry cat. Sickly gray smoke perfumed the air with an acrid stench.

"Got to give this place a good sage smudgin' when you leave," Tia mumbled.

Lily coughed and waved the smoke from her face. "What's the significance of that song?"

"I d-don't know," Annie said in a thin voice. "It came to me." She fidgeted with the hem of her shirtsleeve. "Maybe it's somehow connected with the killer."

"Impressive. But I don't see how it can help me nail the woman unless I take you everywhere I go."

Tia gave a reassuring squeeze to Annie's shoulder before gathering up the tarot deck. "Oh, she's much too valuable for me to let her go traipsin' off with folks. Besides, the spirits have revealed all they want on the matter."

Lily couldn't complain, had found out more than she'd expected from the visit. She'd learned that Nash definitely had an enemy, one that had killed before and now sought her out. And that the killer was a female who enjoyed distorting children's songs into creepy messages of doom and death. Lily dug into her purse for the love offering.

A soft knock sounded at the door—so soft they each paused and eyed the door, as if unsure someone was on the other side. Another rap sounded, a bit firmer.

'Wasn't expectin' nobody but you," Tia said.

Lily arched a brow. "Your psychic powers slipping?"

Tia ignored the barb. "Get that for me, Annie."

But her granddaughter was already at the door, eager to slip away.

"I'd like to see Miss Tia, please."

Lily tensed at the familiar drawl, a habitual response to Twyla Fae's voice. She slapped a couple of twenties on the table for Tia and scrambled for the entrance.

Annie silently opened the door and Twyla and her son crossed the threshold, pausing when she saw Lily. Her child's eyes were a dull blue and he hiccupped, the kind you got from crying hard and long. His thin arms and legs dangled listlessly.

Twyla looked like she'd been sucked dry by a pack of rabid vampires. What should have been the whites of her eyes was so threaded with broken capillaries they appeared pink. Her arms were pasty and limp, as if she'd undergone rapid weight loss and lost muscle tone.

"Oh, hello again, Lily." She jostled the child on her hips and shifted her feet.

Tia stood slowly, knees creaking. "What's wrong with that poor young'un?"

"I don't know." Twyla slid a glance at Lily, clearly not wanting to speak her business in front of her.

Lily perversely crossed her arms and planted her feet. The ceasefire of hostility from Twyla was still too new, too fragile for her to feel comfortable in her presence. But a reluctant sympathy cut through her unease. She nodded at the boy. "You feeding this child enough? He's too skinny."

"That's why I'm here." Twyla looked hopefully, desperately at Tia Henrietta. "Please, is there anything you can do?"

"May I hold him?" Annie held out her arms.

So she wasn't shy when it came to children, Lily noted.

Twyla handed him over with pitiful haste and sank onto the sofa, deflating as quickly as a punctured balloon.

Annie went to the rocker in the far corner of the room, humming softly and running fingers lightly against the boy's face. He stopped crying, fascinated by the stranger cradling his body.

"That boy need a doctor," Tia pronounced. "Can't be using no herbs on a child. Too risky."

"Can't you say a prayer or do a chant or something?" Twyla asked in a whoosh of breath. "Please?" Teardrops spangled her pale eyelashes.

"If you can't afford a doctor, I'll pay for one," Lily offered. She pulled two one-hundred-dollar bills from her wallet and regarded them thoughtfully. "Is this enough for a doctor's visit and some medicine?" she asked doubtfully. She'd never set foot in a doctor's office.

Twyla stiffened. "I *have* taken him to the doctor in town. He don't know what's wrong. Said he had some sorta failure to thrive. He made an appointment for us at the Children's Hospital in Birmingham next month for more testing and evaluation."

Tia handed Twyla a tissue and patted her back. "I'll light a candle and say a prayer for him every night. What's his name?"

"Kevin. Kevin Leroy."

"That's it?" Lily asked Tia. "There must be something else you can do."

Tia's chin rose an inch. "Prayer can be powerful."

There had to be a way to help. Lily tapped her foot, thinking. "I've got an idea," she said suddenly.

Everyone in the room regarded her expectantly, making her instantly sorry she'd thought aloud. "I'll have to check with someone first," she said hastily. "It's kind of a long shot." Twyla might even laugh at the idea.

"I'd do anything," Twyla said. "As long as it doesn't hurt Kevin, of course."

Lily nodded. "All right, then. I'll check on it and let you know."

Twyla scribbled on a piece of torn paper and handed it over. "Call me anytime. And…thank you, Lily. I know I've been mean and petty in the past and I'm sorry."

"Nothing like a sick child to change a hard heart," Tia said with a cluck.

Lily accepted the apology silently. Twyla needed her help, that was all. Once the crisis with the child was over, she'd probably revert back to her mean old self. "I'll be in touch," she said, heading out. She had her own problems to take care of.

"Hurry!" Twyla called to her back.

Lily strode through a thick wall of humidity and eased into the Audi, blasting on the AC, mentally mapping out her errands and priorities. Concern for Twyla and Kevin added an unexpected mix to the day's errands. Her visit to Tia's hadn't yielded a name, but the clues all pointed to a spurned lover. Given Nash's past, that didn't exactly limit the suspects to one or two women. Lily considered questioning Opal about his past lovers, but decided it would put Opal in the unfair position of tattling on her boss.

She eased onto the sandy lane, making her way toward town. There was no hope for it. She had to talk to Tillman and Landry. With their training and contacts, they could help solve the mystery. And then Nash would be free from the guilt and burden of his past, clearing a path for their own relationship to progress. Right now, she sensed he held back, unwilling to draw her into his mess.

And they didn't have all the time in the world. When Nash finished this current assignment, he'd set off again, working a job that would keep him from the bayou. And her mother couldn't be put off forever. She knew her duty. It was time to stop fooling herself. If she couldn't find true

love with a human male, she might as well return to sea
and be with her own kind.

"What do you mean, 'keep this under our hats'?" Landry
bellowed from behind the desk. "Didn't it ever occur to
you that this Nash Bowman might be responsible for the
deaths of his former lovers?"

"No freaking way," Lily said stiffly. "Tia Henrietta said
the killer was female and motivated—"

Landry snorted. "You can't expect us to take the word
of a psychic."

Tillman slashed his hand at Landry, indicating silence.
"Lily," he began reasonably. "Of course we're going to
look into this right away, but we can't promise not to contact Nash if we need more information. Your safety is our
main concern."

Lily did battle with her pride. "Please," she said, hating
to beg. "It will ruin everything if you tell him."

"Why don't you want him to know about the latest call?
If he cares about you, he'll want to protect you," Tillman
said.

"Unless he's the one behind these deaths," Landry added
quickly.

"He's not behind them. I've known him for years."

Landry glowered. "Jet told me about him. You used to
see him summers when you were kids. But people change."

"He's not a killer," she said, hot anger burning her
cheeks. Tillman and Landry were each cut of the same
cloth—typical law enforcement types, suspicious of everyone. She regarded their tense expressions and crisp brown
uniforms with the polished silver sheriff's badges over
their left front pockets. Landry was a bit more hard-edged,
probably because of the violence in his family's past.

At least they'd never hit on her like most every other
man in Bayou La Siryna. Lily stood and grabbed her purse.

"I know neither of you has ever cared for me. You tolerate me because of Shelly and Jet. But I'm begging you for this one favor. Say nothing to Nash."

They exchanged glances and shuffled to their feet.

"I can't promise, Lily," Tillman said. "If I see something suspicious about Bowman, all bets are off."

She considered turning up the volume on her siren charm, but the thought of it made her squirm. These men were off-limits. She might be a lot of things, but she'd never betray her own sister and cousin that way. And these two were strong and decent enough men that they wouldn't let the sexual pull deter them from doing their jobs.

Landry extended a hand. "Be careful," he warned. "Let us know if anything else happens."

She shook his hand and turned away until she remembered there were two people that were dangerous. Lily whirled around. "I almost forgot. Tia mentioned to be on the lookout for Carl Dismukes. Y'all ever hear from your old deputy sheriff?"

Landry shrugged. "I've never met the man."

"Yeah, every now and then I run into him." Tillman ran a hand through his short brown hair. "He hasn't come right out and threatened me, but he insinuates that he'll bring up my father's crooked dealings when he was sheriff. Guess he's saving that news-media bombshell for the upcoming sheriff's election."

"This fall?" she asked.

He nodded.

"So what are you going to do about it?"

He raised both hands palms-up. "Nothing I can do. He knows he can't blackmail me like he did your sister. I'll have to ride out the storm if it comes."

It was no less than what she expected of Tillman. He was as honest as his dad had been corrupt. No wonder Shelly had fallen for the guy.

"What specifically did Tia Henrietta say about Dismukes?" Landry asked, voice roughened around the edges and arctic-blue eyes narrowed. He wasn't as fatalistic as Tillman, and Lily bet he wanted to confront Dismukes head-on. Somebody had to. If not, that was another item to put on her to-do list.

"Oh, so *now* you're interested in what Tia had to say?"

The jibe hit home and Landry's lips tightened.

"Typical psychic revelations," Lily mocked. "Nothing specific, other than he was a danger to all of us."

"Forget Dismukes," Tillman cut in. "We're going to check out this Nashoba Bowman. In the meantime, why don't you stay with me and Shelly until we know you're safe?"

"You have enough to worry about with Eddie," she cut in quickly. Even though Tillman's mother was several months sober, he still spent lots of time with his autistic younger brother. "And Shelly's busy with her job. It's not like either of you would be around for protection."

"You could stay with us."

Lily stared at Landry in surprise. A muscle in his jaw twitched. "Your mother's already staying with us. You might as well, too."

She laughed, guessing at the effort it took for him to extend the invitation. "No, thanks."

"You shouldn't be alone," Tillman insisted.

"I only want you to look into the records of Rebecca and Connie's deaths. I'll get their last names from Nash's assistant." Lily opened the door and the noisy hubbub of the sheriff's office filtered in—ringing phones, citizens shuffling about in the waiting room, a line of people at a desk paying tickets.

She stepped into the fray and heard Tillman call out a warning.

"Be careful."

Chapter 9

Nash threw another dried oak limb on the bonfire.

"Thank you," Lily whispered in his ear, shooting sparks of hot desire to his groin. She'd come to him yesterday, asking for his help in arranging a healing. She was acting as if his rejection on the hike hadn't happened, as if they were only two old friends.

Nash didn't know what to make of that. He should be pleased she accepted they weren't going to become lovers, but his body and heart weren't happy. Not in the least.

He forced his attention on the fire. First things first. It had been years since he'd attended one of his grandfather's healings, and Nash was curious to see if it affected him as deeply now that he was a grown man and long removed from his tribe's customs.

His grandfather had agreed to perform the healing ritual today despite the toll it would take. Physically, it exhausted Sam to do the twenty-four-hour fasting necessary to prepare. And then, once begun, the ceremony itself drained his energy. Also, he didn't like exposing his practice to those outside his tribe. Even within the tribe, a few grumbled that his work wasn't strictly according to Choctaw customs, which really ticked Nash off. Their particular band of Choctaws was a blending of many tribes anyway—Choctaw, Chickasaw, Creek, Apache, Cherokee—and Sam Bowman combined techniques from various tribes within and outside of their mixed band.

It usually worked.

"I can only honor what my spirit guides have taught me," his grandfather always said. "If someone doesn't like that, they shouldn't join the healing circle."

Sam emerged from the back door of the cabin and nodded briefly at the small group standing outside the medicine-wheel circle. The outer edge was lined with conch shells and gay granite rocks. In its center, the small fire lit the late afternoon shadows and contributed to the humid, muggy air. Nash had everything prepared according to his grandfather's instructions. By a large chair, he'd placed a mortar and pestle, several glass vials and a small empty mason jar.

Sweat and smoke stung his eyes, but Nash knew better than to complain. The sweat provided purification for the ceremony. Through the heat glaze, Lily, Twyla, J.P. and Kevin appeared distorted and fuzzy. His gaze lingered on the husband, surprised the guy had shown up given his history with Lily. Hell, it had shocked *him* when Lily had told him the healing was for Twyla's son. But J.P. had acted civil, although he was clearly on the skeptical side and careful to avoid giving Lily much attention.

Smart husband.

Sam entered through a small gap in the circle border on the south side. He cupped a golden bowl half-filled with dried ground corn. Close to the fire, he raised it above his head. "Great Spirit, hear the prayers of your children.

We stand before you humble and grateful for your many blessings. We ask a healing for Kevin." He walked a few steps to the north and lifted a handful of the dried grain, letting it slip through his fingers. His head tilted back and he closed his eyes, gathering the wisdom offered from the north. Satisfied, he repeated the same process three more times—east for gathering birth, south for growth and west for healing.

Nash fought the impulse to stand at his grandfather's side and hold his arm. Sam's face was haggard, his movements slow and slightly unsteady. He was too old and sick to fast and then endure the outside heat coupled with the mental intensity of the ceremony. He shouldn't have asked his grandfather to do this, but Lily's plea had overcome his misgivings.

At least Sam had agreed to the chair inside the sacred circle. With the supplication finished, he sank into it. His gnarled, wrinkled hands gripped the wicker arms so tightly that Nash knew its pattern would be imbedded in his palms. His back was straight as an arrow, tensed and poised for action, and his eyes were closed.

No one dared speak. Nash imagined his own face was as still and intense as the rest of the party. Even Kevin was silent. The wind carried off his feeble whimpers as if to clear the circle for the needed silence. Nash closed his eyes, too, in a long-shot attempt to help his grandfather in the shadowy spirit realm. If such a thing existed. And if he had any power to lend.

The fire popped and crackled, the sound unnaturally loud above the faint ocean waves and the more immediate rustle of birds finding their roosting spot before night settled in. The sweet smell of maize mixed with the scent of the burning sage his grandfather had asked him to place on the fire, a protection from any evil seeking mischief.

Nash's body felt light and barely rooted to the ground.

The sky darkened and a hot breeze lifted hair at his nape. Muffled voices carried in the wind.

Had the heat caused his mind to play tricks? Nash opened his eyes and caught his grandfather's eyes fixed on him. Sam nodded, the movement barely perceptible. His grandfather cocked his head to the side, as if listening to the voices. Nash couldn't make out what they were saying; it was as if they were speaking some ancient language.

A piece of burning oak fell off the woodpile, sending embers spiraling upward. The sparks coalesced for a moment in the form of a starfish before melding into the shadows and losing their glow.

This was no trick, no mind game, no simple prayer request, no empty symbolic gathering. The starfish represented rejuvenation ability and lent its essence for healing the child. Nash couldn't explain how he knew this. He just did. His grandfather truly connected to actual spirits. Nash let that truth seep into his soul, obliterating his skepticism. He believed in it again as purely as he'd done in his youth.

Sam nodded, as if understanding and accepting otherworldly guidance. His hands eased their grip on the chair and he unfastened the small medicine pouch looped at the waistband of his pants. He withdrew a couple pinches of a green herb. He picked up the empty offering bowl and dropped in the herbs. Next, he opened the larger medicine bag strapped across his waist and pulled out the head of a dried cattail, a withered root, fresh silvery-green sage and a single, sharp leaf from a saw palmetto. In the mortar and pestle he emptied a vial of liquid and slowly added snippets of the herbs and roots, crushing them to form a paste.

"What's he making?" Lily whispered by his side.

Nash laid a finger against his lips, not wanting anything to disturb his grandfather's concentration.

Sam ladled out the paste with an index finger and

scooped it into the mason jar. He screwed on the lid and signaled Nash it was time for his part in the ceremony.

Nash stood and felt heat rise at the back of his neck when everyone stared. *Buck up. This is for Grandfather. For a sick child.* He undid his own medicine pouch from the waistband of his jeans and opened it, conscious he'd never done so in front of another person before. His grandfather had insisted he be a part of this healing. Had told him that when the time was right, he would be called upon to use an item from his own pouch and he would know what to do.

But what if he failed? What if *he* was the reason Kevin didn't heal? The soft brush of feather against his fingers stilled his hand. A whooshing came from above, with all the force produced by an eight-foot wingspan. Nash looked up but could barely discern a solid shape in the shadows. Citron-colored eyes surrounded by white feathers pierced through the shadow realm. The large chocolate-brown body of the bald eagle blended into the deep purple sky. A shrill piping escaped its golden beak.

Kuk-kuk-kuk. I will help you.

Nash grasped the tip of the eagle feather he'd found as a child, never realizing its discovery had been planted for this future moment. He withdrew it from his pouch, meeting Lily's curious eyes. Twyla, J.P. and their child focused on him, as well. No one looked above. No one else saw or heard what he did.

Except his grandfather.

Sam cocked his head toward the child and Nash knew what to do. He went to Kevin and the child reached out a hand, grabbed the feather and clutched it to his chest.

Nash returned to Lily's side and Sam rose from the chair, opened a sealed plastic pouch and sprinkled the brown leafy contents at each circle direction. Nash knew from times past this was tobacco, a sacred herb offered in gratitude to the spirits for their assistance.

Sam exited the circle holding the lidded jar. He ambled over to Twyla, who held her son against her right hip and arm, and placed it in her left hand. "Rub a pinch of this on his stomach every night for the next week."

J.P. eyed the green mixture with narrowed eyes. "What all is in that?"

"Nothing that will harm your son. A mixture of cattail, galangal, fresh sage and saw palmetto. His stomach ails him," Sam explained. "This will balance his digestion."

"Couldn't hurt, I guess." J.P. reached for his back pocket. "How much we owe ya?"

Sam stiffened. "I take no money for spirit work."

Twyla shot her husband a warning look. "I've already got it covered." She dug in her purse and pulled out a sealed pouch. "Will you accept this gift of tobacco?"

Sam nodded and stuffed it in his large medicine bag. "And this is for you." He produced a small dream catcher, the size of a salad plate. Feathers were attached to its wooden hoop with leather strips. "Place this by his bed at night. It will help his guardian spirits keep away those spirits who would steal your son's energy."

Kevin grabbed the dream catcher and tugged it to him, giggling as feathers tickled his face.

A look of mutual admiration passed between Sam and the child. A ping of understanding hit Nash. Little Kevin was going to be okay. The sallow skin looked pinker and the listless eyes held a newfound spark.

"You think he's cured?" Twyla asked in a rush, her voice a mixture of hope and desperation.

"The spirits have confirmed your son is fine. But I always recommend people follow up with their doctors to be safe."

Nash shook his head. Even mystical healing these days required a "cover your ass" disclaimer.

"Would save us a boatload of cash if we didn't have to travel to Birmingham," J.P. observed. He hung his head and shoved his hands into his pockets. "Not that we wouldn't do everything possible for Kevin."

"Of course," Lily agreed. She shot Nash a look of such awe and gratitude it made him squirm.

He'd done nothing to earn this respect. For years he'd barely acknowledged Sam's or his own abilities. Nash saw how selfish he'd been, even if he still wanted no part of shamanism or further development of his own earth magic.

Perhaps Sam had agreed to the healing partly to show Nash why he should respect and honor his heritage.

He moved to his grandfather's side and addressed everyone. "I think my grandfather needs a good meal and rest now. This kind of work is tiring."

Twyla and her family offered profuse thanks and hurried away. Twyla clutched the jar of green salve as if her son's life depended on it. Perhaps it did.

Lily hesitated. "Can I fix a meal for y'all before I leave?"

"Not necessary," Sam objected. "I have a pot of stew on the stove. I'll eat and then head off to bed. You two can go about the rest of your evening."

"You sure?" Nash asked. "Today's been tiring and with your—"

Sam cut him off. "What are you going to do? Hold my hand while I sleep? I'll be fine."

Nash grasped his grandfather's hand and gave it a firm shake, hoping it conveyed his love and respect. He'd been away from the bayou too long, had neglected the person who best understood him. Somehow, he had to atone for the thoughtlessness.

Sam squeezed his hand. "I am well pleased with you, Nashoba. Always knew you'd return when the time was right."

Nash covertly watched his grandfather as they made

their way back to the cottage. Sam's steps were slow but sure. He'd make it up to him, would arrange to stay in Bayou La Siryna until his grandfather's heart beat for the last time.

"What did he mean about returning when the time was right?" Lily asked in a low voice.

"I'm not sure," he admitted. "Sam often speaks in riddles."

They waved goodbye to Sam and climbed into Nash's truck. Lily snuggled against Nash as best she could, considering the truck's bucket seats that separated them.

"Thanks again for talking Sam into helping them." She shot him a sideways glance. "Think it worked?"

"My grandfather says it's up to the spirits to decide if there's to be a healing, especially with babies and young children. But I believe Kevin will be fine."

"You sensed the spirits, didn't you? That's how you knew what Kevin needed from your medicine bag."

"It's not easy to explain," he hedged.

Lily tapped her fingers against her lips. "Will you take Sam's place one day as a healer?"

"Hell, no."

His answer surprised her. Nash had acted like a natural at the ceremony. She stared out the window at the dense clumps of saw palmettos and the occasional one-story cottage. After spending months at a time undersea, this was the one constant place in her life—this bayou where generations of Bosarge women had shape-shifted and found a second home of sorts. In Jet and Shelly's case, it was their primary home.

Nash turned sharply onto Main Street and drove past the drawbridge where large shrimping vessels returned with the day's harvest. "The healing art will probably die with my grandfather. Speaking of which—" Nash hesitated.

"Go on."

The sharp planes of his face grew sharper. "Sam suspects he won't make it to the Green Corn ceremony later this month."

Damn. "Can't he call on the spirits to help himself?"

"He says it's his time and he's ready."

"Surely the doctors can do something. He doesn't look so bad for his age."

"He's already had one bypass surgery and refuses another. At first, I thought he looked fine myself, but after spending time here, I see how easily he tires."

"Is that why you really came home? To help him and to say…goodbye?"

"Pretty much. Finding this assignment was easy. Gave me an excuse to hang around indefinitely."

Lily guided a hand underneath the leather cord that pulled back his long black hair and rubbed the stiff muscles at the nape. "Bet he's glad for the company."

"Mmm." He softened under her touch. "That feels incredible."

Lily reached up with her other hand and kneaded the top of his shoulder blades. "How about a full-body massage when we get to my house?" she whispered.

Nash moaned. "You do that and I might never leave."

The words lay between them, heavy and tantalizing.

"My plan is working," Lily said hoarsely.

"Sweetheart, if that's an invitation, I'm in." He laid a large palm on her bare thigh.

Her flesh burned and rippled, heat spreading upward like a current to her core. Nash slid her a molten look and shifted uncomfortably in his seat.

She cast a feverish glance out the window at the tree-lined street. Another mile. She groaned and nestled her head into his chest. Nash threaded the fingers of one hand through her hair, while the other hand gripped the steering wheel like a lifeline.

He wanted her. Really wanted her like she wanted him. It was time. She wanted to be with him as much as possible, in every way possible. The thought of him eventually leaving the bayou pinched her heart. She wouldn't think of it now. Anything could happen in the next few weeks. Tonight was for exploration, and she intended to make love to every inch of his body.

Nash hit the accelerator and she grinned into the soft cotton of his T-shirt. Soon. She sniffed, heady with the earthy male scent that belonged to him alone. "Nashoba." She whispered his name, a muffled sound that warmed his shirt against her lips.

"We're here." Truck tires crunched against the ground shells of the driveway.

Lily raised her head. Through a haze of lust, something tickled in her consciousness, a feather prickling warning sensors in the deep, primitive cerebellum. A distant warning that the world had shifted in a minor, yet important way. She cocked her head to one side, considering. No unusual sounds or smells or out-of-place objects. She scanned the yard, but nothing ominous hovered in the gathering twilight.

Ring around the rosie…

Annie's voice flashed in her memory, singing in that high-pitched creepy cadence.

Pocket full of posies…

Da duh da duh da, it chimed in a familiar singsong pace as Lily searched the shadows.

Evil surrounds me…

The evil had something to do with shadows. It was too dark—

We all fall DOWN.

Down.

Down.

At the crescendo of *down*, Lily's mind heaved like the

turbulence of a strong undertow, pulling her down into its dark depths. Darkness—that's what was wrong—the house was too dark. The porch floodlight was off again.

Nash stopped the car and shot her a wary glance. "Is something wrong?"

"Looks like the porch light must have burned out." No sense alarming him until she ran out of options. Damn it, they'd been minutes away from the ultimate intimacy, and now this.

"I'll check it out."

Nash got out of the truck with the silent, fluid motion of a cat. Hands on hips, he surveyed the yard and house. Lily was certain he could sniff out danger, see and sense what she could not. Undersea, she had the same ability. Echolocation allowed her to perceive the shapes and natures of moving creatures at far distances.

Lily climbed out the passenger side and quietly approached, not wanting to disturb his concentration.

Without looking at her he raised an arm and drew her into his side.

"Go back in the truck and lock the doors." He pressed a set of keys into her hand. "I'm going to take a look at the porch light."

"I'll go with you."

He leveled her with a stern gaze. "As stubborn as you ever were." But he held her hand and proceeded forward.

"The porch light's in that corner." Lily pointed to the far right wall, and Nash picked his way through the white wicker rockers and potted ferns.

He reached up and turned the bulb, which fell immediately into his hand.

"Must have come loose?" she asked, relieved to see it hadn't been smashed.

"Must have been deliberately unscrewed."

He returned the bulb to its socket and light burst upon them with shocking intensity.

"Hand me your keys," he commanded.

Lily turned them over, thankful she wasn't alone.

"Stay behind me. And this time do as I say."

Lily snapped him a salute. "Aye, aye, sir."

He scowled, not amused. "And keep quiet."

A familiar click of the lock and he eased open the door, stepping cautiously over the threshold. Lily placed her hands on either side of his waist, face almost pressed into his back. She inhaled the earthy sandalwood scent that made her feel protected and safe. Once inside, she let go and took two steps toward the kitchen.

The iron band of his forearm blocked her path.

"Behind me," he hissed. "Light switch?"

She pointed to the left interior wall of the kitchen.

Nash flipped it on and a massive chandelier cast brilliant prisms of amber, coral and teal light into the kitchen.

Lily exhaled and spoke without bothering to keep her voice low. "I must have forgotten to turn it on when I left earlier."

"There's still the matter of the front porch light. I don't like it. Not after you told me about the phone calls."

"I'm sure it's nothing." Yet she glanced around the pristine room where everything appeared in place.

"Let's check the rest of the house to be sure," Nash said with a frown.

Lily led him through the downstairs rooms, which showed no signs of disturbance. She was beginning to feel foolish. Maybe that trip to see Tia Henrietta had done more harm than good, had put unwarranted suspicions in her mind. They proceeded upstairs and did a walk-through of the bedrooms, saving hers for last.

The closed door to her bedroom gave her pause. The only time she'd ever kept this room shut was after Jet's dog,

Rebel, had chewed on a pair of her designer shoes. Now that her sister and the dog were gone, there was no reason to shut it. Lily halted, hand on the knob, a faint echo of a child's song bouncing in her mind. *It's okay. Nash is here.*

Nash laid a hand over her own. "I'll go in first."

She stepped back. "No argument from me this time."

He snapped on the light and a fusillade of color bombarded Lily. The worst damage was at the back wall where her easels and paintings were stored.

Slashing X tears ripped through her latest watercolor. An explosion of acrylics had been smeared across her other works mounted on a drafting table in the far right corner. Angry rainbows of blues, greens and purples marred her delicate artwork. Paint tubes lay scattered on the floor, twisted and empty. In the middle of her lavender-flowered bedspread was a huge blob of red paint in the shape of a severed heart.

Her ears buzzed as if a cacophony of ricocheting bullets had been fired.

Someone hated her. Hated her with a primal fury that wouldn't be sated until her own heart was gutted and bared like the painted one on the bedspread. *Why?* She stepped forward, dazed, fingers outstretched and trembling, wanting to touch the red acrylic, wanting to prove this was real.

"Don't touch anything," Nash said harshly. "The police will want everything undisturbed. I'm calling them now."

"What if someone's still here?" She glanced at the frilly lace bed skirt, wondering if the childhood bogeyman she imagined living underneath might have morphed into the real thing—ready to snake out a hand and grab her ankles if she neared its lair. Her gaze shifted to the open closet door and then the attached bathroom.

Nash stopped mid-dial, fingers poised above his cell phone. "Right. Better check first." He stuffed the phone into his back pocket, grabbed a broom that leaned against a wall and strode to the closet. He ran it through the rows of clothing as if he were wielding a weapon, ready to impale anyone hiding among the clothes. "Nothing there."

Lily jumped out of his way as he headed to the bed; the fury on his face was wild and primitive. She wouldn't want to be on the receiving end of such raw anger.

Nash lifted the bed skirt and slashed through the underbelly of her bed with the broom. "All clear there."

He straightened, eyes unfocused, as if sensing something beyond the immediate.

"Let's get out of here," Lily urged. "What if there's someone here? Someone armed?"

He was past reason, intent on finding the culprit. Nash acted as if he didn't even hear her.

"There's something here," he murmured. "Something alive and deadly." Ever so slowly his neck swiveled toward the bathroom door. "There."

Lily raised a hand and laid it over the vulnerable, exposed carotid artery and windpipe beneath her neck. "Don't go in there," she rasped.

But Nash lifted the broom in his right hand and didn't turn. "Stay where you are."

As if. This was her house, after all, and she needed to know how far this violation of her space extended. Lily followed.

He jerked open the shower curtain and the top rings screeched and clanged against the metal rail. At eye level, the baby-pink tile was visible and she uncurled her fists, relieved not to find…someone…a monster in hiding. A loud machine-gun rattle erupted and bounced around the tiled room. She'd never heard a rattlesnake, but its dry buzz of warning sent an instinctual chill down her spine. Her scalp prickled with awareness. Despite the heavy dread thickening her threat, Lily inched closer.

A diamondback rattler wriggled inside a large black

mesh bag attached to the faucet head. Coiled into an S shape and fangs bared, it signaled attack mode. She bit back the high-pitched scream burning inside her lungs. "That's one pissed-off snake," she said, voice thin and reedy.

"More terrified of us than we are of him."

"I doubt that," Lily muttered.

Nash leaned in closer to the tub and she tugged the back of his T-shirt. "Don't get in striking range."

"I'm not stupid. What's it doing in that bag?"

"Whoever left it didn't want it crawling off. They wanted to make sure you saw it."

Nash chanted words unintelligible to her. Probably Choctaw, she guessed. His deep baritone underpinned the snake rattle like a bass in a macabre war song. The rattler retracted its fangs and the striped tail lowered fractionally.

Lily gave a shaky laugh. "What are you—a snake charmer?"

He didn't bother answering but continued chanting until the snake uncoiled and lay flat. Lily didn't let go of her grip on his T-shirt. Nash would keep her safe. He was solid as the earth itself. Dependable. Even at age twelve when he'd found her in the woods. She'd heard his voice first, calling her name, and had known immediately that all was well. As long as she held on to him, no striking snake could sink its fangs into her, no evil could befall her. Nash wouldn't allow it. She let the knowledge sink in deep, let it warm her chilled body and stay the shivering and chattering teeth.

"Get me a bedsheet," Nash said, eyes never leaving the snake.

Reluctantly, Lily released her hold on his shirt and raced to her bed. She hesitated. What if another snake was coiled beneath the bedspread? She kept her body as far from the mattress as possible, leaned over and yanked off the bedspread. So much for not touching anything. Thankfully, there was no nasty hidden surprise. An exterminator would have to do a thorough sweep of the house before she ever set foot in it again. She quickly stripped off the cover linen and rushed back to the adjoining bathroom.

Nash grabbed the sheet and spread it on the tile floor. He resumed chanting, lifted the mesh bag with its deadly bundle and placed it in the middle of the sheet. He gathered the cloth and tied it at the ends. "This is only for a little while," Nash said, addressing the bagged snake. "You'll be released in the woods later." He set the bag by the door and Lily backed away, giving the wriggling bundle a wide berth.

She went to the bedroom and stared again at the ruined paintings. All that work, all that painstaking detail she'd created with such hope and pride—gone. She barely listened as Nash placed the emergency call.

Nash came by her side and placed the heavy weight of an arm across her shoulders. "All your beautiful paintings," he whispered.

Her chances of entering and winning the prestigious art competition lay destroyed among the slashed watercolors. Her hopes and dreams were destroyed, too, detonated by some anonymous bomb of fury. A few more days and she'd have had them packaged and in the mail. The sharp edges and harsh lines of ripped paintings blurred.

"I'll never win that competition now." She raised her hands to her eyes, trying to staunch the ridiculous tears. Her nonexistent art career should be the least of her worries.

"What competition?"

"Some dumb event that I hoped would get my art noticed." No doubt he'd think her twice as vain as when he'd first come back to the bayou. "It's not like I had a real chance of winning anyway."

Nash studied what remained of her work. "Sure, you had a shot at winning. These are amazing."

"*Were* amazing."

He enveloped her in his strong arms.

It undid her. Lily sobbed into his chest, mourning the loss of her dream.

"There'll be other contests," he whispered into the top of her scalp, his breath warm and comforting. "Other paintings."

"I know," she agreed, crying all the harder. Stupid to let the paintings matter more than the threat to her life. More than Nash's feelings. She swallowed hard and gazed up. "You're right. We need to focus on what's really wrong, on discovering this enemy."

He disentangled from her arms and lifted her chin. "*I* need to figure it out. Not you."

"No." She couldn't let him pull away from her now. Not when they'd drawn so close. "We'll do it together."

"I should have known this would follow me." Nash slammed a fisted hand into the palm of the other. "The past hounds me. I'll never be free."

His wounded fury hurt worse than anything else that had happened. He'd suffered more than anyone should have to endure. Regret and guilt pricked her conscience. She hadn't used Sam's sage for days. If she'd smudged the house like he'd instructed, maybe none of this would have happened. "It isn't your fault. Some crazy, obsessed woman is to blame."

"Why the hell would you say that?"

"I went to see a woman who…sees things, *knows* things. You met her a few times when you were little. Tia Henrietta?" she questioned.

Nash folded his arms, unresponsive and withdrawn.

"Tia told me I'm being harassed by a woman motivated by love and that she's killed more than once."

He paced the bedroom, consumed with his own thoughts, working out the facts.

"Don't shut me out, Nash," Lily implored. "I know this is hard for you to accept. But deep down, haven't you always suspected Rebecca's and Connie's deaths weren't accidents? Even without evidence?"

He stopped pacing and faced her. "Of course I have. Makes the guilt a million times worse."

She moved to him, wanting to cross the distance between them, to comfort him. "There's no reason for you—"

Nash held up his hands, blocking her advance, stopping her words. "Tia give you a name?"

"No."

A siren blared in the distance. Lily glanced out the lace-curtained window, where flashing red-and-blue lights strobed through oak and cypress limbs. "I should probably warn you about my brothers-in-law. They're the sheriff and deputy sheriff in this county. I spoke with them this morning about my…situation."

Nash nodded. "Good."

"I told them because there've been more calls."

His eyes hardened. "And you had no intention of telling me, did you?"

She'd promised him and now he took her omission as a betrayal. "I didn't want you to worry. I—I was afraid you'd leave me."

Headlights beamed through the window, casting his face in sharp focus, luminous against the darkness.

He was in no mood for apologies.

But she at least had to warn him of what was about to burst upon them. "There's something you should know," Lily continued miserably. "Tillman and Landry—my brothers-in-law—immediately jumped to the wrong conclusions. You know how suspicious and jaded cops are."

"They think I'm responsible for Rebecca's and Connie's deaths and whatever befalls you now." His words were hard and scratchy, like two granite rocks scraping against one another.

Reluctantly, she nodded.

"It won't be the first time I've been under suspicion. And here we go again."

The empty resignation in his voice, the flatness of his eyes, bruised her heart. "I know you've done nothing wrong. I'll make them listen."

The trill of her recently purchased cell phone made her jump. Probably the cops wanting the front door unlocked. The text on the flat screen glowed with two words.

He's mine.

Chapter 10

It was happening again, Nash realized. Past and present merged into a maelstrom of despair, anger, regret, frustration. Who was behind this? Why?

He rubbed his temples, trying to stamp out what felt like a swarm of stinging bees beneath the sensitive flesh.

"You must have some guess as to what's going on here." The sheriff cut him a hard stare and gestured at the slashed paintings. "This is the third woman who's been harassed after being involved with you."

"If I had a clue, I'd tell you. For the last time, I don't know." He kept his tone as flat and neutral as his interrogator. Sheriff Tillman Angier and his deputy, Landry Fields—or the BILs, as Lily liked to call them—did nothing to conceal their distrust of Nash.

The sheriff held up an index finger. "First, it's Rebecca Anders. She crashes her car weeks after a string of harassing phone calls with a message to break it off with you." He held up a second finger. "Then, two years later, Connie Enstep has a drug overdose. Again, after receiving a mysterious phone call warning her away from you. And now—" he waved a hand at the vandalism "—this."

Damn. It sounded incriminating as hell. He'd tried to convince himself with the first two that it was coincidence, even when his instincts had rejected the notion. But with a third occurrence, there was no denying it any longer. An unknown evil was wreaking havoc in his affairs, crushing out any woman he'd tried—however casually—to let into his life. "You're not telling me anything I don't already know."

"Leave him alone." Lily spoke up from behind. "I wish I'd never told you about the calls."

"You did the right thing," Fields admonished. "We looked into the records today and I don't like what we found." He leveled glacial blue eyes on Nash. "You have quite the reputation as a ladies' man."

"And I have my own reputation in Bayou La Siryna," Lily cut in. "Doesn't mean I'm a killer. Besides, he has the perfect alibi. We were together when someone crept in and destroyed my bedroom."

Nash's lips curled up involuntarily. Lily's swift defense was a relief. She understood him and didn't judge, a rare occurrence in his experience. Her belief in his character and innocence was absolute. All anger at the broken promise evaporated.

"No one's accusing Mr. Bowman of murder or even conspiracy to commit murder," said Angier. "We're trying to protect you and find out who's behind this."

"Then get your fingerprints from my room and trace the calls or whatever it is you do to find the bad guys."

A look passed between the BILs and, as if in unspoken agreement, Fields took Lily by the hand, subtly guiding her to the opposite side of the large bedroom.

"Now, look here," Sheriff Angier said in a hushed voice.

"Lily is family. I can't let anything happen to her like the others. If you have any ideas who the culprit might be, spit it out."

"For the hundredth time, I don't know."

Angier studied him. "Tell me about these two other women. Were they serious relationships?"

Nash gritted his teeth. No matter how he answered, he was damned. If he said they were serious, the sheriff would think he had arranged for them to be killed because he got cold feet. If he said they weren't serious, the sheriff would think he didn't care they'd been killed or, worse, that he had tried to get rid of them permanently. Might as well tell the truth.

"More serious on their part than mine," he admitted. A familiar twist in the gut tugged at Nash. They'd deserved love and commitment. Instead, his job had always been the top priority. "But it was devastating. Especially wondering if their deaths were connected to me in some way."

"No doubt about the connection now. Not with a third person threatened."

"I won't let anything happen to Lily," Nash vowed, mind racing on the best way to keep her from harm. It needed to be someplace remote, somewhere that allowed him to use his gifts to advantage.

Angier's lips pressed to a grim line. "And how are you going to do that?"

How, indeed. He should never have gotten involved in another relationship. But since he had, it was too late to end it now and still keep Lily safe. An image of swaying sea oats and a knell of cypress trees arose. "I'll take her to Herb Island with me."

A sharp gasp came from behind.

"You will?" Lily's face suffused with a glow, as if he'd presented her with an unexpected present. She was the one beautiful, perfect thing in this nightmare of an evening. The thought of her meeting one of those mysterious, unfortunate accidents twisted his guts. A pressing urge screamed inside him to whisk Lily up and instantly escape to the island.

"Is there anything else?" he asked the sheriff. "We'd like to be on our way."

Sheriff Angier addressed Lily. "You don't have to go with him. Shelly would love to have you stay with us until the investigation ends."

"Or you could stay with me and Jet," the deputy offered. "Your mom wants to spend more time with you, anyway, during her visit."

"I'm going with Nash. I'll pack while you finish up in here." She turned and looked over her shoulder. "How long do you think we'll be gone? Oh, never mind. I'll pack a bunch and come back later if I need to."

"Impulsive," said Deputy Fields. "Just like her sister."

"Stubborn as Shelly," Angier said with a rueful shake of his head.

Nash raised a brow. "Runs in the family, I see?"

Angier snickered. "Better get used to it."

Nash couldn't blame them for their concern. If he were in their shoes, he'd have the same misgivings. "I'll protect her," he vowed again.

Angier held out a hand. "I'm holding you to it. Your grandfather is one of the finest men I've ever known. And Lily obviously trusts you."

Nash shook the proffered hand, humbled and relieved at the overture. "The island should be safe. I'm the only one out there at night. Even during the day, there are few tourists. If any woman from my past shows up, I'll know it right away."

"I approve," Angier said with a nod. "And Ned Brock, who operates the ferry, can keep a log of everyone that boards for the island."

Deputy Fields opened a notebook and scribbled. "Here's our cell phone numbers if you need us. The ferry's closed for the day. Where will you spend tonight?"

"We can stay with my grandfather." But the idea stirred a qualm of unease in his gut at placing the old man in jeopardy. If he and Lily avoided his grandfather's place, Sam would be safer.

Angier was already pressing buttons on his cell. "No point drawing Sam into this mess. I'll have Ned make a special run tonight. He's made them before for emergencies."

Lily dragged over two suitcases. "We can grab some provisions from my pantry. Should I bring linens, too?"

"No. There's plenty at the lodge," Nash said. "Opal arranged everything before we arrived."

"Who's Opal?" Angier asked.

"Opal Wallace, my photographic assistant. She was here a week or so when I first arrived, but she left on another assignment."

Deputy Fields wrote down the name in a small notebook. "Opal Wallace. Tell me about this woman." He snapped the book shut.

Nash shrugged. "What do you want to know? I've worked with her on and off over the past several years on various projects. She's an excellent photographer in her own right, but works with me as an assistant between her jobs."

"Opal's my friend," Lily said quickly. "She's been gone for days, so she couldn't have anything to do with this break-in."

"Better safe—" Angier began.

"—than sorry. Yeah, yeah. We get it." Lily waved a hand dismissively and faced Nash. "I'm ready."

The sun called him. Fire rays of warmth that beckoned Nash to arise and greet the new morn. Even lying in bed, eyes closed and head cradled in clean-smelling cotton linen, he divined the sun's energy had risen.

He'd lain in bed awake most of the night, stiff and tense, unable to relax after the evening's hellish events. But sleep had briefly claimed him unawares in the darkness. Nash pushed aside the sheet, untangling his long legs, and walked to the window. Drawing the curtain, he took in the dawn's ascension over the brackish water, its light shimmering in bits of silver, as if the Great Spirit had tossed chips of clear quartz crystal across the sea. Clouds of violet and magenta danced in the sky. It felt like a sign, hope for a new beginning.

Time to confront the past and stop the killer. Time to seek help from any source. Time to accept any comfort offered and mentally prepare for what was to come.

He'd traveled the world and seen thousands of majestic sites, but nothing sang to Nash's soul like his homeland. Like this moment of peace and promise in the land of his ancestors.

Don't fight it, his grandfather had said. *Listen to the land and its creatures and the spirits of your ancestors in the piney woods and the Gulf breeze.* Sun heat invigorated his body with a glow of energy. For the Choctaw, his tribe and nation, the sun endowed life, was the epicenter of the world that illuminated Mother Earth and Father Sky.

I will fight no more. For the first time in two decades, calm washed his mind, cleansed his quibbling and unease with his extraordinary connection to nature and earth's creatures. Accepting the gifts didn't mean he'd have to end up like his grandfather, stuck in the bayou and serving as some ad hoc medicine man. No matter where the next assignment led, he'd keep a piece of home in his heart. His talents were a gift and, if possible, he intended to use them to help keep Lily safe.

The need to be outside and greet the sun gripped him

with a passion as fervent as the animalistic urge to mate in spring. Quietly, so as not to awaken Lily in the adjoining room, he pulled on a pair of loose drawstring pants and gathered the needed tools to bless the morning—a ritual he and his grandfather had shared in days past. Arms laden with a woolen blanket and totems, Nash tread barefoot across the sun-warmed oak floor and opened the screen door, pausing at the rusty screech of its hinges.

He stilled, ears attuned to the slightest sound from the next room, but Lily didn't stir. Still barefoot, Nash walked down the porch steps until his calloused feet sank into the white sand that held the warmth of yesterday's sunlight. Cerulean warblers chirped a welcome that seemed a personal greeting for him. *Chirrup. Chirrup. Come into the light.* As if he had done it all his life, had walked this path before. Nash picked his way to shore until he arrived at a mound of sand dunes. In between the dunes he spotted a level middlemost point where the sand mounds surrounded him on all sides like a private oasis.

Here.

He climbed a dune plumaged with sea oats and arrived at a consummate ceremonial spot. At once, he spread out the turquoise, red and yellow blanket with a woven symbol of the sun and the crossed kabocca sticks. Carefully, he arranged the materials—his ever-present medicine pouch, a leather-sheathed hunting knife, a bag of cornmeal and bald-eagle and turkey feathers. He grasped the waistband of his pants and tugged, shedding the cloth that separated his body from all that was natural and free.

Unencumbered, Nash stretched his arms toward the sky. An ocean breeze lifted his long hair to the winds; the salty air swooshed every inch of his skin in blessing. He lifted his head, closed his eyes and fully experienced creation. The eternal crash of the tides pulsed through blood and bone and sinew, the sun caressed his naked body and, through the blanket, the soles of his feet yoked to the earth's core, grounding and centering. He inhaled the clean scent of water and salt as savory as a bountiful feast to a starving man.

This was what he'd been missing for years, what he'd unknowingly sought in wild African safaris, in the chill, lonely splendor of the Arctic, the high mountains of Nepal and the valley of the Grand Canyon. Ancestral land held a sacred belonging unparalleled anywhere else one roamed. To walk among one's forefathers and behold the place where they'd once breathed and loved and struggled and eventually died and returned to dust.

Incredible. Nash dropped his hands and opened his eyes, eager to express his gratitude, his blessings, all the more precious from the guilt and regret he'd suffered the past three years. He dropped to the blanket and sat cross-legged, the totems within arm's reach. He opened the suede medicine pouch and emptied its treasures: the tip of an eagle's feather, a vial of dirt from the backyard of his grandfather's cottage, tiny perfect shells he'd collected as a boy, a sand dollar, a smooth carnelian pebble and a narrow beaded bracelet crafted and handed down from some unknown female relation. He let the sunlight bathe and bless the relics, renewing their energy and spirit.

Nash held up the turkey and eagle feathers to the light before braiding them into his hair, framing both sides of his face. And this might be what helped him heal and find answers. After bubbling burst from deep in his throat, he chanted, *I seek and accept all that is offered.*

This was good. This was right. This was his heritage. No more would he shut out the gift or resist what was so freely offered. Nash again stood, lifting the bag of corn-meal. He opened it and grabbed a fistful of the golden maize that had been the sustenance of his people over the ages. With a powerful thrust, he released the ground corn, scattering it in the Gulf wind. Turning in all directions, he tossed more cornmeal in private thanksgiving. An offering to the earth in thanks for its power and bounty. Grains of yellow corn mixed with the pristine white sand. In a final movement, he emptied the bag in one fell swoop, watching the swirl of it rise upward and then fall to the ground.

Over and beyond the dunes, a woman with silver-blond hair stood and waved. Her blue nightgown fluttered in the breeze like an errant pool of water, and then it pressed against the feminine curves of her body.

Lily.

She approached with a dignity and purpose he admired. He wouldn't let anyone hurt her. She possessed an inner strength and beauty that called to him as strongly as any ancient spirit. He'd never experienced this call with anyone else. Never been drawn to want to completely possess a woman. This longing to be with Lily felt as natural and as deep as his connection to earth and sun. As before, an otherworldly message heralded her presence. A lone seagull screeched. *Two spirits.* Another squalled, *but your destiny.*

She wasn't what he'd thought he wanted in a woman. Nothing about her was normal. Lily was as mysteriously tied to the bayou as his spirit was bound and connected. Lily accepted and believed in his Choctaw roots, his connection to the land and its creatures. And he wanted her with all his heart. Mind, soul and body yearned to be one with Lily and discover all her secrets.

And so he stood, naked and unashamed and open.

Unbounded black hair fluttered wildly in the wind like a constable of ravens, alerting Lily to where Nash had disappeared. The screeching of the screen door had awakened her from restless dreams of exploding cars, empty pill bottles and a dark menace hovering in the mist.

She walked closer until she was near enough to see past the dunes and view his body.

His naked body.

Bronzed and muscled, Nash stood as proud and powerful as a warrior. *Her* warrior. For as long as he stayed and wanted her in return. Anticipation quickened her pace. She ached to be one with him.

The first ferry ride to the island was hours away. They were alone on this paradise and Lily intended to make the most of it. They'd arrived late last night, somber and weary. Nash had matter-of-factly showed her around the small wooden lodge, pointing out where supplies and toiletries were kept. He'd immediately retired to a separate bedroom, obviously wishing solitude after the grueling realization that the past's evils had followed him all the way to this remote bayou.

Two seagulls screeched as they dove down and flew between her and Nash.

As before, Lily fancied their arrival was intentional and that they mysteriously communicated with Nash. Not that any of that mattered at the moment.

She would greet him as unafraid and bold as he stood before her. Lily slipped off her nightdress and held it casually bunched in one hand. Nash was still as a sturdy oak, but his eyes darkened with a need that matched her own. She stumbled in the sand but regained her balance and kept walking, undeterred. Nothing could stop her from joining with Nashoba. Nothing. Even if he broke her heart when he left. If she returned to sea with her mother and rejoined the merfolk, she'd do so knowing her heart would forever stay with Nash no matter where he wandered the earth.

No. She wouldn't think of it now. Wouldn't allow the unforeseeable future, or last night's events, to rob the present.

She was so close. A few more feet. Nash held out his arms and she stepped into his embrace, his strength. They clung to each other, the breeze whipping around their bodies. She buried her head in his smooth, broad chest as her hands explored the hard, silky skin of his back, stretched taut over lean muscles coiled tight as a loaded spring. She didn't want to move. Ever. Not even for a millisecond to let go and raise her face for a kiss.

Nash's hands entangled in her hair and cupped the base of her neck. He lifted her face as he lowered his own. Lily closed her eyes, her last sight the full lips coming to press against her mouth. A whimpering rumbled in her throat until Nash's tongue invaded and quieted her cries.

Oh, he was skilled. A master kisser. Just the right pressure, just the right amount of teasing and claiming. The press of his need against her stomach fevered her core and she rocked her hips against him. She didn't know how it happened—there was a sensation of falling—and then she lay on a blanket, Nash's body covering her own. The delicious heaviness of his weight anchored her so there was no escape. Not that she ever wanted to be anywhere but here, making love with Nash.

His erection pressed against her womanhood and she lifted her hips, aching for him to fill her as she signaled her readiness.

Nash rose up on his elbows and stared down, eyes harsh and stern with desire. "Are you sure about this?" he asked, his voice as hoarse as the screeching seagulls that had flown between them earlier.

Lily marveled at the contrast of her voice compared to Nash's. Where hers flowed, liquid and beguiling, his rumbled in a deep baritone, as powerful as an earthquake, the low notes vibrating deep in her core. "I want you," she moaned. "So much."

Nash sank and lowered his head until their foreheads touched. "I'm nothing but trouble. I've brought pain to anyone I've been close with."

"Even if that were true, I don't care." Lily ran her fingers through his long hair, which was smooth and fluid as water.

"I won't let anything happen to you, Lily," he said, his breath fierce and hot upon her face. "I promise."

She'd never felt so protected, so safe. *Everything will be fine.* "I know you won't." She kissed him and again rocked her hips against his stiff manhood, ready for him to claim her as his own, to be as one.

Nash planted a series of featherlight kisses down her neck and shifted his body back as he edged lower. He cupped a breast in his large, calloused hand and Lily sucked in her breath. His mouth came down and suckled one nipple, then another. Wet heat flicked her sensitive buds until she pushed at his shoulders. "Let's do it," she said raggedly.

"No way."

He shook his head, obsidian hair falling over the sides of her face, neck and shoulders, a velvet veil that obscured everything, as if they formed their own private island that excluded the world. There was only this moment, this passion, the exquisite sensations that left them both trembling and consumed. Lily could see nothing but the harsh planes of his jaw and high cheekbones and burning stare. The green of his irises darkened, lasered through her defenses until she was stripped clean—raw and trembling and desperate for Nash to claim her body. To be so filled deep inside that the soft curves of her body melded into his muscled strength and hardness.

"Now," she insisted.

He grinned, a pure male smile of pride. "No. Not for all the pirate treasure supposedly hidden in Bayou La Siryna."

Lily would have laughed if she hadn't been so frustrated. She was used to calling the shots in everything. *Everything.* But this time, Nash wielded control.

It pissed her off. And excited her.

Nash shifted his weight until he lay alongside her and cupped her breasts, fingers kneading the soft flesh. Eyes still on her, he rolled a nipple between his thumb and index finger.

And squeezed.

Lily moaned as her core tightened and inner thighs pressed together. Nash lowered his hand past her rib cage until it rested over her belly. The warmth of his fingers and hand splayed over her stomach was tender—and a pregnant pause that foretold more to come.

She'd waited long enough. Lily shifted in the sand until she also lay on one side. Gently, teasingly, she ran a finger down his hard shaft and cupped the tight, hard sacks at its base.

And squeezed.

This time, it was Nash who groaned with need.

"Now, please," Lily breathed, face pressed into his wide chest.

In one fluid motion, Nash lay on his back and pulled her so that she straddled his midsection. Lily threw back her head and closed her eyes. The sun shone down on her exposed skin, seeping into every pore like a blessing. The tide surged, crested, broke and then surged again, timeless and powerful.

I'll never be the same. Another moment, and my life changes. Lily knew it, as if the universe sang the message in her ear.

No more begging. Nash seemed to want her as badly as she wanted him. He guided her over his shaft and entered, filling her, claiming her in a way she'd never experienced.

They moved, slowly at first and then faster. Harder. She locked eyes with his, studying the awed, determined darkening of his dilated pupils. The blue of her irises was reflected in his like round orbs of water in a pool of blackness. Mind, body and soul joined and bound together until they melded in a fire as bright and hot as the risen sun.

Talk about backfire. *Stupid, stupid, stupid.* Opal clawed the right side of her face, her sharpened fingernails abrading the skin around the scar. She'd driven that bitch right into his bed, his heart.

Lordy, she hated this stinking bayou that reeked like rotten fish. And the heat! It was smothering and thick as sickly sweet syrup that coated your skin until you were constantly sticky and nasty-feeling.

The cheap motel room was as tiny and constricting as a jail cell. She'd suffered it for days now, venturing out only at night—scurrying about like a rat searching for a bite to eat. The only daylight she'd been out in was when she'd gone to Lily's house to execute the final warning. Sneaking in had been as easy as leaving a utility room window cracked when Lily had invited her over for dinner before she supposedly left the bayou.

Easy entrance, but no fun. There was a faint herbal scent that was off-putting, yet not strong enough to keep her away. She'd spent hours rambling about the house, seething at the opulence. Rich bitch.

Opal held out her hand—the blue sapphire mounted on the gold ring gleamed mockingly under the fluorescent light. Lily would never miss it. She had dozens of jewelry boxes stuffed with such baubles. Opal had opened each one, fuming at the pearl bracelets, ruby necklaces, emerald brooches and precious stones in every rainbow color, every shade and hue of expensive stone.

And that closet, row upon row of expensive, lacy and satiny concoctions. Opal ran a hand down the bubble-gum-pink nightgown she'd lifted. Lily would be breathtaking in it. But on her, the ultra-feminine gown was a mockery.

This was supposed to be *her* time with Nash on Herb

Island. She'd undergone three plastic surgeries until the idiot doctors claimed the scar was barely noticeable and was as good as it was going to get. Damn liars. She was a Frankenstein. She'd wanted perfection before telling Nash she loved him, but now would have to do.

Lily was ruining everything. That woman could have any man she wanted in the bayou, yet she selfishly had to claim Nash.

It was so unfair.

Why didn't they ever listen to her warnings? Lily was as daft as Rebecca and Connie had been. You tried to play fair with people, you gave them a warning, and they continued to go their own selfish way. Just once, Opal wished she'd been given more warnings growing up. But no, she was never given advance notice of when the next move would take place. One day a social worker would pull up in a government-issued sedan, tell her to pack her bag of belongings and that would be that. On to a new foster home.

At first, Opal had been terrified of a new family and new school but always hoped *this* time would be better. That *this* time they would love her. *This* time they wouldn't find her strange. This time she'd be well-fed. This time she wouldn't be beaten.

The memory of the last family haunted her. They'd been kind initially; the foster parents were gentle and their son had...liked her. Liked her *lots*. Tommy would sneak into her bedroom in the dead of night and show his love. It had been glorious up until the moment his mother had caught them. She'd shrieked and shaken Opal so hard she'd wondered if it was possible to die of adolescent-shaking syndrome. Her head had whipped back and forth so forcefully Opal had been sure her neck would break.

The shrieking had stopped, followed by a venomous hiss. *Don't you ever come near my son again, you filthy slut. What would the neighbors say?*

That had been the first and last warning.

She and Tommy had been oh-so-careful after that, knowing their time together was limited since his mom had told the social worker to take her away at the end of the month. But there wouldn't even be that if they were caught again; she'd be out on the streets immediately.

Opal had learned to school her features, to give the appearance of calm and nonchalance, even when her inner world roiled with self-loathing and despair. The external could be controlled if she was very, very careful to mask her pain.

On the last night with them, the foster mom had evidently been lying in wait for the creak in the hallway. Again, Opal was jerked up in the woman's vise and the shaking and shrieking had started again. *I warned you! I warned you!* Opal was disoriented, the room blurry and spinning. Why didn't Tommy help her?

With a mighty thrust Opal never would have guessed the petite foster mom had in her, the pinching, bruising hold on her arms was gone and she fell forward, toppling into a dresser. Her face smashed against a mirror. An explosion of glass shards pricked her face and wet goo inched down her neck. She sank to the floor, palming the shredded flesh of her right cheek, her screams mingling with the foster mother's.

She'd escaped the system at age eighteen. It had been rough but better. The thing was to keep moving, keep on the run, keep to yourself. And always, always maintain.

She'd survived. Opal hated the platitude "What doesn't break you makes you stronger."

No. Her life was nothing but brokenness, even if the only evidence was the scar on her cheek and the ones on her forearms from the self-induced cutting. The blessed cutting that allowed a small portion of the pain to seep out with the blood. A minidetox for the soul.

Opal rushed inside the motel bathroom and unwrapped a new razor. The thin edge of the blade flashed like quick-silver in the afternoon rays before sinking into her skin. The sharp bite of pain was so bittersweet, pain and plea-sure intermingled like animal sex. Hurting so good she moaned. A ruby rush of liquid ran down her arm, sticky and hot. With the letting came clarity.

She'd handle Lily. Take her rightful place in Nash's arms. He loved her, she knew it. If he didn't realize it, he'd learn to. Rebecca, Connie and Lily bound them together. He'd know he was at fault for their deaths as much as she was—and that death and secrets yoked an unbreakable tie.

He'd be her forever love. Her forever home. And if he left, she would follow him to every square inch of the globe and poison any other woman he ever looked at. She would warn him of her intention, too.

Because you had to be fair about it. If you didn't play fair, you were as bad as the rest of them, deserving of hell and vengeance and death. Those filthy sluts deserved to die.

As did Lily.

Chapter 11

Nash stroked the curve of Lily's hip as she lay on her side, one arm stretching out, head cradled on her forearm, eyes closed. He wished he had his camera to capture the image of his dark, rough hand as his fingers rested on the fair plane of her hip. Lily's skin wasn't a pure vanilla-white. Pinpricks of pink and silver and green and blue pastels shimmered, as if she'd been dipped in crushed mica. A black-and-white photo alone couldn't capture the nuances of Lily's beauty.

One day he'd have to ask her permission to photograph her nude. Not for public view, but for his own nostalgic remembrance when he was alone again far from his bayou home.

Home. Nash eased up on an elbow, determined to move past such sentimental musings. Special as it was, the bayou was not home. The world was his home. He'd achieved a slice of fame, and a milder portion of fortune, but he was in his prime, beginning what could be a long, profitable career. He could maybe even become the best wildlife photographer ever.

Better yet, he would leave Bayou La Siryna with the issue of the mysterious stalker resolved and be here for his grandfather in his dying days.

If this morning was no hallucination—no trick of the mind—if Lily was truly his destiny, then she would have to follow him. But he couldn't imagine her uprooting from this place and her family.

Nash ran his hand up and down Lily's right thigh. "Hey, sleepyhead, you'll burn up if you stay naked out here with no sunscreen."

Blue eyes popped open. "True. My skin burns in no time."

"I remember."

Even as a kid, Lily had been fastidious about applying sunscreen and avoiding direct sun at midday. Nash grinned as Lily retrieved and shook out the now-wrinkled nightgown. She pulled it on and began braiding her long hair, the colorful beads of her friendship bracelet highlighting the graceful bend of her wrist.

"Allow me." He took hold of her hair, gently teased it into three parts and weaved them into a thick plait, enjoying the feel of shifting satin in the roughened skin of his palms and fingers. He tugged gently at the end. "You have anything to fasten it with?"

"No, but this will do to keep the wind from whipping my face until we reach the lodge."

Nash kissed the exposed nape of her neck and an unexpected tenderness twisted inside. It would be hard to leave Lily. And he wouldn't until the killer was found and she was safe.

With effort, Nash brushed aside the worry that invaded his peace. This morning was for exploration and he wanted to prolong the lightness from his burdens. He couldn't recall the last time he'd felt so free, so light and open.

Inspiration struck. "How about a morning swim?"

"You know I can't swim." She stood and stretched, the thin nightgown so transparent he could trace the rosy nipples and thatch of hair between her legs. He imagined the gown wet and plastered against her skin.

"C'mon, I'll teach you," he said past the thickness of his tongue. "It'll be fun."

"I don't want to learn."

Lily stepped off the blanket and dug her pretty pedicured toes in the sand. "Shouldn't we head back to the lodge for breakfast?" she asked.

Nash rose. "We're on an island. Now's the perfect time to learn to swim."

Impatience swept across her face. "Maybe later."

"Okay." He dropped a kiss on her forehead. "No swim lessons. But let's bathe in the ocean. You don't have to go farther than waist-deep. I'll hold you."

Lily turned up her exquisite nose and he laughed, feeling as playful as he had in childhood. On impulse, he scooped her into his arms and twirled her around. Lily threw back her head and giggled. The sound enchanted him.

"You trust me, right?" he asked.

She lightly brushed her fingers along the side of his neck. "With my life. After all, you saved me once before." She grew serious. "I never thanked you properly."

"No need," he assured her. "I think you just did."

Lily kissed him on the mouth, a hard press of lips that left him wanting a repeat performance of the morning's activities. But if he did, he'd lose all track of time. Nash strode to the water. A quick skinny-dip, and then they needed to get dressed before the ferry arrived.

"What are you doing?" Lily shrieked, craning her neck toward the sea. "Put me down."

Nash hesitated. Did the water scare her that badly?

She leveled him a gaze that meant business. "Now."

Wordlessly, he released her. Lily hit the sand running, bits of white sand puffing at her heels. Near the dunes she turned and waved, face sunny again.

"Beat you to the lodge," she shouted.

Would he ever understand her? The woman was even more of an enigma than most. But he liked that she stood up to him, not afraid to express her feelings. He was used to women fawning over him, seemingly grateful for his attention.

It wasn't as fun as you'd think. Not after a few years, anyway.

Nash gathered his treasures, placed them in the medicine bag and sheathed the knife, everything now blessed and cleansed by the sun. He shook sand from the blanket and made his way back to the lodge, wondering at Lily's changing mood.

A hiss of pipes sounded as he climbed the front steps, announcing she was in the shower. He debated joining her but decided it'd be best to wait for Lily to offer such invitations. Their rustic accommodations didn't include a large supply of hot water and he doubted there would be any left when Lily finished. With a sigh, Nash set his things on the porch and headed back to shore. He'd bathe in the ocean alone.

Cleansed, he returned to the lodge and was greeted by the smell of bacon. Sex had kicked his appetite in gear and he followed his nose to the kitchen. A pot of cheese grits bubbled on the stove and three crisp bacon slices lay on a paper towel.

Nash opened a pine cupboard and got a bowl. "Lily?" He ladled the gooey orange goodness into the bowl and rattled around the drawers for a spoon. "Lily?" he called again.

No answer, but he was too hungry to wait. He spooned

up a mouthful of the grits, and the melted cheddar and butter was hot, creamy heaven. He looked out the kitchen window, eating grits and taking bites of crisp, salty bacon. Where had she gone? He was used to the solitary life, but an unexpected pang of disappointment hit him, as well as worry for her safety. Would have been nice to share breakfast. She must already be out with her watercolors, searching for a subject to paint.

At least he wouldn't have to worry about keeping her amused while he worked. But he'd caution her from now on to let him know where she was before other people arrived on the island. He wanted to keep a close watch.

Nash's fingers tightened on the counter. In the excitement of the morning, last night's events had slipped to the background of his mind. Now they burst forth again, the ripped canvases, angry slashes of paint and, worse, the hissing snake.

Who?

Nash circled around the long list of women he'd ever been involved with, inwardly wincing. Sex had been too quick, too easy for him in his youth, and he'd done little to resist the women who'd made advances. Eventually, he'd grown bored with the easy pickups and ashamed of the casual flings. Both Rebecca and Connie had been longer-term relationships; they hadn't seemed to mind his frequent trips and lack of exclusive affection.

Nash mentally shook off the painful reveries. This didn't do anybody any good. He stretched, stiff muscles alerting him he'd been reminiscing more than a few minutes. He went to the fridge, poured a glass of orange juice and took a sip, the sugar hitting his veins with a pop of instant energy.

Faint splashes and voices drifted through the open window. Nash checked the stove clock and frowned at the time—almost 7:30 a.m. Ned was usually predictable in his scheduled ferry arrivals: 8:00 a.m., noon, 3:00 p.m. and 5:00 p.m. People had arrived and he didn't know where Lily had run off to. Nash set the glass of OJ down on the cheap laminate countertop so hard he was surprised the glass didn't shatter.

He started to run out the front door in his underwear. "Damn it," he muttered, hand paused on the door handle. He snagged a pair of jeans hanging on the back of a chair in his bedroom. Zipping and buttoning the waistband, he took off in the direction of the voices, somewhat molli-fied that there only seemed to be a few voices and the tone was light. No screams or angry words signaling danger.

Past a bend in the curve of a shallow inlet, he found an older woman with hair the color and length of Lily's slip-ping on a pair of jeweled sandals. She wore a long coral sundress and her eyes widened when she caught his glance, then cut quickly out to sea.

Nash followed her gaze and saw two clones of the woman as well as another with short, dark hair. Was that—? His eyes narrowed and he shaded them with one hand until he made out the delicate planes of Lily's face.

Lily—who repeatedly claimed she couldn't swim and had refused to even get her toes wet with him this morn-ing. She was too far out in the ocean for her not to be swimming or doing some sort of dog paddle that kept her torso above water.

She lied to me. Disappointment warred with anger and confusion. Why lie about such a trivial thing? More impor-tant, what else had Lily lied about? Even after the morn-ing's intimacy, he noticed a secrecy, a holding back on her part.

The older woman on shore let out a shrill whistle and three startled faces turned as one in his direction.

A seagull shrieked overhead. *They all are of two spirits.* Whatever the hell that meant.

"Hello," said the woman, walking toward him with a confident smile. "You must be Nashoba Bowman. I'm Adriana Bosarge, Lily's mother. We've met before when you were a little tyke."

She took his arm and started leading him back to the lodge. He glanced over his shoulder, but Lily and the others had vanished.

"You've placed my daughter in danger," Adriana admonished, drawing his attention to her once again.

The tone was light but the reprimand was there, sharp steel wrapped in delicate silk.

"Yes, ma'am, but I'm watching her and won't let anyone hurt her."

She cocked a brow. "Watching her so well that her family arrived and you didn't even realize it for several minutes."

Nash's face burned, but not from the summer heat. "What did you do—bribe Ned to ride out early?"

"Ned's an old friend," she answered, sweeping past him and up the porch steps.

Which didn't really answer his question.

He followed her inside, where she settled in on the old, faded sofa. Her dress billowed out with a coral glow that attracted the room's light and energy. What an arresting photographic subject she'd make. He'd develop the photograph in black-and-white; the only spot of color would be the dress. Nash shook off his professional wanderings. This moment could be an opportunity. Lily and the others might traipse in at any moment.

"Great to see Lily in the water this morning," he said, settling in a chair opposite Adriana. "Considering her childhood trauma."

"What?" She straightened, alarm flickering across her placid face. "Oh, that." She jiggled a set of thin gold bangles on her right arm. "Lily told you about it, then."

"Yes. Must have been a difficult time. How did she escape?"

"Escape from what?" Adriana's smooth brow furrowed and her jaw dropped a fraction until she regained her composure. "I really don't like to talk about it. You understand."

"Escape her fear of the water," he insisted. He understood he was being fed a load of bullshit. Secrecy must be a Bosarge family trait. Privacy and reticence Nash understood from his own childhood warnings not to broadcast his grandfather's healing abilities outside their tribe. But outright deception was an altogether different kettle.

"No. I really don't understand."

Adrianne crossed her legs and smiled. "That's because you don't have children and understand how hard it is to talk about their problems. Be a dear and fix me a glass of cold water or iced tea. Whatever's easiest."

He rose reluctantly, but Southern manners had been drilled into him too deeply to refuse her request or to continue challenging an elder. And this was Lily's mother, after all. No point in antagonizing her family.

Nash entered the kitchen, poured a glass of iced tea and returned.

Adriana thanked him demurely and nodded at the chair opposite the sofa.

"I'll be direct with you, Nashoba. I am not thrilled about your relationship with my Lily."

I bet you aren't. His fingers dug into the soft, worn leather of the armchair. Bitterness peppered his mouth and stomach, but he kept his tone civil. "Because we're so *different*, right? Our backgrounds and heritage are too far apart." Which was the polite way of saying he was the wrong color, the wrong ethnicity for her lily-white daughter. Like he hadn't heard that before.

"Oh, not that." Adriana shrugged and gave an I-know-something-you-don't smile. "Although the two of you are monumentally mismatched in every way. But that's not my greatest concern. I've spoken with Tillman and Landry. Your last two girlfriends didn't fare too well."

"I would do anything to change what happened."

"I'm not blaming you. But of all humans, I would have wanted someone at least safe for my daughter."

Humans? What an odd choice of words.

At the creak of the porch steps he turned to look out the front window. Lily and the other blonde looked so alike it was startling. Jet was the odd duck with the black hair and eyes. All had damp hair and T-shirts that clung to their sea-slick skin. They laughed and chattered like tourists on a vacay.

Lily entered first, wearing an insouciant smile like armor. "Mom's not giving you the third degree, I hope." Her tone sounded deliberately chirpy. She sank into the chair next to him and began twirling fistfuls of hair.

"She's your mom. She has the right to speak her mind," he said flatly.

The other two scampered in, sat on either side of the sofa by Adriana and began chattering away in earnest.

"I'm Lily's cousin, Shelly," the blond said, introducing herself. She turned to Adriana. "How long are we staying this morning?" she asked. "I'm teaching a water aerobics class at noon."

"And don't forget you're supposed to take me shopping today in Mobile for nursery stuff," Jet piped in.

It dawned on Nash that they wanted to spare him the mother-dragon act by engaging Adriana's attention on them. He faced Lily.

"Have a nice swim?"

"I don't know what you mean." She crossed her legs and her right knee jittered back and forth.

He pointed to her damp hair. "You're all wet. Besides, I saw you out there swimming."

"No, you didn't." Lily's eyes were steady, her gaze steadfast and true. "I only stepped into the water a few feet, and my hair's wet because Jet splashed me."

Jet nodded their way. "That's right. Sorry, Lily. I do still like to tease my little sis."

"Lily's afraid of the water," Shelly said. "Ever since that time she almost drowned."

The girls had evidently concocted a story on the way in. "Of course," he agreed, folding his arms across his chest. Unbelievable. Nash frowned, but he wouldn't call Lily out in front of her family. A frisson of disappointment gnawed his gut. After the earlier intimacy, a chasm now separated them and he felt further from Lily than the day he'd bumped into her at Winn Dixie.

"Excuse me a moment," he said, walking out of the room. He'd had enough of their chatter. The minute he and Lily were alone, he'd get some answers.

Adriana's long hair tossed wildly in the sea breeze as they stood on the shore, saying their goodbyes.

"Sweet seven seas, Mom. What did you say to him?"

Adriana lifted her chin. "That the two of you are totally unsuitable."

Jet stood behind Adriana and rolled her eyes. "No one's good enough for Lily."

Lily inwardly winced at the slight bitterness in Jet's voice. Having their mother's favoritism growing up had complicated their sibling bond. Things were better between them these days, but Lily realized she'd often been insensitive in the past, especially last year when Jet had won her event in the annual Poseidon Games. Her sister had trained relentlessly for months, yet when Lily had entered and won the Siren's Call event, as she effortlessly did every year, the family and merfolk had excessively lauded her instead of Jet. Yet she'd only done what came naturally.

Lily made a mental note to have a private talk with Jet to apologize and try to set things right. She couldn't change her mother's behavior, but she didn't have to encourage it.

Shelly, ever the peacekeeper, hugged Lily's neck. "We need to get a move on. If Ned sees us, he'll wonder how we got here without his ship."

Adriana didn't budge. "Leave, Lily. You don't have to stay here and put yourself in danger. Come out to sea and take your place where you belong." She stepped forward, face softening. "You can have your pick of any merman."

Her mother would never understand. She wanted to be joined heart and soul with a man, wanted someone to share her life with. With mermen, sex was enjoyed and encouraged for the propagation of the species. That held little appeal to Lily. She saw what Shelly and Jet had and it was far superior to pair bonding with a merman for an occasional mating, the spawning of merbabies and then raising the increasing fry of merbabies alone.

If Adriana hadn't wanted her to live in the bayou, she should have kept her daughters at sea more growing up. Although, to be fair, her mother had done it to try to protect Jet from discovering some ugly truths about her true biological parentage.

It had almost worked. Lily hadn't known that Jet was actually her cousin, not her sister, until last year. Even though the tragic past had been dredged up, Lily would always consider Jet a true sister in every way.

"Maybe later I'll return and find a suitable merman." Lily drew a circle in the sand with the tip of her big toe. She was too emotionally on edge to have this confrontation with her mom right now. If things didn't work out with Nash…life at sea was a possibility. No sense in drawing a line in the sand over a man who probably was going to leave her by summer's end. "Give me a few more weeks. You want to stay until Jet's baby is born anyway."

Adriana placed her hands on Lily's shoulders. "I can't make you go with me like I did when you were a child. But at least promise me you'll be careful."

"At the first hint of danger I'll head out to sea," Lily promised, fingers crossed behind her back. "Now y'all need to scoot before Nash comes searching for me. I'll hide more clothes for you again in the same hidey-hole in case you return underwater."

One by one, they each disappeared behind a rock, disrobed and dove underwater. Lily cast anxious backward glances, sure Nash would pop up at any moment.

"I'll come back later with your paint supplies," Shelly called out from behind the rock. Three distinct splashes and the island was a party of two again—just her and Nash.

Everything was so much simpler with the outside world held at bay. No murders, no meddling family, no job assignments to foreign lands. Lily picked her way back to the lodge to fetch the sketchpad and pencils she'd brought last night. Being caught lying unsettled her in a way it never had before. She was used to lying about everything to the land dwellers and even kept a tiny part of herself hidden from her family. For all they knew, she reveled in her siren powers, enjoyed the adoration of the merfolk and was amused by her dalliances with the local bayou men.

None of that was true now that Nashoba Bowman had returned.

Lily quickened her pace, eager to draw. She'd immerse herself in art and forget Nash's condemning stare when she'd entered the lodge. She'd been having such fun, too, until she'd spotted him on shore. Splashing, diving, the water invigorating and salty, her mer fin whipping in the Gulf current.

Impossible to live on the island for days or weeks without swimming. Lily resolved to be very, very careful until she could tell him the truth. When Nash fell asleep in the evenings, she'd slip out in the moonlight and swim under its silver orb, connected even deeper to the tide by the pull of the moon. In some ways, Mom was right. She and Nash were opposites. He was of the sun, dark golden and grounded to the earth, whereas she was of the moon, moored to the fluid sea and bewitched by moonbeams.

In no time, Lily gathered the needed supplies and one of the rolled woolen blankets Nash kept on the porch. She meandered down narrow trails with blizzards of cypress, pine and saw palmetto. That was one of the things she loved about the bayou—the varied landscape. You had the white sandy shore and the sea, but you also had green woodland heavily scented with pine that mixed with sea brine in the breeze.

The millions of mosquitoes and gnats were the only undesirable trade-off for such paradise.

Lily found a patch of Southern seashore mallow in full bloom cheerfully waving their delicate pink petals surrounding a sunshine-yellow corolla. She spread out the blanket and opened the sketchpad. Such a shame she hadn't packed colored pencils last night, but she'd make do with her pencils and paint a watercolor of the flowers later.

"What you got there?"

Her heart exploded, pulsing and pounding *danger danger danger* to her brain and limbs. The instinctual command to flee was immediate and she lurched forward, scrambling to her feet.

A strong hand gripped her right forearm, preventing escape.

"It's me, Lily. Nash."

She drew ragged, painful breaths. She was safe. Last night had rattled her more than she'd realized.

"Hey, I'm sorry." Nash wrapped his arms around her waist from behind and she melted against him, wilting like an uprooted flower needing to bury into soil.

"I've got you," he whispered into her hair.

"I thought you were angry with me."

"I am. But I'd never scare you on purpose. What kind of man do you think I am?"

"A good one. The best," she said softly. Lily closed her eyes and enjoyed the heat of his skin pressed against her back, the comfort of his arms circling her waist.

"So why did you lie about swimming?"

Nash wasn't going to let this go. Lily swallowed hard. Normally, lying was no problem, something necessary to keep hidden in the bayou and protect her family and all the other merfolk—what remained of her kind. But now the unspoken lies soured on her tongue and she struggled to explain with at least a modicum of truth.

"I only swim with my family," she offered lamely.

"Why?"

Damn. As if she didn't know that would be the next question. "I'm a terrible swimmer—all leg kicks and thrashing arms. It's embarrassing."

"Hmm."

The vibration of his voice rumbled deep in his chest and radiated the length of her spine.

"But you didn't have to go in deep. I only wanted—"

"Sorry," she interrupted, turning in to him and kissing the hollow of his throat. "What were you doing naked out there this morning? Not that I'm complaining."

Nash studied her and a muscle in his jaw twitched. Lily's breath stilled. Would he let the matter go for now?

"I know what you're doing." His voice was husky, thick with either anger or desire. Possibly both, Lily wasn't sure.

"Did it work?" She gave him her most dazzling smile. He didn't return her smile. "I'll let it go for a moment."

Nash guided her shoulders forward and dipped his chin onto the top of her scalp. "To answer your question, when I was young, my grandfather and I had this dawn ritual where we greeted the sun and thanked the earth for its blessings."

"Naked?"

"No." He chuckled. "I'm not sure why I took off my pants. It seemed the right thing to do at the moment. When Grandfather and I used to do this, we'd open our medicine bags for the sun to bless the contents and sometimes we'd chant or dance to the beat of his drumming."

"Like a moving prayer," she whispered. Exactly how she felt during moonlit swims. "I know what you mean."

A comfortable silence descended, and, emboldened, Lily ventured another question. "Sometimes, like today with the seagull, I imagine birds are talking to you. Really talking."

His hands, which had been stroking her forearms, stilled. She hardly dared breathed while she awaited his response.

"And if I told you they were?"

"I'd believe you."

His heart thudded against her back and his muscles tensed. "They do."

The admission hadn't been easy for him. "Thank you," she said, encouraged he felt safe to open up. "One last question. What do they say?"

"I knew that was coming," he said ruefully. "Actually, this is new to me and it's only happened twice. Both times while I was with you."

"Go on," she breathed.

"They say you are of two spirits."

Chapter 12

Two spirits.

Lily pondered the mysterious words, her spine tingling with wonder. Two spirits—as in she was two-faced? A liar? That she was, and so much more. And to think all this time she'd never suspected her secret would be betrayed while she walked on land, least of all by one of earth's creatures. Instead, she'd always feared being spotted at sea by human eyes.

"What does it mean?" Nash asked. "Assuming, of course, you don't think I'm crazy and hearing imaginary voices."

"No!" Lily moved out of his arms, sat cross-legged on the blanket, took hold of his hands and drew him down with her. "You're the sanest person I've ever met."

He ran a hand through his long hair. "Have to admit, I've doubted myself at times, especially since coming here. Everything's intensified."

"Your connection to the land and animals?" she guessed.

Nash stared. "You've always intuited it, haven't you?"

"I sensed it when we were kids. The way you would grow still and cock your head, as if listening to whispers in the wind. I knew it for sure the time you found me when I was lost. How did you do it?" She shuddered, remembering the horror of the day and night she'd spent alone in the woods.

She'd gone looking for Nash and, not finding him in their usual hangouts, had meandered down obscure trails until she'd realized nothing was familiar, or rather everything was the same in all directions. Merely clumps of pine trees and knotty dirt trails with no distinguishing marks. She'd tried to imagine what Nash would do if he were lost. Inspired, she'd ripped one of her socks with a sharp rock and unraveled the threads, deciding the best course was to pick a direction and stay with it. She'd walked along and, every few feet, tied a string on a low-lying branch to mark her progress.

Hours later, exhausted, thirsty and increasingly panicked, Lily spotted one of the knotted cotton strings and realized she'd been walking in circles. Defeated, she strategized that the next best course of action was to stay put. She built a bed of pine needles and sat to wait for help.

And waited, waited, waited. Until the sun had sunk below the horizon and complete darkness had shrouded the woods. The only flicker of light came from fireflies randomly darting above dense shrubbery. If only she'd had a jar, she could have collected the fireflies and kept them encased by her side like a lantern in the gloomy pitch. She'd imagined the woods would be a quiet place, but she'd been wrong. Owls hooted and insects buzzed. Unseen animals scrambled about. Lily had forgotten her hunger and thirst as fear filled her stomach and lungs.

The worst had been an eerie high-pitched caterwauling. Bobcats weren't unheard of in those parts. What if one stalked in the trees above, ready to pounce the instant she drifted to sleep? Lily had hoped the wail was from the ginger-colored feral cats that peppered the bayou. Nevertheless, she'd resolved to stay awake.

She fought sleep, remembering Sam and Nash's Choctaw tales of mysterious beings in the bayou. If there were supernatural creatures roaming the forest, she hoped it was only the Little People—Kowi Anukasha—known for their mischievous pranks, like throwing sticks to try to scare humans. They meant no real harm. Unlike the Hoklonote, an evil spirit who could assume any shape and read people's thoughts. If so, he'd know she was alone and frightened. Even worse, there was Nalusa Falaya, the dark being who could eat your soul.

Eventually, her eyes had ached and her mind had fallen into sleep's blankness.

Twigs snapped and pebbles crunched, jerking her awake. An oval of light beamed on her face, blinding in the sudden brightness.

Lily?

Nash's voice had slashed through the haze of alarm, and relief washed over her. She was safe.

A gentle squeeze of her hand jolted Lily from the memories.

"You were a pitiful sight, but a welcome one," Nash said.

"So how did you find me when no one else could?" She tilted her head, wistful. "Let me guess. A little birdie told you."

"Nothing that dramatic." His lips twitched at the corners and then he sobered. "I figured you'd gone out looking for me at the usual places. When you weren't there, I retraced my steps until I neared the felled oak seat." A heartbeat's pause. "It's hard to explain, but something in the air's energy shimmered…as if it had been recently disturbed. The soles of my feet tingled and a *knowing* slammed my gut that you'd walked the path behind the rock. I plunged ahead and found the bits of string you'd tied on the trees and shrubs. After that, it was easy."

"My hero," she said simply, with no trace of irony.

Nash snorted. "Some hero. I've brought you nothing but trouble and danger this time around."

Nothing but love. Instead of bursting fireworks, the realization settled on her soul with the tranquility of still waters—deep and pure and abiding. It had always been there and would always remain.

"Nash, I..." She hesitated. The time for confessions could come later. He was consumed with guilt and anger over the stalker who hurt any woman he'd had a relationship with. The last thing he wanted to hear right now was that she loved him. She wouldn't add to his burdens.

He released a hand and stroked a finger along the curve of her jaw. "What?" he prodded.

"Just... None of this is your fault."

His face darkened and he dropped his hand into his lap. "Maybe it is. Maybe I've played fast and loose once too often with a woman's affection. Now I must suffer for past wrongs."

"Look who you're talking to." She thought of Gary, of all the men she'd dated and dumped. What would it do to her if Nash didn't return her love? She hadn't meant to hurt anyone, had been seeking love in her own way and breaking it off before they fell too deep—at least that was how she'd justified it. Shame burned her cheeks. If there was such a thing as karma, she was doomed. Lily ducked her head.

"Hey," he said, gently brushing back her hair. "I don't care about your past. All that matters is the future."

"Then cut yourself a break, too. Goes both ways."

A muscle worked the side of his jaw. "At least none of your boyfriends died."

"It's not your fault," she repeated.

"If I'd been more careful, if I'd even loved them a little in return..." He closed his eyes.

"There was nothing you could have done. You aren't responsible for the actions of a crazy person."

Dark eyes snapped open. "Don't you get it? It's probably some ex-lover I disposed of as casually as a used paper plate."

"Stop it." She gave his hands a shake. "Tillman and Landry are good cops. They'll find who's responsible. And when they do, you're going to have to find a way to let it all go."

"Yes, ma'am." He gave a mock salute.

Garbled voices drifted over. "Seems we have some bird-watchers about. Why don't we grab lunch? I'm starving."

"Good deal." He arose, seemingly as relieved as she was to drop the self-flagellation over ex-lovers. He pulled her up and planted a quick, fierce kiss on her mouth.

"You're all right, Lily Bosarge."

Lily beamed as if he'd bestowed a grand compliment. "You, too. Now let's get out of here."

She bent down to retrieve her sketchpad.

"Whoa, let me see this." Nash took it from her and stared at the drawing. "This is really good."

"You think so? You're not saying that to be nice?"

Nash whipped a sharp glance. "How can you be so self-assured in everything except your art?"

"Because it wasn't handed to me at birth." Unlike her looks and her voice. "Plus..." She hesitated, but if Nash could open up about his gift, she should in return. "It's important to me that it's worthy. I want to be noticed for something other than my looks. Everybody in Bayou La Siryna thinks of me as the slutty blonde whose only talent is styling hair."

His brows screwed together. "Styling hair?"

Lily picked up the blanket and rolled it, tucking it under

an arm. "I used to own a beauty shop in town. I closed it down a few months ago to paint more."

"To hell with what others think."

"Easier said for a guy, especially one that doesn't live in a small town."

"I suppose," he agreed with a slight shrug.

She shot him a sideways glance. "Aren't you curious about my past? My reputation?"

"No," he answered shortly. "You're not guilty of anything that I haven't done. I don't believe in double standards for men and women."

They returned to the lodge, holding hands in companionable silence.

"You made breakfast, so I'll make lunch," Nash said. "Just going to wash up first."

Lily stretched out on the sofa, absorbed with a rare feeling of lazy contentment. What a perfect day. If only they could share every day together. She tucked a pillow under her head and closed her eyes. She'd worry about the future later. Her mind drifted to slumber. A little nap while Nash made lunch...

"What's this?"

Lily jerked awake at the loud voice and sat upright.

Nash carried in the straw basket she'd carelessly laid in the bathroom. Her mom's coral dress was bunched in his right hand, the basket with the rest of the clothes in the other.

Lily blinked, mind momentarily fuzzy from sleep. "It's, um, Mom's dress."

"I recognized it. Shelly and Jet's clothes are in here, too. What'd they do? Board the ferry naked?"

"Don't be silly. They brought a change of clothes with them."

He frowned. "That doesn't make sense. This is what they wore after they finished swimming."

She shrugged and faked a yawn. "They decided to change again." She had to get his mind off those damn clothes. Lily got to her feet and walked to him, smiling. "What are you fixing us for lunch?" She put her arms around his neck and brushed her body against his.

Nash stepped backward, frowning. "No. They were wearing these when they left the lodge."

"Were they?" She tapped her index finger against her lips. "I can't remember."

"I do."

"Oh, stop making such a fuss over nothing," Lily groused, pretending to be cross. The man was too damn observant. She'd have to be more careful with the two of them confined to such close quarters.

"Something funny's going on here," Nash insisted.

"You don't see me laughing." Lily headed to the kitchen. "I'm starving. Let's eat."

She heard Nash return to the bathroom as she opened the fridge and took out a pack of crabmeat and mayonnaise. The bathroom door creaked open and she felt his eyes on her back. Lily ignored him and rummaged for the loaf of bread and a bag of chips.

"Lily," he said, a command to face him.

She continued puttering with the food. "What?"

Nash pulled at her right elbow, guiding her to turn around. The implacable, sober set of his jaw warned that this conversation wasn't over.

"You're keeping something from me."

She opened her mouth, but Nash placed a finger on her lips.

"Don't bother to deny it. I've told you things I've never told anybody. Can't you trust me in return?"

Lily froze, conscious of the utter stillness. The only sound in the kitchen was the mechanical hum of the refrigerator. Guilt spiraled in her mind like an eddy. Oh, how she wanted to tell him everything, but she couldn't. Sure, he'd confessed to some supernatural abilities, but it wasn't like he shape-shifted into another kind of creature.

His eyes stared into her own, open and pure. "All I ask from you is honesty. I've learned from my past that if you can't have that with someone, then there's nothing real between you. So what about your past, Lily? Have you been honest with the men you've been with over the years? Or did you keep a part of yourself hidden while secretly enjoying their devotion?"

His words seeped into the dark corners of her heart and mind, slipping through years of denial and justifications. Shame scalded and she glared at him, angry he brought it into the open. "That's not true," she denied, not wanting to see the truth. 'I can't help it if men fall in love with me."

"But it pleases you, doesn't it? Heady stuff, having all the men chase you, wanting to be your lover."

Lily pursed her lips. "Is that how it feels to you when all the women fall at your feet?" she snapped.

"It used to," he admitted quietly. "Gets old, though, over the years. And I'd give anything if I'd never encouraged Connie and Rebecca. They wanted more from me and I had nothing to give. I should have ended it with both of them when I knew I wasn't in love."

She thought of Gary, how he had dropped his steady girlfriend when she'd crooked her finger his way. She remembered all the men she'd enticed. True, it hadn't taken much effort on her part, but she could have kept to herself. But no, loneliness had driven her to pursue men for the momentary excitement and temporary satisfaction.

What perfect cosmic justice if she'd fallen for the one man who couldn't love her in return.

"Have you ever been in love?" she asked wistfully.

"For the first time, I think I could be."

Lily sucked in her breath, dizzy with joy. It could really happen for her; she could love and be loved in return. "Nash—"

"So tell me what's going on around here. What are you hiding? I need the truth."

"I—I can't," she stammered. "If it were only me…perhaps I could. But too many people could be hurt."

An entire race, to be precise.

His eyes shuttered and his lips compressed. "I see."

Nash turned and walked away, taking all her hopes and dreams with him. Lily raised a hand to catch his arm but let it drop by her side. There was nothing more to be said except…

"I'm sorry," she said to his retreating back.

He kept walking.

Lily gripped the edge of the countertop. She'd been so close… Pain lanced her heart. *So this is love. Damn, it hurts.*

The screen door squeaked open and then banged shut. Nash's footsteps sounded across the wooden porch floor and then all was silent again. Lily peeked out the window and watched him settle into a rocking chair, feet propped on the railing.

Day one alone with Nash and she was blowing it. Lily numbly put up the uneaten food, appetite gone. She returned to the den and sank onto the sofa, acutely conscious of Nash on the porch, probably brooding on what a disappointment she was.

The trill ring of his cell phone went off and he answered, voice low and muffled. Had there been any developments in finding the stalker? Lily strained to hear.

Nash unfolded his feet and jumped out of the chair; his voice had risen to a louder, faster rate, but she couldn't make out the words. Whatever it was, the news wasn't good. Nash propped an arm against a column and dropped his head.

Lily scrambled to her feet. It had to be news from Tillman or Landry. Was someone else hurt? She opened the door and saw Nash let the cell phone drop to his side.

"What's happened?" She edged between him and the porch column. "Nash?"

He lifted his head, eyes dead with pain. "It's Grandfather. He's had a heart attack."

"Is he—?" Lily faltered, unable to go on.

"He's in the hospital. Critical condition."

She stepped into his arms and rubbed his back. "I am so, so sorry."

He clutched her close for a heartbeat and then set her aside. "I've got to go."

"Of course." She took the cell phone dangling loosely in his left palm and checked the time. "Fifteen minutes until the noon ferry. Let's get packing."

His face was rigid, his spine stiff as a column of stone. "You don't have to come with me."

Lily bit her lip. She couldn't let him freeze her out of his life, especially not now, when he needed a friend. "Don't be ridiculous."

He shrugged. "Suit yourself."

The pungent scent of antiseptic cloyed at Lily the moment she entered the hospital lobby. It followed her down a maze of tight passageways and into the crowded ICU waiting room.

She rubbed her temples, wishing she were a lady in the days of yore with a hanky doused in rosewater to hold over her nose. Hours of this olfactory torture and her head would hurt so badly she'd be admitted as a patient.

As if. No telling what kind of funky biology the docs would flush out of her mer body.

Denim-clad legs brushed against her bare knees.

"Excuse me, ma'am," someone mumbled.

Lily looked up at the same moment the middle-aged man caught her eye. His mouth widened slightly and he didn't move.

"No problem," she mumbled, lowering her face to gaze at the white linoleum. She didn't want to deal with any advances right now. With a swish of denim, he moved on and she surreptitiously watched as he poured a cup of coffee into a foam cup.

Her mouth salivated with the need for a drink. Her body required at least twice the amount of daily liquid intake needed by humans. Unfortunately, she hadn't noted any water fountains or vending machines en route to the waiting room and she didn't want to risk going to the cafeteria to buy a bottle of water.

Coffee it was, then. No sense taking a chance on missing Nash when he finished his visitation. She couldn't stand his anger and disappointment. There had to be some way to appease him while protecting her family. Lily got up and poured a cup of the hospital-provided coffee. Maybe it would help take the edge off the chill in the cold room.

She wandered over to a back window and sipped, taking in an uninspiring view of the parking deck. Somewhere in the cavernous lot, they'd whipped into the nearest empty space and hightailed it inside, arriving breathless and flushed. Nash was assured his grandfather had survived the ordeal but was weak. They'd ushered Nash down a hallway and through a set of double doors that locked behind him and she had no idea when he'd return.

The cold sterility of the room made Lily want to shrink into herself for warmth. Harsh light bounced around gleaming walls alternately painted white or a sickly institutional green she associated with prisons or morgues. She'd never been inside a hospital before and sincerely hoped to never again have to enter its artificial, claustrophobic confines. Lily longed for the open sea, enveloped by the primordial water dancing with life in every microscopic drop.

As she waited, she absorbed the special subculture of an ICU waiting room. A few people sat alone, staring at a book or their cell phones, clearly giving the message they wanted to be uninterrupted with their misery. Most everyone else huddled in small groups, talking of trivial matters while continually caressing one another's shoulder or offering little kindnesses. Lily turned again to look out the window.

Elevator doors constantly pinged open and shut behind her as staff and families alike scurried about their business. An unexpected hush descended and Lily turned, curious at the sudden silence. Her gaze followed the crowd and she spotted the reason.

The Bosarge women—Mom, Shelly and Jet—emerged from the elevator. Lily noticed their striking beauty in a way she never had before. Jet's dark hair and eyes created an exotic panache, while Shelly and Mom bookended either side of her with their pearly skin and Nordic blond hair streaming in thick waves down to their hips. Jet wore a scarf, and Mom's and Shelly's hair was artfully arranged over their necks' gill markings. But more than their beauty, they possessed an energy about them that was deep and flowing and magnetic.

"There she is." Adriana gracefully floated to Lily's side, leaving a ripple of male interest in her wake.

"You got here quick," Lily said, grateful for their company.

Jet rolled a small suitcase along the bare linoleum. "And armed with provisions."

Ever the nurturing one, Shelly placed an arm across Lily's shoulder. "How is Nash's grandfather? Any word?"

"He survived, but they want to keep him longer. Nash is with him now."

Jet unzipped the suitcase and pulled out a pink cotton sweater. "Landry warned me that hospitals are usually as chilly as a meat locker."

"Bless you." Lily donned it at once and accepted the bottle of water Shelly held out. She guzzled it down immediately, parched throat allayed from thirst.

"The smell in this place is atrocious." Adriana frowned and scrunched her forehead. "It's giving me a headache."

"Try sitting in here for an hour and see how you feel."

Mom rubbed Lily's arm. "Poor baby. See what happens when you mix with—" She darted a furtive glance at everyone studying the four of them from the corners of their eyes. She lowered her voice to a whisper. "When you get mixed up too long with humans."

"It's not all bad," Jet muttered.

Shelly slipped Lily a wink. Those two were clearly happy to be "mixed up" with their human husbands.

Adriana addressed Jet with an imperious lift of her chin. "Now do you believe me when I say an underwater birth is the right way to go?" Lily grinned. At least Mom's attention was distracted by Jet's pregnancy.

As if sensing her daughter's unspoken thoughts, Adriana rounded on Lily. "And you must realize that the proper thing for you do is to—"

"—take my rightful place with my own kind," Lily groaned, careful to keep her voice down.

"How much longer are you going to stay here?" Adriana asked. "If Nash is visiting with his grandfather, is there any need for you to remain?"

Lily bristled. "I want to be here when Nash comes out. I can't walk out on him."

"Write a note or something. Too much longer in this hospital and your head will explode from the noxious smell. You need fresh air."

Really, Mom was so obvious in her attempts to steer

her away from Nash. Lily pursed her lips to staunch an angry retort.

Adriana's face softened. "Don't be angry. You've always been overly sensitive to odors, even more than the rest of us. I'm only looking out for my only daughter."

Jet's sharp inhalation drew Lily's attention. Their Mom's remark had hit a painful spot. Technically, Jet was Adriana's niece, but Mom had raised her since she was a newborn when her sister—Jet's biological mother—had died in childbirth.

"Really, Aunt Adriana!" Shelly's normally serene face reddened in anger.

Adriana's eyes filled with tears and she placed a hand over her mouth, as if to take back the words.

But the damage was done.

Jet placed a hand on her protruding belly, as if calming her own baby from distress.

"Excuse me."

The older gentleman in jeans who'd brushed against Lily earlier approached with tentative steps. "I don't mean to intrude but I couldn't help overhearing you mention the need for fresh air. The hospital has a lovely outdoor garden area for families."

"I can't leave," Lily protested. "I'm waiting for my boyfriend to finish his visitation."

"Send him a text message to call when he's available," Shelly said. "The break will do you good."

Lily wavered.

"You'll be better able to comfort Nash if you don't greet him with a splitting headache," Shelly added.

Some fresh air *would* be renewing. "Okay," Lily agreed. "For a little bit."

The man smiled kindly. "Take the elevators to the lobby and turn left. You'll see a door on your right marked Therapeutic Garden."

"Thanks," she said, giving him a grateful smile. They headed to the elevators and snagged one with no one else inside.

"We didn't drag you away for your health," Jet said as the elevator doors clanged shut.

Lily's heart quickened. "Have Tillman and Landry found out something about the stalker?"

"I wish," Adriana cut in. "I'm afraid it's more trouble. Carl Dismukes is turning into a real problem."

Chapter 13

Lily's shoulders sagged in disappointment as they exited the elevator. How she'd love to have good news for Nash after all his worry over Sam's health.

An orderly pushing a steel cart loaded with surgical supplies stopped in the middle of the hallway and blocked their path, staring at them as if hypnotized.

"We're looking for the therapeutic garden. Could you direct us?" Adriana asked, attempting to break the spell.

He limply raised an arm and pointed like a marionette doll, never breaking his stare. "Th-that way."

Lily and Shelly moved to the orderly's right, while Adriana and Jet passed to his left, like a wave bypassing the solid boulder formed by man and cart.

"There it is. Hope no one else is about so we can really talk." Jet pushed open a glass door, allowing Adriana and Shelly to pass through.

Lily stopped at the entryway. "I'm stealing Jet for a moment. We'll be right back." Ignoring Adriana's frown and Shelly's knowing nod of approval, Lily pointed at an empty alcove banked with a row of chairs. "We need to talk a minute."

Jet scowled. "If this is about what Mom said earlier, there's no need. I'm used to it."

"This is between us." Lily walked to the alcove and sat, patting the empty chair beside her. After a moment's hesitation, Jet came. Her tall, athletic frame and normally fast, purposeful gait somewhat marred by the bulk of her pregnant belly, she settled into the chair butt-first, a hand holding the back of it for support. Lily still couldn't get used to the idea that her wayward, fiercely independent sister was the first of them to make the leap into motherhood. Shelly she could buy, with her nurturing nature. Being only half-merblood, her cousin's need to be at sea was easily satisfied with the occasional full-moon swim.

But Jet?

"You seem to get a little bigger every day," Lily remarked.

Jet settled her hands over her swollen abdomen, a satisfied smile transforming her face with tender grace. "Landry likes to tease me about it, but he's so proud and excited he's about to burst."

Lily marveled at the changes in her sister these past months. "Are you happy, Jet? Truly happy?"

Jet's brown eyes narrowed and snapped. "Of course I am. Did Mom put you up to this little talk? She doesn't believe I'm capable of making my own decisions on how I want my baby delivered and raised. I suspect she even wants me to return to the sea, as well. But there's no going back to my old way of life. And, thank you very much, I couldn't be happier."

Now *that* sounded like the old Jet she knew.

"Mom goes about showing it the wrong way, but she wants what's best for you."

Jet huffed. "Fooled me. And if she makes one crack about my child being a TRAB, I'll never forgive her."

For merfolk, a TRAB, or traitor baby, was the result of mixing mer and human races and was increasingly considered taboo. Centuries of interbreeding had reduced their pure-blooded population to dangerously low levels.

Lily nervously tugged and twirled the ends of her hair. Jet's baby had more than the TRAB stigma. The child would also inherit her paternal grandfather's Blue Clan blood. That clan was mostly shunned in the merworld because of their ferocious nature, not just toward humans, but also to their own race. They were an aggressive, power-seeking tribe that sought to overtake and rule the undersea kingdom.

As if Jet could read her mind, she scowled at Lily. "Even if I mated with a merman, our children would still be considered tainted. You are her pure-blood, true daughter, not me."

Lily swallowed hard, wishing they were kids again with none of the emotional baggage that had driven a wedge in their relationship.

Once Lily had hit puberty, a shadow had darkened their former childhood camaraderie. Lily had been slammed with attention from all sides, and not only from males of both human and mer species. She'd had the adulation of all the mermaids for her siren's voice and beauty. Worst, Adriana showed a partiality that must have deeply hurt Jet.

"No matter what happens, Mom does love you."

"Not as much as she loves you."

There. It was now a spoken thing between them.

Lily didn't deny it. "I'm sorry." She bit her lower lip, trying to quell its tremble. "Truly," she added miserably.

"It doesn't matter." Jet's gaze dropped to her belly.

"Of course it matters." Lily's face burned with shame,

recalling the many occasions when she'd made the situation worse with her selfish need for attention.

She placed a tentative hand on her sister's knee. "I'm sorry," she said again.

Jet looked up and arched a brow. "You've certainly changed."

"I'm trying to be a better person. Hopefully a little older and wiser."

"It's Nash, isn't it? I do believe you've fallen in love for the first time in your life."

"Yes," she whispered. For once, someone else's needs and happiness outweighed her own. Even if he returned to his travels and she returned to the sea, she was forever changed. "It's scary," she confessed.

Jet slowly nodded. "Even scarier than the stalker threat, I'll bet. Is he worth the danger?"

"Oh, yes." Lily's answer was swift, unequivocal.

"Then fight for him."

Understanding and affection flowed and crested between them in a new way.

"Thank you, Jet. Forgive me?"

"You're my sister."

Lily grasped her hand and Jet squeezed it in return.

"Are you two finished?" a voice called from the doorway. Adriana waved them forward.

"We're coming," Lily answered, helping Jet rise from her chair.

Adriana disappeared behind the door and Jet gave Lily a rueful smile. "Don't worry about me and Mom. We'll make our peace. She is who she is. Now that I have Landry and our baby's on the way, I'm satisfied. And very, very happy."

"I'm glad."

In spite of the unresolved danger, the sadness at Sam Bowman's health and the uncertainty of Nash's feelings toward her, Lily felt a lightness in her body and heart. Whatever problems she faced, she had her family behind her. The Bosarge women stuck together.

"We have a huge problem," Adriana announced as they seated themselves at a round picnic table in the shade of an old oak tree.

Lily scanned the tranquil outdoor area that featured a bubbling water fountain and a labyrinth of blooming flowers. Therapeutic indeed, a real sanctuary from the artificial, intense hospital world fraught with illness and death.

With a sigh, she faced her family. "Okay, what's Carl Dismukes done now?"

"The man won't go away," Shelly said. "We thought that after Tillman forced him to retire, that would be the end of his threats. But no, he's going to make trouble in the sheriff's election next month. Last week, he went to Tillman's office with a stack of papers documenting the money Tillman's father embezzled when he served as sheriff. Dismukes says he's going to drag his father's reputation through the mud."

Lily leaned her elbows on the table. "I don't get it. Carl was in on the whole embezzling scheme, too."

"He's doctored all the documents to cast blame solely on Tillman's dad," Shelly explained.

"That's rough, but Tillman's dad has been dead for years. I don't mean to be rude, but it's not like the scandal could hurt him."

"Its guilt by association," Jet cut in. "People will think 'like father, like son.' It would ruin Tillman's chance at reelection."

"Maybe." She considered Jet's agitation. "And if Tillman goes down, your husband's job as deputy is jeopardized."

"Right. He could probably get back his old FBI job in

Mobile, but that would be…problematic. I don't want to leave Bayou La Siryna."

Lily nodded. Here in the bayou, Jet could come and go as she pleased without detection. She came to their homestead almost daily and slipped out to sea through their secret portal.

But the situation didn't seem all that dire. Not compared to the life-and-death dramas going on in the hospital or her own danger from an unknown enemy. Easy to see why Jet and Shelly were upset, but why was her mother taking it so hard? It wasn't as if she were especially fond of her human sons-in-law.

She faced Adriana. "What's got your tail twisted in a knot?"

"You haven't heard the worst part. I thought once Jet quit illegally selling marine treasure on the black market, the past would stay buried. But the ever-resourceful Carl is threatening to expose that little secret, as well."

"But—" Lily frowned at Jet. "I thought Landry had taken care of all that."

Jet nodded. "He did. Dismukes can't prove anything from my past. But that's not the point."

They all stared at Lily expectantly. She was obviously missing something here. Lily threw up her hands. "Spell it out for me."

Adriana took charge. "Carl wants us to start providing him more marine artifacts to sell. If we do, he won't expose Tillman's father during the election. And even though he can't prove Jet once was involved in shady business, he's lived here long enough that he knows influential people in Bayou La Siryna. He'll trash Jet and Landry's reputation."

Dread curdled in Lily's stomach. Would they never be free of this man?

"I don't care about my reputation," Jet said.

Adriana stared pointedly at Jet's belly. "You're starting

a family. Do you want your children to grow up here and be stigmatized for your past mistakes?"

Jet's hands fisted so tightly her knuckles turned white. "This is all my fault. If I wasn't pregnant, I'd take care of him right now."

"Carl is a disgrace." Adriana shook her head. "Blackmail and betrayal to fellow humans, I understand. But he has merblood in him and our kind is bonded together to protect one another from exposure. I could return to sea and alert the merfolk. There are some who would be willing to travel here and take care of the matter. They'll force Dismukes to stop...or else."

"That might work," Shelly mused. "We can play along with him, give him a few trinkets and buy time until help arrives."

"You can't be serious!" Lily said. "We can't buckle under to his demands. Not even once. And contact the merfolk to do our dirty work? Unacceptable."

Her mother fixed her with a pointed stare. "Then what do you propose we do?"

"We need to confront him at sea, on our own turf." Lily's thoughts whirled as she stared at each mermaid relative across the table.

Shelly. Being only half-mermaid, her cousin was the weakest link. And her nature was much too kind for dirty business. When Shelly had had her own crisis with a serial killer, Melkie Pellerin, Lily and Jet had been forced to handle the matter.

No help there.

Jet. Much as she was willing, and the physically strongest of them all, her sister was in no condition to take any risks for several weeks. She shouldn't even have to endure this emotional strain while carrying a baby.

Mom. Adriana was mentally tough and had no compunction enforcing the merfolk code of secrecy. But even though she was in good shape, Mom was getting on in years and it wasn't fair to expect their mother to protect them anymore. She'd already aided them once before when Jet's ex-boyfriend, Perry Hammonds, had kidnapped Jet and held her hostage.

Which left...

"I'll take care of Carl Dismukes," Lily said at last. She knew exactly how to get him alone at sea. It should be easy enough to scare the wily old bastard then. Frighten him so bad he'd realize the Bosarge women were out for blood.

His blood.

"How?" Jet asked bluntly. "Dismukes isn't a criminal fugitive like Perry was. If he disappears or dies like Perry, there'll be questions and a lengthy investigation." Jet's stare was hard, accusing. "You can't kill him."

Murder? Lily sprang to her feet, outrage crackling through her spine. "I'm not going to kill Dismukes! Why would you say such a thing?"

No one answered. Silence pounded her eardrums and swished through her brain like the pressure from floating at the bottom of the deepest ocean.

"Well," Adriana said drily. "We've always wondered exactly how Perry died the day you rescued Jet. You were alone with him undersea when Jet swam away. And you were the last person to see him alive."

They think I killed him.

The thought reverberated in her mind, loud and forceful as a whale's bellow. Lily inhaled raspy and loud, her panicked lungs unable to suck in enough oxygen. She pressed her trembling lips together and tried to paste on her Mona Lisa smile, a reflex built from years of masking emotion.

It didn't work.

How could they believe her capable of murder? Lily couldn't take their avid stares. She sat down and picked at a small sea-glass chip on her bracelet, staring down as if she'd never seen it before. Churned and battered by the currents, it had been buffed from a shard of broken glass—garbage—to a piece of art. The muted teal absorbed Lily's attention. Perhaps she could capture that tone in a watercolor, mix the blues and greens together, followed by an opaque wash...

A warm touch on her forearm startled Lily out of her reverie.

"No one's judging you," Shelly said. "We're curious about what happened down there."

Lily met the kind eyes of her cousin. They might look almost like twins, but they couldn't be more different in temperament. Whereas Shelly was a soft-hearted peacemaker, Lily was rigid and unyielding in her ideas of justice.

Evil deserved no mercy. But she'd never made herself jury and executioner. Except that one time...

"An eye for an eye," Shelly nodded, as if reading her mind. "Like when you clawed out one of Melkie Pellerin's eyes that night we captured him for the police."

"But I didn't kill the killer." Lily jerked away from Shelly's touch. She shuddered, remembering the serial killer that had stalked the bayou for several years. He'd gotten away with murder until Shelly observed him dumping the body of a victim one night at sea. "He was fortunate to only lose one eye. His victims suffered far worse."

Shelly crossed her arms. "If I hadn't stopped you, I believe you would have killed him."

"Then you would be wrong." Lily rubbed her face, feeling as weary as an old woman. If her own family believed her so cold-blooded... Well, she had nothing.

Jet thrust her face within inches of her own. "Did you kill Perry or not?" she asked in her forthright manner.

That bastard. Perry of the roving hands, who'd groped and leered at her every time Jet left the room. Yet she would never tell Jet. That little secret was as dead and silent as Davy Jones's locker at the bottom of the sea.

"'Cause if you did—" Jet ran her hand through her black hair and exhaled loudly "—I don't care. You saved my life."

No, she hadn't laid a hand on Perry. But she hadn't helped him, either. Guilt and shame scalded her nerves at the memory of Perry under the ocean, swallowing handfuls of sea water, panicked from oxygen deprivation. Her only crime was one of omission. She'd drifted nearby, observing his agony for a couple of seconds before rushing in to save him. Had those two seconds made the difference between life and death? Her brain said no, but the question haunted her.

"I didn't lay a finger on him," Lily spat out, immediately on the defensive. "He drowned."

"Sure, he did." Jet drummed her fingers on the picnic table. "Very convenient. Had Perry lived, he would have blackmailed us to bankruptcy…or worse."

"Worse?" Shelly asked, brows furrowed.

Jet stood and paced. "We were probably worth more to him alive. As a circus act." She stopped and faced Lily again. "Thank you."

They don't know me at all. Damn her famous composure. "I didn't kill anybody!" Lily's scream echoed like a receding wave in the stunned silence.

"Shh." Adriana put her index finger to her lips and glanced about the garden.

Lily pushed away from the table, eager to flee, but her knees shook and she slowly stumbled past them, feeling invisible—like the ghost from Christmas past in a roomful of strangers.

Death stalked her in the tight maze of hallways as patients were wheeled by in stretchers. It haunted the fearful eyes of family members in waiting rooms. Life was so fragile, so fleeting.

Lily quickened her pace, overcome with an urgent need to see Nash, to feel tucked into the haven of his embrace.

Stubborn, stubborn, stubborn. Sam Bowman was worse than a headstrong mule when it came to modern medicine. Nothing Nash or the doctors said earlier today could shake his resolve at refusing another heart operation.

"I done tried it before and I'm not doing it again. The spirits told me the end is drawing near and I aim to spend what's left of my life fishing and roaming my own property and dying in my own bed."

Nash unwrapped a barbecue sandwich, knowing he needed to eat but not having much of an appetite. Nothing was more physically and emotionally draining than sitting for hours and hours at a hospital. He'd rather brave climbing a Peruvian mountain in a sleet storm.

Lily appeared equally exhausted. Her face was drawn and pale and she kept rubbing her temples.

"Headache?" he asked.

"The worst. I think I'm allergic to hospitals."

"You didn't have to come." He was surprised she had after their argument. But he had to admit her presence had been comforting, even if he was still angry. And at least he knew she was safe as long as he was with her for protection. "Let me get you some aspirin." He half rose from the sofa but she waved him to sit back down.

"Um, no. I don't take pills. I have a weird metabolism. A little food and wine will help."

She picked at her basket of fried shrimp, appearing to take as little enjoyment of the takeout food as he did.

A few more bites of the barbecue and Nash gave up on it. He took a long swallow of beer and stared moodily out the window of his grandfather's cottage.

"It's his decision, you know," Lily said quietly. "And who's to say it's the wrong one? Seems like he's outlived all his family."

Irritation spiked his gut. "I'm still here. Dad and my brother are still alive."

"But he hardly sees y'all. You're spread all over the country, living your own lives."

"He could come visit us. Over the years, I've sent him dozens of invitations to join me. Places like Hawaii and Alaska and South America, all at my expense. He refuses to leave the bayou." Nash realized he was shouting and calmed himself. "It's like he's obsessed with this damn place."

"It's his home. And you've told me he's held in high regard by your tribe. They come from Mobile and farther for his help when they're sick or need council."

"All the more reason to live as long as possible," he snapped. "He helps everyone except himself."

Nash had brought up that exact point in his futile attempt to convince his grandfather to undergo another heart operation. But Sam was having none of it.

"Another healer will take my place," he'd said. "Someone who can be guided by the animal spirits and Mother Earth better than I ever could. A man born to this destiny but who has yet to discover all his gifts."

There had been a certain directness in his grandfather's eyes when he'd spoken those words that had shivered through Nash like the burning cold of frostbite. *He couldn't possibly mean— No way— I don't want this— No, no, NO.*

But Sam hadn't pushed the point. He'd closed those burning black eyes and murmured, "I need to rest. Come back in the morning."

Lily set down her glass of wine and strolled over to a small gallery of black-and-white photos mounted above the fireplace. She pointed to the largest, a woman in her mid-thirties with long black hair braided in two plaits, dressed in a plain white shirt adorned with a beaded and feathered necklace. The woman's expression was sober, intense. "Your grandmother, right?" Lily asked.

"Momma Nellie," Nash confirmed. "She died when I was quite young. I only remember her as a quiet woman, always cooking and doing her beadwork."

Lily idly traced a finger over the beaded bracelet on her wrist. "How did she die?"

"Boating accident. She'd gone out fishing alone one morning and the boat capsized. Her body was found three days later. Grandfather doesn't talk much about it, but I believe he's mourned her all these years. As far as I know, he's never even looked at another woman."

Lily's arms hugged her waist. "Drowned. How horrible. She couldn't swim?"

"No. I can't understand how someone can live near the ocean all their lives and never learn. Like you."

She ignored the jab. "Perhaps staying in Bayou La Siryna makes Sam feel closer to his Nellie."

"Maybe. And he places importance on living in the land of his ancestors."

She turned and pierced him with a direct gaze, an arrow that fissured his soul. Nash recalled the intensity of his sun ritual, when he'd felt the love and protection of all who had come before him and walked the same path in the same place.

"Don't you feel it, too?" she asked.

Against the backdrop of the darkened window, her hair glowed in a tangle of golden curls, bright as lighthouse beams in a storm.

Your destiny.

The seagull's message slammed into him anew.

"No," he denied peevishly. "There's nothing special about Bayou La Siryna."

This was all a trap. He was being hemmed in on all sides—his grandfather's expectations, the communion of his ancestors, but most of all, by the call of Lily. It was too much, too fast. He was being sucked in like quicksand. The longer he stayed in the bayou, the deeper he was drawn into the pit until the roots of the prevalent majestic oaks tangled around him deeper, tighter, until at last there would be no escape. The swampy miasma would swallow him up until it smothered and choked him into surrendering his freedom.

She walked to him and stopped an arm's length away. "You don't mean that," she said, her voice all honey and harmony.

"Why do you stay here? You have enough money to live anywhere. Why this marshy swampland?"

"It's been home to my kind—I mean, my family—forever."

Not knowing better wasn't a valid reason for exploring the world. He'd traveled it for years now, made a name for himself, been successful in a tough, crowded field. His life had been fine until some unknown enemy had slithered into his personal life, silent and deadly as a water moccasin.

Nash couldn't shake the feeling that the unknown woman was nearby, lying in wait, coiled and poised to strike. And this time—the third time—she would kill Lily, sink her poisonous fangs into that fair skin. His brain ran in circles again—that endless groove of searching his past romantic relationships for clues. If only he could read people like he did animals and nature.

"I should leave," he said, his voice guttural and harsh. "And so should you."

"You're thinking of the stalker again."

"Not a stalker—a killer. Call it what it is."

"Your grandfather needs you," Lily reminded him. "*I* need you."

He studied her sea-blue eyes. So blue and bottomless he could drown in them if he let himself dive into those tempting deep pools. She was like the bayou—mysterious, full of secrets and a living link to memories of his carefree childhood.

Lily stepped closer, toe to toe with him. "Did you hear me, Nash? I need you. Don't go. Not yet."

And then she kissed him, her soft flesh pressed against his, reminding him of their joining earlier this morning. But this time, instead of the purity and openness and sunlight of the beach, it was night and moonbeams and a sweet seduction into an unknowable magic.

One day she would regret he ever returned to the bayou. They were hurtling toward some dangerous day of reckoning; he sensed it with every glimmer of a gift that had been passed on through his Choctaw ancestors. If only she could trust him with her secrets, the way he had shared his own.

But for now, it was night and she was life and feminine energy and alive—and he'd spent all day with sickness and death and worry. So he drank in Lily's comfort, rejuvenated by her essence. Nash returned the kiss, marveling at how perfectly they complemented one another in every way.

He abruptly pulled away and took her hand. A pause— a look, that unspoken communication that was timeless between men and women—and she followed as he led her to his bedroom. They undressed slowly under the flickering moonbeams pouring through the window. Her naked body filled him with awe—he'd never tire of the sight as long as he lived.

And this time their joining was tender. Nash took his time, determined to postpone his ultimate pleasure until he'd touched and tasted every part of her creamy, sleek body. He didn't stop until her moans of demand could no longer be denied. He covered her body with his own and entered, sinking deep into her core, until they both found their release.

And so the night went on. He made love to Lily many times, as if it were the only night they were promised to spend together. When the first light of morning dawned, Lily lay in his arms, her mouth slightly curved upward in an innocent, trusting smile.

Whatever it took, Nash vowed to protect her from the danger that stalked.

Chapter 14

Gusting winds trembled the Spanish moss in the tall oaks, making the trees appear like old bearded men shaking their heads. The sky dulled from turquoise to smutty gray and scented the breeze with an electric charge that promised rain.

Not great weather for deep-sea fishing. Which meant that her chances of confronting Carl Dismukes alone on his boat were probably slim this morning. But she had to try.

Giving Nash the slip hadn't been easy. She'd sat with him and his grandfather most of the morning before announcing she had a few errands to run. Nash made her promise that she would keep a family member with her for protection.

She'd lied, of course. This job was something she needed to do alone.

Lily parked her car next to the storage shed, got out and glanced back at her house. The old Victorian appeared the same as always—solid, feminine in its curved lines, inviting. Grand without being so majestic as to attract undue notice from the townsfolk. No hint that it had been trespassed, yet Lily wondered if it would ever seem as safe and secure as it once had.

How had the intruder broken in? All their doors were double-bolted, had been since the incident with the serial killer last year. They'd all believed their world was secure again, their haven in the bayou permanently restored. Until someone had trespassed yet again.

And then there was Dismukes.

The first raindrops sprinkled as Lily unlocked the shed. As she quickly secured it behind her after she entered, the familiar musk smell of enclosed spaces washed over her, comforting in its familiarity. This space had never been violated by outsiders. To the rest of the world, it appeared to be an ordinary detached shed, a stainless-steel safeguard against strong winds and the occasional hurricane.

Inside, the room was empty save for a shoe rack and a pegged rack for clothes, bags and robes. In its center was a hole about the size of a manhole cover on a paved street. Lily stripped naked and hung up her clothes, glad to be rid of their lingering antiseptic scent.

She picked up an oilcloth sporran from one of the pegs and discarded the items in it that she wouldn't need for this trip—a few scavenged pearls and antique coins, a couple of seashells that had caught her eye, a small golden trinket to remind her of the sun while in the darkest realms, seaweed string for tying fish together and pulling back her hair while hunting, a mirror and various other knick-knacks. Her sea purse was nearly as stuffed as the leather one she toted on land.

Lily carefully drew out a slender abalone vial and unscrewed its coral stopper. Excellent—it was more than half-full with a liquid neurotoxin harvested from sea-snake venom. This she would bring. She withdrew her knife from its leather case and examined the edges, satisfied it was sharp. This she would also bring. Last, she unclasped an airtight clamshell, ensuring that it was filled with sand. The shell was secured on a leather chain that could be worn like a necklace. She placed it in the sporran and belted it around her waist. These three items were all she needed to carry.

The sound of the ocean was louder inside than outdoors, the crash of waves reverberating off the steel walls. Splattering rain echoed on the tin roof, casting an illusion that the storm was already in full swing. During heavy rainfall, the effect was like being trapped inside a steel drum during an air raid.

Compacted sand squished between her toes as she approached the portal. Generations of Bosarge women had used this same portal for shifting from land to sea and back again. Curiosity about land dwellers had always run high, and many mermaids and mermen had chosen to live among humans over time. Many of Bayou La Siryna's citizens unknowingly carried distant merblood in their veins. Lonely, remote bayous had always appealed to merfolk as a portal because they afforded the needed privacy to mingle undetected.

She entered the water feetfirst, legs instantly melding into a fishtail that shimmered with a glow that cast rainbow prisms on the shed's walls and ceiling, as if someone had switched on a jeweled candelabra. Down she went, until the narrow tunnel widened. Lily swam out of the tiny undersea cave and into the Gulf waters.

Briny tang coated torso and tail in welcome and Lily luxuriated in its caress, as if the ocean were lover and mother and friend. She flipped and rolled, playful as a dolphin. Bubbles and billowing hair swilled about her body, drawing the attention of a few rainbow runner fish that brushed against her arms and tail. The eternal swish of the currents roared in her ears, a muffled static to the chirps and hums of sea creatures teeming below on their eternal quests for food and mates.

Too bad today wasn't a mere joy swim.

Lily quit the acrobatics and used her sonar senses to set her course. Past experience had taught her where Carl best liked to anchor down for fishing. With his enforced retirement, the man's passion for fishing was indulged almost daily. An impending storm wouldn't deter him as quickly as most humans. He was one-eighth merman, so in any boating disaster he had the advantage of being an exceptional swimmer and could even stay submerged underwater for a good length of time. Perhaps as long as ten minutes, Lily guessed from various accounts she'd heard from other mermaids.

Still, he was no match for her at sea. Especially with her advantage of surprise.

Distant churning vibrations signaled a boat ahead, exactly where Carl preferred to fish most days. Lily swam closer, the roaring of the motor louder, more strident, churning a thick maze of foamy bubbles.

Abruptly, the motor cut off and silence reigned. A fishing cable plunked in the water ahead with a bit of shrimp dangling at the end as bait.

Lily circled underneath the boat and studied the hull. Made of white fiberglass and at twenty-five feet long and eight and half feet wide, it fit the dimensions and color of Carl's vessel, which she'd observed many times in previous swims. She swam near twin one-hundred-fifty horsepower motors with their ominous black blades, careful to keep a safe distance in case it roared to life. She read the Yamaha label, which was the brand Carl used. Yet she had to be 100 percent certain this was Dismukes and that he hadn't brought a friend out on this expedition, although that was a rarity.

She sped out fifty yards from the boat and calculated the risks. First, the location was too far from shore for anyone to spot her from land. Two, she'd only raise her head above water for an instant. Three, she'd perform this final check on the boat's stern. More than likely, Carl's back should be to her while he cast his fishing lines.

With a mighty swoosh of her tail, Lily wiggled up and broke surface. The nictating membrane in her eyes instantly adjusted to air and she spotted Dismukes's profile. His white hair fell in a damp, untidy mess about his long, angular face. He was bare-chested and she was surprised that despite his age, he had good muscle tone in his chest and back.

No matter. This was her chance and she was taking it.

Lily sped forward, deadly and silent as a torpedo, slowing only as she neared the boat's low-sided stern. She took one last quick peek at Dismukes, who was absorbed in baiting the troll lines. The opportunity would never be greater than this moment. She slithered up and over the low side as soundlessly as possible, tail instantly morphing to legs. Lily curled into a ball, casting an anxious eye to the boat's bow.

Dismukes's back was to her. Success! No doubt the low rumble of thunder now tumbling in from the west had helped shield any noise from her landing. Heart hammering, she glanced around the interior for something to throw over her naked body. She shouldn't give a damn about modesty, but couldn't bear the thought of his crude leering.

Lily spotted a beige cotton shirt on the floorboard underneath an empty cooler. Carefully, she pried it loose. Fish blood and slime were smeared across the front and it smelled as awful as it looked. But it was long and oversize, which was what mattered. She slipped it on, grateful that it fell midthigh. It was damp on one side from the steadily increasing rain, but it would have to do. She unsheathed the buck knife from her sporran, hung the clamshell necklace over the front of the shirt and left the sporran flap open in case she needed quick access to the poison vial, her last desperate weapon for self-defense.

Lily padded forward on bare feet until Dismukes was within six feet. "Are the fish biting?" she called out.

Carl jumped and swung forward, jumbo shrimp scattering down his legs. A fishing pole clattered to the floorboard.

"Wh-What?" he sputtered, the whites of his eyes exposed in fear.

Lily took momentary pleasure at his terror. After all he'd put her family through over the years, he deserved that and so much more.

He looked past and around her, evidently checking for any more unpleasant surprises. "How?" Carl shook his head. "You swam out here." His gaze swept the sea. "Alone?"

"Maybe," she brazened. "Or maybe there are a dozen mermaids below, ready for my signal to sink your precious boat."

Carl's spine stiffened and his face resumed a cunning edge she always associated with him.

"Nah, you're alone." His lips curled into a sneer as he pointed at the weapon held loosely in her right hand. "Gonna take more than a buck knife to scare me, little girl."

Show no fear. "We'll see." Lily kept her voice cool, face composed. She raised her right hand and waved it loosely, the sun sparkling on the knife's metal surface. "Nice vessel. Folks around here always wondered how you could afford a sixty-thousand-dollar boat on a county deputy's salary. I'd say you owe me and my family a huge thanks for past services rendered."

"That what you sneak on board for? To force me to be

polite? Okay, then. Thank you. Now get the hell off my boat."

"Not until I get what I came for."

"Which is?"

"To make you understand my family won't be blackmailed anymore."

"Jet and Shelly put you up to this?" He spat off the boat's side. "Bitches. Shelly's a weakling. And now that Jet's knocked up, they elected you to do the dirty work."

Crude old bastard. "The balance of power has shifted in the bayou. Tillman and Landry are the head honchos now, and you're a nobody. Stay away from us."

"Or else?" He raised a shaggy gray eyebrow and grinned, as if she'd delivered the punch line to a joke.

"Don't underestimate our kind's ability to protect one another. We're not without our own defenses. Once we spread the word to other merfolk about your threats, these waters will swarm with some pissed-off mermaids and mermen."

"So what?"

"Look at you. You're out here almost every day—even in *this*." Lily raised a hand skyward, indicating the storm. "Keep messing with us and you'll have to give up your passion for boating. You will never be safe at sea again."

"Passion, you say?"

His words came out garbled, husky—not his usual raspy bark. Carl's face had gone funny, too. His eyes were glazed and he wouldn't meet her gaze. Lily glanced down, following the path of his eyes, and immediately realized what had distracted Carl.

Rain had plastered the grimy cotton shirt to her breasts, exposing the outline of her nipples and the thatch of hair between her thighs. She needn't have bothered putting on the filthy rag, for all the protection it offered.

So much for modesty.

"Look at my face, you pervert."

Instead, his gaze drifted lower. Lily fought the impulse to cross her hands in front of her thighs. *Don't let him know it bothers you. He wants to humiliate you, gain the upper hand.* "Enjoying the view?" she asked, acting as if she could give a rat's ass.

"I ain't looking at nothing that half the men in Bayou La Siryna haven't done seen."

Fury lanced, as sharp as if her mermaid tail had slashed against needle-pointed coral. She'd been offended when her family thought she'd murdered Perry, but now Lily believed she truly had it in her to kill. The knowledge of the poisonous vial in her sporran made her hands itch to fling it in Dismukes's lecherous face.

Stay calm. Think. "Too bad you'll never get further than the looking stage, asshole."

He chuckled and gave a wink. "I've had my eye on you for years. Maybe we can work out our own little deal."

"No deals." She gripped the knife tighter. "I'd rather die than let you touch me."

"Methinks you protest too much." He stepped forward. "I could satisfy you more than that Indian dude you're sleeping with. Slut like you probably likes it a little on the rough side, I bet."

"Shut up." She was getting nowhere talking.

"Does he know you're a freak of nature? Play nice with me and it'll stay our little secret."

"I've told him," she lied.

He grinned and advanced another step, almost in arm's reach. "You're bluffing."

Lily scooted backward and fumbled with the necklace clasp, not daring to break his stare. She emptied the clamshell and cupped the sand in her left palm.

Carl's bushy gray brows drew together. "What the hell you got there?" he asked incredulously. "Sand?"

Lily mentally tested the wind. It was blowing against her back, right in Dismukes's direction. *Perfect.* She flung it into his eyes as hard as she could.

Carl stumbled and rubbed at his face, grinding the gritty sediment farther into the tender tissue of his eyeballs. "You little bitch!"

Now was her chance. Lily lifted a knee, preparing to kick him in the groin while he was blind and helpless.

Damn. She couldn't do it, not yet, anyway. At one time, Lily wouldn't have hesitated. Behind the mesmerizing voice and serene face lay a steel determination no one suspected, save her family. It was why she was here, after all. But she remembered how calmly, and with such dignity, Nash had dealt with Gary and his friends at the restaurant. Maybe there was a way to get Carl off their backs without resorting to violence. Quickly, she gathered up a length of coiled rope on the deck and tied Carl's hands behind his back. By the time he realized her plan, she had him good as handcuffed.

Tears streamed down his face, his body's natural reaction to the irritant in his eyes. Lily waited until his vision returned and then slowly curled her lips into that Mona Lisa smile she'd perfected over the years. That mask that hid all traces of inner turmoil. *Be strong. Show any mercy or weakness and it's game over.* She had to do this or none of them would ever be free from his greed. He would ruin her family and Lily couldn't bear it if that happened.

"Look at me, Carl. Here's how it's going to be. You aren't going to destroy my family. We'll never work for you again. You're going to go away quietly because to expose us is to expose yourself. Understand?"

"Why should I listen to you?" he said with a sneer.

"You have one week to leave Bayou La Siryna."

He raised an eyebrow. "And if I don't?"

"You didn't act concerned about me contacting other

mermaids about your threats. But what if I told you I could rally some of the Blue Mermen Clan this way?"

Carl paled and worry lines creased his brow.

"Ah. You *have* heard of them, I see. One of their clan—a particularly vicious one named Orpheous—is quite enchanted with me. He and his friends wouldn't hesitate to kill you. All it would take is one word from me."

"But—"

"No buts. Live out what's left of your miserable life someplace far from here and keep your mouth shut. Because if you don't, the Blue Mermen will find you. And anytime you're at sea you'll always be wondering who's underneath, ready to pull you under, never to be seen or heard from again. Because I promise you, we'll do it."

A bolt of lightning flashed in the gray sky and thunder cracked loud as a shotgun blast. She gathered her knife from the floorboard and circled behind Carl. With two slices, she cut through the rope's binding and tucked the knife back into her sporran. Carl swung around with a fist raised.

Lily waved an index finger in his face. "Not a good idea," she sang in her sweetest siren's voice.

He slowly lowered his hand and his shoulders slumped in defeat.

"Better hurry to land," she added. "The storm has arrived."

And she dove under, heading home.

Nash paused at the closed door, puzzled by the laughter and murmurs of many voices on the other side. He checked the room number—408—which he'd been told was his grandfather's new room after being moved from intensive care. He pushed open the door and entered, surprised to find a dozen or so men and women packed inside.

Raymond, his grandfather's closest friend, stepped forward and shook his hand. About Sam's age, Raymond was tall and gangly. Just as Nash remembered as a kid, he still sported the same turquoise bolo tie whether dressed in a business suit or jeans.

"Thanks for calling me last night, Nashoba. I alerted the rest of the tribe that he was at the hospital and many wanted to come pay their respects."

Nash nodded at the assemblage, deeply touched by their concern for Sam. He glanced around at the unusual bevy of gifts—no flowers or fruit baskets in sight. Instead, a few eagle and crow feathers were strategically placed by the window and at the foot of Sam's bed. A colorful dream catcher adorned the standard-issue medical cot and on the nightstand sat open bowls of fresh crumbled tobacco and sage. The rich, earthy aroma mingled with the scent of food. Lots of food. Every square inch of flat space on the dresser, shelf and windowsill was stacked with aluminum-covered casserole dishes.

Sam sat up in bed, looking much healthier. He'd changed out of the hospital gown and wore a short-sleeved denim shirt and cargo pants. He was down to just one IV stuck in his arm. Although his color was better, Nash could read the fatigue in his eyes, and the lines in his face seemed more deeply etched, as if the heart attack had aged him overnight.

Nash approached the foot of the bed and nodded. "How are you, Grandfather?"

"Better," he answered. "Ready to go home."

Nash knew not to bring up the operation in front of present company. To argue the point would insult his grandfather's dignity.

"Docs say he can be released in the morning," Raymond piped in. "I'd be honored to stay at Sam's cottage a few days or as long as he needs to regain his strength."

Nash clenched his jaw to refrain from arguing that his

grandfather should undergo further surgery. Raymond was not to blame for Sam's stubbornness.

"Thank you for your kindness," he said, clasping Raymond forearm to forearm.

Sam spoke up, his voice proud. "This is my grandson, Nashoba. Many of you have not seen him since he entered manhood."

Shame gutted Nash, quick and deep. He should have visited more often instead of insisting his grandfather travel to meet him.

Raymond raised his arms at the crowd. "Time to go and let them visit in private. Sam needs to get some rest, as well."

A scraping of chairs and the whoosh of people gathering their belongings, and then one by one they shook Nash's hand and waved goodbye to Sam.

Alone, he stared at his grandfather and shook his head. "Is there no talking you into having another operation?"

"My mind is set and I'm at peace," Sam said firmly. "I have prayed to my God and the spirits have answered."

Nash conceded defeat. Sighing, he pulled up a chair close to Sam's cot. "Then I suppose I have no choice but to accept your decision." His throat constricted, remembering how kind his grandfather had been on those summer visits long ago. The bayou had been his childhood refuge, a place to escape his parents' constant bickering and the hustle of city life, which he'd detested. All during the long school years he looked forward to exploring the Alabama backwoods and hearing his grandfather's tales of the Choctaw.

"I'm sorry," Nash said, throat burning with regret. "I should have visited more." He swallowed painfully. "Come sooner."

Sam grasped his shoulder with surprising strength. "None of that now. I understood the circumstances."

He'd been thirteen when his parents divorced, and his mother had spitefully refused to let him visit his paternal relatives in a misguided attempt to punish Nash's father for his many infidelities. For his part, Nash's father was too wrapped up in his own life to want to return to Bayou La Siryna. To him, the place he grew up in was dull and he couldn't wait to leave at the soonest opportunity.

Still, Nash wished he hadn't been so set on traveling and building his own career. He should have visited more once he was older and on his own.

"I, um, spoke to Dad last night. He'll be flying out in the next couple of weeks, as soon as he wraps up his latest business trip." Nash had urged him to come sooner, but his father was insistent he had other matters to finish first.

"It will be good to see him again," Sam said, removing his hand and settling against his pillows.

Nash hoped that whatever distance had come between his father and grandfather could be healed before it was too late.

The room seemed too quiet now after the earlier crowd of well-wishers. Sam's eyes had closed, but Nash didn't think he'd fallen asleep yet. "Grandfather?" he asked tentatively.

Sam's eyes opened. "Yes?"

"Tell me one of your stories again like you used to." Nash didn't want to ever forget them. He yearned for the closeness they'd once shared. "Unless you need to rest," he added quickly.

The deep lines on his grandfather's face softened and he smiled softly. "Which one?"

"You choose."

"The most important one is that of the Okwa Nahollo."

"The white people of the sea."

"With skin the color of trout," Sam said with a nod. "There are places deep in the swamp where the water changes to a clear white color. That's where they live. It is said that if you near this mysterious pool of clear water, they will take you down below to their home under the sea. Should you stay with them more than three days, you may never return to land."

"I wonder how this legend came to be," Nash mused.

His grandfather regarded him with a profound intensity. "Legend? It's true."

Surely Sam didn't expect him to believe these old tales like he once had as a child. "Okay," Nash said mildly. Now was no time to scoff.

"They exist. And a day will come soon when you see this truth."

What kind of medication was his grandfather taking? He seemed lucid enough—but mermaids? Really.

"Since you've returned, haven't you felt and seen things more deeply? Haven't the land and its creatures revealed anything to you?"

Nash immediately thought of the crows and seagulls telling him Lily was of two spirits. "I have," he admitted.

"I'll tell you more of the Okwa Nahollo, things that aren't part of the general legend. It's a truth that the waters have whispered to me over the years."

Nash's skin prickled. "Go on."

"As our people were being rounded up for the Trail of Tears, the sea dwellers heard their wails. Those who chose, those who believed, escaped capture and removal. The Okwa Nahollo allowed them to come live with them undersea. There they were free, far from the government men who hunted them down."

Nash said nothing. His grandfather would never lie to him, so he must truly believe this had happened. It was probably what came with old age, a great imagination and too much time alone in the bayou.

"It's true," Sam insisted. "But you must discover this for yourself."

"Sorry, but you're right. To believe such a legend, I'd have to see a mermaid with my own eyes."

Sam closed his eyes once more and whispered, "Maybe you already have."

Chapter 15

"Where were you all day?" Nash had asked the moment she arrived at the hospital.

"Family business," Lily offered cryptically. "How's Sam?"

"Downgraded from ICU to a regular bed. He may even be released in the morning." Nash delivered what should have been good news with an air of impatience.

"I see. So you couldn't talk him into the operation?"

"No. His mind is good and made up."

Lily squeezed his arm in sympathy. Privately, she couldn't blame Sam for opting out. He'd lived a long life and deserved to meet his end on his own terms.

It had taken a long time to load up Nash's truck with the avalanche of food. Sam Bowman would be set for at least a couple of weeks. Even though it was human food and not her preference, the combined scent of turkey, corn bread, dressing and homemade pies created a homey, cozy kind of smell.

The truck jostled over the bumpy road to the Bowman cottage, which was worse than usual because of the earlier downpour. Although the storm had passed, it was dark for late afternoon, courtesy of a few lingering clouds that muddied the sky to a potash gray. Lily kept a check on the backseat, making sure none of the packaged food overturned. A comfortable silence settled in, for which she was grateful. The confrontation with Carl had left her exhausted and anxious. Had she done enough? Too much?

The jangling ring of her cell phone startled Lily and she scrambled in her pocketbook to find it. "Hello?" she answered breathlessly.

Click.

"Hello?" she repeated.

Silence.

"Who is it?" Nash asked sharply.

"Could just be a bad signal out here." Her fingers trembled as she pulled up the recent calls menu. It was a local number but not one she recognized. She pressed the number and waited.

"Whoever it is, they aren't answering," she said flatly. *Oh, hell, here we go again.*

"Let me see." Nash grabbed the phone and frowned at the screen. "Recognize the number?" he asked.

"No," she admitted.

"Son of a bitch." Nash handed the phone back to her and slammed a hand against the steering wheel. "I'll call Tillman as soon as we reach the cottage. See if he can do anything."

"It's not the same phone number from the last incident." Lily tried to infuse some optimism in her voice. But the memory of the slashed canvases sent a renewed surge of anxiety rippling down her spine. At least with Dismukes, the enemy was in the open.

"Big deal. It'll turn out to be from a throwaway phone again."

Nash's frustration and bitterness was palpable, his body rigid with anger.

It was so much worse for him, even though the threat was directed at her. He'd been dealing with this for so long, Lily couldn't fathom the pain he must have endured, was still enduring.

"Tillman and Landry will find whoever—"

The phone rang again and Lily dropped it in her lap as if it were a live thing with the power to sting. "Same number as before," she said, inhaling sharply.

Nash scooped it up and pressed the answer button. "Who are you?" he demanded. "You fucking coward." He dropped the phone in the console in disgust. "They hung up again." He accelerated the truck, branches and shrubs scraping noisily against its sides. He drove as if speeding to an encounter, desperate to confront danger head-on.

"At least she knows I'm not alone," Lily offered. "Maybe— do you suppose—we could set a trap? We could make her think I'm alone one evening while you secretly lie in wait."

"Not a chance."

Nash's tone was implacable, but Lily couldn't let go of the idea. If Nash wouldn't do it, perhaps she could talk her brothers-in-law into it. The sooner, the better.

"I don't like waiting for her to catch me," she insisted. "This might be the safest option."

"Absolutely not." Nash pulled up to the cottage and abruptly slammed on the brakes. He turned to face her, dark eyes gleaming with intensity. "Get it out of your head. Understand?"

I understand what needs to be done. "Okay," she agreed at once.

Nash narrowed his eyes. "I mean it," he ground out in a voice hard as diamonds.

"I said *okay.*" Lily scrambled out of the truck and

slammed the door. He didn't have to be so testy on the subject.

With an impatient sigh, Nash got out and they each gathered armfuls of the gifted food from the back of the truck. In a silence that was no longer peaceful or comfortable, they climbed up the cabin steps.

A sheet of notebook paper was pinned to the door with a message written in large red block letters.

"No trespassing. Go Home Lily."

She stared at it stupidly, the words sinking in slow, burning like hot lava. The roar of thousands of crickets and cicadas buzzed in her brain. What was it Sam used to say? Something about crickets signaling that bad prayers and wishes were being cast upon you. She glanced behind her and then to the tree line past the yard. Was there someone out there now, waiting for a chance…one unguarded moment to snatch her into the darkness?

Nash swore under his breath, and she caught the sentiment, if not the exact words. He set the casserole dishes on a porch rocker and took the load from her arms, as well. Nash grabbed a large tree branch that had fallen near the porch steps and roughly pulled her behind his body as he tested the lock. "Stay behind me," he ordered.

"Be careful," she whispered against the soft cotton of his T-shirt. She pressed her head between the hard blades of his broad shoulders, inhaling his musky sandalwood scent.

The door was securely shut, so he fished keys from his jeans pocket and unlocked it. They entered, Nash's palm curled tightly on the branch, ready for battle. Lily peaked around his shoulder. The small den appeared undisturbed, same as always. She let out a whoosh of relief as some of the tension unfurled from her tight muscles. "It looks okay," she ventured, stepping to his side.

"Stay close," he said shortly.

Lily willingly followed as he walked, silent and deliberate, into every room, checking closets, windows and under beds.

Nothing.

"Looks like she wasn't able to break in," Lily said. "We're safe."

"For now."

Frustration laced his words and Lily suspected he was disappointed not to uncover an intruder. He wanted to find the culprit and end her deadly games.

"Let's get the food put away and leave," he said, glancing at the clock over the fireplace. "We can catch the last ferry out to the island if we hurry."

"You think she'll come back tonight?"

"I'm not taking any chances while you're with me." Nash abruptly pulled her to him and wrapped her in a fierce embrace. "I won't let anyone hurt you. Ever." His breath was fiery and fervent as he kissed the top of her scalp.

He released her as quickly as he had gathered her close. "Stay in the kitchen while I bring everything in."

They made quick work of storing everything, placing a few casseroles in the fridge and most everything else in the freezer. Lily opened a large plastic bin, grateful to find it filled with a fish stew. They could eat this tonight on the island.

Supper in hand, they returned to his truck. Lily stared back at Sam's cabin, a new worry wiggling in her brain like a worm. "If Sam's released in the morning, you'll need to stay with him while he gets his legs under him."

"He's got a friend that's going to stay with him."

"Do you think they'll be safe?"

"I do. The killer only came here to find you. But I'll warn them to be careful. My grandfather has several shotguns and the two of them are both excellent hunters."

"He shouldn't have to worry. The stress can't be good for his heart."

"I know. I've done him more harm than good coming back."

She studied his profile, noting the grim set of his jaw. "I don't believe that. He's thrilled you're here. Besides—" she pointed at the warning note he'd carefully removed from the cottage door and placed in the backseat "—that might give Tillman and Landry a clue to the woman's identity. With any luck, they'll find her soon."

"Doubtful. But we'll pay them a visit in the morning after I check on my grandfather."

His mood stayed somber as they again traversed the muddy potholed road, rushing to catch the last ferry ride of the day. What a nuisance having to depend on a boat when she could easily swim to the island alone. If he only knew… Lily reached out a hand and placed it on his thigh, wondering what he'd think if he saw her shape-shift to mermaid form. When this ordeal was over, and if he decided to stay in Bayou La Siryna, she would have to reveal her secret. He'd been so open with her about his own supernatural abilities—maybe he had it in him to accept hers, as well. *Lots of ifs and buts and maybes.* No point borrowing more trouble with speculations on the future when the present swirled with danger.

The moon beckoned like the call of a long-lost lover. Lily stole a glance at Nash, sprawled on his back, chest moving rhythmically up and down in deep slumber.

Their evening had been subdued, each absorbed in their own troubles. Their earlier rift over revealing secrets remained a wedge between them. She'd tried to cajole him out of his gloom, but he stayed reserved and she'd felt so removed from him, at least until they'd made love. Their shared passion remained unmarred from the outside world and all its problems. One pure thing, intimate and open. And she'd come oh-so-close to telling him she loved him. But when she did, Lily wanted the timing to be perfect, unfettered by secrets and danger.

She stared out the window, the moon tugging at her restless thoughts. How she craved a swim. Night was the best time of all undersea, when silver beams danced on the water's surface and starlight flickered above with pinpoints of light.

Dare she chance it?

It would be a relief to go undersea and erase the memory of today's harassment and especially the underwater confrontation with Carl. A reclaiming of her territory of sorts.

Ever so slowly, Lily disentangled her legs from beneath the sheet while keeping an eye on Nash. She eased off the bed and padded across the hardwood floor to the kitchen, then paused at the open doorway.

He hadn't moved. She could see him in the darkness, her mermaid nature accustomed to vision in the ocean's dark depths, the same eyesight that allowed her to see at night while on land. Nash's eyes remained closed, his breathing regular. Lily silently passed through the kitchen and to the separate bedroom on the other side of the lodge. He'd be less likely to hear any squeak from the other room's door. Gently, she crept out and waited to hear if she'd disturbed his slumber. If he sought her, she'd tell him she'd stepped out for some fresh air.

A few minutes of silence passed, and she was confident he hadn't heard anything. Lily ran sure-footed to the shore, tossing off her silk nightgown in the island breeze. Not even the softest of material felt as freeing or soft as the night wind against bare flesh.

She ran and ran until shore met sand, then slipped into sea, the transition to siren seamless and instant. Sediment and seaweed swirled, roused from the day's storm. Tonight the ocean was all astir, tumbling with power. Lily absorbed its energy, became one with its vital force. She drifted with the strong undertow, allowing it to draw her farther, deeper. Not fighting, not thinking, not plotting nor scheming as she had to do on land. Here, she was queen of the sirens, the pride of the merfolk, secure in her power.

Could she really give all this up? Did she want to?

Niggling doubts crept in, disrupting her mindless swim. The easiest path would be to leave the bayou with its endless problems and dangers. Her mother would be delighted and her own kind would welcome her return. With them, there would be no secrets or need for subterfuge. She could mate freely and do her duty in helping repopulate their dwindling species. Why resist her natural siren's call?

Lily propelled upward, fishtail beating back and forth, arms lifted, parting a path through the Gulf current until she was within a foot of the water's surface. She floated on her back and sought sight of the moon.

There. It shone a pale green, full and ripe in a pregnant beauty. Dark clouds drifted over its face, giving an illusion that it winked at her, sharing a secret, acknowledging its very own child of the waters.

The same ink-black clouds hid the stars, blanketing their beauty. Even so, Lily felt their burning presence, which refused to be muted by mere puffs of drifting nebula.

This must be how Nash experiences Earth. The very soil sings to him, and all land's creatures recognize he is one with them, a fellow brethren of land. He has more power than he knows, if he would but accept his gifts.

Nash's face flashed in her mind's eye, obscuring the moon. It was strong—harsh, even—sporting high cheekbones, an aquiline nose and a squared plane along his jawline.

I love him.

Totally, completely, unequivocal as any law of nature.

Every cell in her body craved his touch, whether on land or at sea, as human or as mermaid. Nash was anchor and home in the world.

Could he learn to love her, as well? Or would he leave one day soon and return to his travels? Much as she loved him, she couldn't follow him down that road, even if he asked. To leave Bayou La Siryna and her portal was unthinkable. The bayou straddled land and sea, allowing the freedom to shape-shift between two worlds. She was a mermaid and needed the sea, even if it was restricted to this slice of the Gulf of Mexico.

Fight for him, Jet had advised.

And so she would. But only if he loved her, too, and could be satisfied keeping Bayou La Siryna as a home base. Nash was worth every danger. Always and forever.

Peace came with resolution and Lily swam for shore, longing to return to his bed, to feel his body pressed against her own. At the shallow sand bed that marked the meeting of ocean and earth, she glided in, tail fin dissolving as her body rolled onto shore. She arose, human legs wobbly at first until the adjustment to solid footing on ground, the earth steady and sure beneath the flesh of her soles.

The white of her nightgown whipped in the breeze at eye level, and a ghost cloud descended from the heavens. Lily narrowed her eyes and saw that the gown was attached to a human arm. Her gaze traveled the length of the arm to the man standing less than six feet in front of her—solid and strong as an oak tree.

Nash.

Oh, shit. Not now, not like this.

"Enjoy your swim?"

Angry disbelief surged through Nash and he marveled that he could even speak. *What the hell?* Was this a mirage or some kind of magical illusion? His world shook as if an earthquake rumbled beneath, tectonic plates shifting the natural order of the universe. He inhaled deeply, grounding himself against the maelstrom of this revelation.

No, it was real. He'd seen what he'd seen.

"You're a—" He sputtered and halted. Lily was— He couldn't bring himself to say the *M* word, much less think it.

She stood before him, eyes wide, wet and sleek as a dolphin, bits of seaweed clinging to her golden hair and pale skin. *Pale as trout.* His grandfather's tale of the Okwa Nahollo rang in his head, leaving him dizzy and disoriented. *Maybe you've even seen one and not known*, he'd said.

Lily took a tentative step forward, hand outstretched, pleading. "Oh, Nash. I didn't mean for you to find out so soon. And not like this."

He steeled himself against the anguish in her voice and eyes and stepped backward. Her hand fell to her side.

"I don't believe you were ever going to tell me," he ground out harshly. "You've lied to me from the beginning." Even as a child, she'd lied. He saw that now.

"I had to. Please try to understand. It's not just my secret. It's one I share with all my kind. Exposure to humans can mean our death."

"So you were toying with me all this time. Playing with me, treating me like a dumb animal you could pet and then abandon." He remembered all the local men and their crude remarks about the easy Lily Bosarge. "I'm the latest in your long string of conquests."

Her face grew even paler, white as the fabric of the nightgown he held in his hands. Nash bunched the silky folds in his fist and raised it toward her in accusation. "I woke up and when I couldn't find you in the lodge I went searching. Do you have any idea how scared I was? I was afraid the killer had found you."

"I—I'm so sorry. I didn't think you would—"

"You're damn right, you didn't think. And when I found *this*—" he shook the gown like it was some vile thing "—I thought maybe there'd been an accident. That you had drowned."

"I get it. You're angry I slipped away." She grew more composed, face smoothing into its usual calm. "You have every right."

"Damn straight."

"Now can we discuss the real issue?"

Her voice was sensible and matter-of-fact, as if she were dealing with an unreasonable child. Anger washed over him anew. "Fine. Let's talk about the fact you're a liar, a sneak."

"That's not what I meant and you know it." Gone was the sorrow and regret in her eyes. They glittered now with defiance as she lifted her chin. "You witnessed the change."

His mind balked at the image of Lily washing up on the beach. At first, he'd been terrified, certain she had drowned. And then a large mass behind her had shimmered, reflecting a rainbow of colors in the moon's light. Enough light to see that the object was a fishtail that began at the curve of her hips and narrowed down to a split fin. The colors he'd seen were pixilated scales where legs should have been. Seconds later, the shimmering mass had dimmed and become two columns of pure white. Lily had arisen on the sand like a ghost in the night.

He'd been rooted. Torn between relief she was alive and dismay at her dual nature and utterly, utterly astonished. Was this what the crow and seagull had been trying to tell him? *Two spirits.* Which was the real Lily? A creature of the sea, or the warm-blooded woman who was his lover?

His mind grappled with the warring emotions and

he chose anger. Familiar, safe, old-fashioned anger that masked vulnerability and powerlessness.

"I don't want to talk about your—*change*," he spat out, mocking her euphemism. "Maybe the real issue here is trust and your lack of it. I opened up to you—told you things I've never shared with anyone. And there you sat with your big secret, never saying a word."

The confident defiance slipped and her chin quivered. "I was going to tell you."

"When?"

"Later. After the killer was caught and everything returned to normal."

"Normal?" He laughed bitterly. "Nothing about my life is normal. You were the one good thing I had going for me."

Tears streamed down her face, almost undoing him.

"I'm still me," she said, placing a hand over her heart. "Lily."

The anger melted, replaced with an unbearable sorrow. "It feels like I don't even know you anymore," he said softly. "What other secrets do you hide?"

"Just one."

His heart took a nosedive off a cliff and he averted his face from hers, seeking balance.

She moved close and touched his arm. "Nash, look at me."

He gazed at her. Even now, wet and covered with bits of seaweed, she was the most beautiful woman he'd ever met.

"I love you."

The truth was there in her eyes. "Don't," he said, broken. "I'm a man who's brought you nothing but trouble."

"That's not true. You've taught me what it truly means to love another. I didn't know before if that was possible for me." She placed both her hands in his. "I don't expect you to tell me you love me, too. You've had a shock tonight. But answer me this—does my mermaid nature repulse you? Do we still have a chance?"

Nash drew in a deep breath. Repulsed? No. There had been beauty and magic in her mermaid body. No matter what form she took, Lily was lovely. Even now, the close proximity of her body made his blood pound with desire.

"You could never be anything but beautiful in my eyes," he admitted.

She dropped her head against his chest and he wrapped his arms around her slender waist.

"That's all I need to hear for now," she whispered.

Another cloud passed over the moon, pitching the world in black shadows. Still, he didn't let go of Lily.

Was this love?

His mind was confused, torn, uncertain of everything he once held as fact. There would be no answer to this question tonight. For tonight, he would keep her close, filled with wonder and an aching need to discover the real Lily.

Chapter 16

Lily tossed aside the sketchpad. She couldn't focus on anything except Nash. Besides, what was the point? Her best paintings had been ruined and her dreams of artistic recognition had been ripped apart as surely as the shredded canvases. It'd been a foolish ambition anyway.

"Problems?" Shelly asked in wry amusement. Her cousin didn't bother opening her eyes as she rocked on the front porch, the wooden floorboard creaking at a lazy pace. "Relax," she advised. "Sit a spell with me and enjoy the breeze. I love this island. It's so peaceful."

"So remote," Lily grumbled.

Shelly cocked open one eye. "Getting a little stir-crazy, are we?"

"You try sitting around here all the time." Lily stood and sighed heavily. "I'll go bring us more iced tea. You want anything to eat? We've got leftover fish stew and corn bread."

"Nah, I'm meeting Tillman for lunch in a bit."

Lily pushed open the screen door and entered the tiny kitchen. The lodge seemed deserted without Nash. *Don't get used to him hanging around forever*, her heart whispered in warning. She opened the fridge, removed the pitcher of tea and returned to the porch.

Shelly held out her glass and Lily poured more tea in it before refreshing her own glass. She sat in the rocker next to Shelly and tried to relax. Images from last night rattled around her brain in photographic clarity: Nash's grim face as he held her nightgown on the beach, their bodies intertwined in the moonlight later that night and the mysterious flicker in his eyes as he'd left on the morning ferry.

Where did they go from here?

She and Shelly fell into a syncopated rocking pattern that soothed her agitation.

"Do you want to talk about it?" Shelly's voice broke the companionable reverie.

Lily stared at her cousin, who was physically almost her mirror image. "Talk about what?" she hedged.

"Nash, of course. And how you've fallen completely in love with him."

"Jet must have told you." There weren't many secrets between the three of them.

"Nope. Figured it out all on my own."

"I'm that obvious, huh?"

"Only because I know you so well." Shelly took a long swallow of iced tea. "The feeling's mutual, right? I've seen the way he looks at you."

"He hasn't said so, but I'm hopeful."

"A man couldn't help but fall for you with that siren's voice."

"It's more than that," Lily said sharply. "He knows me—knows everything."

Shelly's eyes widened. "You mean—"

"He caught me swimming last night."

"Why did you take such a risk?" Shelly stopped rocking and her fingers tightened around her glass. "You must have wanted him to find out."

Lily opened her mouth to deny it, then clamped it shut. Maybe she subconsciously had wanted to force the issue.

Shelly bit her lip. "Hope he doesn't tell anybody."

"He won't," Lily said, bristling. "Nash wouldn't do that to me. To us."

"I hope you're right."

Lily frowned at her cousin's skepticism. "It's not like you didn't spill the beans with Tillman. And Jet did the same thing with Landry. Why shouldn't I be allowed to do the same?"

"But Nash is only here to do a photo assignment and visit his grandfather. It's not like he's staying."

The reminder was like a slap and something in her face must have communicated the hurt. Shelly got out of the chair and gave her a quick hug.

"Forget what I said. I just don't want you to get hurt, Lily."

"Too late." She attempted a wobbly smile.

Shelly ran a hand through Lily's hair. "Whatever the difficulty, the two of you can work it out. You deserve love as much as the rest of us. Don't give up on it."

"Jet said much the same." Lily got out of the rocker, restless. "Isn't it almost time for the noon ferry? I'll walk with you to the landing."

"Are we good?" Shelly asked with a tentative smile.

"We're good," Lily assured her. "Go gather your things."

Shelly scooped her pocketbook from the coffee table and they began the short walk to the ferry landing.

"I almost forgot to tell you some great news," Shelly said. "Your mom called this morning and reported that Dismukes's house has a for-sale sign in the front yard."

Relief washed through her. "One problem solved, a dozen more to go," she quipped.

"How'd you do it?" Shelly slanted a look of admiration.

"We had a little heart-to-heart talk while he was deep-sea fishing. The details aren't important." She didn't want to talk about or think about the encounter. "So what's the game plan for this afternoon? I'm sure Mom or Jet will show up next to babysit me."

"They went shopping in Mobile this morning for baby clothes, but said they'd be on the noon ferry to take my place. Don't be annoyed. You shouldn't be alone until Tillman finds the stalker. Besides, none of us want to face Nash's wrath if we left you unguarded."

Lily stifled a sigh. She'd much prefer to be by herself until Nash came on the last ferry. Mom would get on her nerves about returning to sea and Jet had enough to do running her antiques store. Lily could have gone to the hospital with Nash this morning and helped him get Sam settled back at his cabin, but she'd wanted them to have time alone together.

They arrived at the landing in time to see Ned pulling in the boat with only a handful of passengers.

Shelly frowned. "I don't see Mom and Jet." She dug her cell phone from her purse and entered her password. "Damn. I missed a call. They left a message saying they're running late and asked if I could stay with you the rest of the day."

"It's okay," Lily said quickly. "You go on and have lunch with Tillman. I'll be fine."

"No way. I'll call and cancel. He'll understand."

Lily again stifled a sigh and watched as Ned guided the boat to the small wooden pier where passengers exited onto the island. A flash of red hair blazed like fire in the harsh sun and a friendly, familiar face grinned at her from the boat.

"It's Opal," Lily said with a start, waving back at her friend. "I can't believe she's here."

Shelly paused from punching in numbers on her phone. "Who's Opal?"

"Nash's assistant. I met her earlier, but she left to go on another assignment."

They watched as Opal climbed out of the boat and strode down the short wooden walkway. A camera was slung across one shoulder and she carried a small tote bag.

"Problem solved," Lily said cheerfully. "You can go to your lunch with a clear conscience."

Shelly eyed the redhead pushing past an elderly couple with binoculars and a bird guide book. "You sure?"

"Positive." Lily waved an index finger in front of Shelly's face. "Better watch it," she said with a mocking grin. "You're getting as suspicious and paranoid as Jet."

"Okay, okay. Call me later."

"Stop being a mother hen," Lily said firmly. "I'm in no danger."

After a myriad of paperwork and a last-minute dire warning from the doctor on duty, Nash drove his grandfather home. Once there, Sam insisted on sitting up in his favorite chair on the back porch, which he claimed was the most comfortable spot in the small cabin. Nash pulled up a chair beside him.

"You feeling okay?" He studied Sam's face, searching for signs of fatigue.

"A little tired," he admitted. "But there is no pain and for that, I'm grateful. There will be no suffering when the spirits come to take me with them."

"Let's hope it's not for a long time."

"My time is near. Very near. And I have much to tell you."

Nash shifted uncomfortably in his seat and sincerely

hoped his grandfather wasn't going to spring some shocking revelation. Discovering Lily was a mermaid last night still had his mind spinning. But he straightened in his chair and focused on Sam. He could at least do that much for his grandfather. "I'm listening."

"I have one last story to tell you. But first, why don't you share what's on your mind? Something has filled you with confusion."

Sam was as perceptive as always. Nash rubbed his face. It would help to talk over what he'd witnessed, but he didn't want to give away Lily's secret. "I can't go into specifics," he said carefully. "But last night I saw—" He drew a deep breath. If anyone would believe this wild tale, it was the man seated beside him. "I saw a mermaid."

Sam nodded and kept his face turned to the woods in the backyard. "Here? Or on the island?"

"The island." It was easier to talk with his grandfather's profile to him instead of his direct gaze. Nash also stared straight ahead.

"Then it wasn't the Okwa Nahollo, but some other manner of being that is closely related to our white people of the sea."

"You said you'd seen one of them before, but I didn't believe it. Not that you would lie," he added quickly. "I thought you'd imagined it."

"No one would believe such a thing unless they saw it for themselves. I knew the day would come soon when you'd observe one firsthand."

"Shocked the hell out of me and I'm not sure I handled it well."

"Lily understands this."

Nash leapt to his feet. Sam had known it before he did. "You've known all along about her and didn't warn me?"

Sam calmly motioned for him to sit back down. "Some

truths a man must discover for himself. Didn't the birds deliver a message?"

He slumped back down in the chair, bemused and bewildered. "They said Lily was of two spirits and that she was my destiny. Whatever that means."

"What do *you* think it means? Learn to search your own heart for answers. Be honest and fierce in seeking truth."

The trapped feeling he'd experienced before returned and the screened-in porch was like a cage. His world narrowed to the narrow slab of concrete flooring surrounded by metal screens. *No!* The spirits—fate—some supernatural force—were trying to snare him for their own mysterious reasons and he wanted no part of it. *Screw them.* He was his own man.

Nash rose to his feet again. "I need some space," he said shortly, heading to the door.

"Wait." Sam motioned for him to return to his seat. "Let's finish our talk first."

Reluctantly, Nash returned and sat, folding his arms across his chest. "How did you know about Lily? Oh, wait." He held up a hand. "The spirits told you."

Nash tried to keep the sarcasm contained inside, but the words came out with a sardonic edge nonethcless. Sam had to have picked up on it, but he answered with his usual dignity.

"I've suspected for years that the Bosarge women were of the sea. You must observe and seek signs in the smallest of details, consider the behavior of your subject and keep an open mind. After all that, ask the spirits for help in interpreting all the information you've gathered. I did all three before I reached my conclusion."

Keep an open mind. He would try. The smallest details… Nash struck a palm against his forehead. "The tiny scars on each side of Lily's neck must be some sort of gill markings."

Sam nodded. "Go on."

"The pale skin." He pictured Lily's naked legs with their subtle mica shine. "Pale skin that glitters. Must be a small vestige of her mermaid fishtail." Nash stopped and stared at his grandfather. "I can't think of anything else."

"You're missing the biggest clue, but we'll come back to that. Can you identify any of Lily's actions and habits that could have helped you uncover her secret earlier?"

"Only in hindsight. I see now how she lied, but I thought she was merely reserved, overly private."

"If someone is guarded with friends and lovers, it is wise to ponder why. Here's what I have noticed. The Bosarge women have always lived in an isolated area and kept to themselves. No man has ever lived with them in that house. I suspect that somewhere on the property is a hidden portal where they come and go."

"That's some mighty big speculations based on little that is fact."

"And that's where your spirit guides can assist. But first you must do the groundwork and be open to that which is unlike any other reality you've experienced. If you do, you'll find the bayou is filled with magic."

Despite his reluctance to entertain the supernatural, a stirring of wonder fluttered in Nash's gut. "You told me you once saw the Okwa Nahollo. How did it happen? You must have caught one unaware, like I did with Lily."

Sam rocked in his chair, silent, his profile stern and unyielding as carved granite. But to Nash's astonishment, salty tears flowed down the deep crevices of his lined face.

"I didn't come across one unaware," he said. His grandfather's voice was gruff but sturdy. "Many, many years ago, she came to me. I was out fishing late one afternoon by the small nearby inlet, as is my custom. I grieved for my loss and she heard. My Nellie came for me."

Nash's breath caught and the skin on his arms and legs prickled. "Grandmother?"

Sam closed his eyes, reliving the moment. "I heard distant chanting in the old Choctaw tongue. It didn't come from the sky or float across the wind, but from underneath a clear white pool of water. As I stared at this calm patch, a mass of black tendrils drifted near the surface. I walked into the water up to my knees for a closer look." Sam paused and swallowed hard, opening his eyes again. "It was my Nellie, her long dark hair swirling about her pale, pale face, so different from the olive color I remembered. Her deep brown eyes were darker, too, like large, black pearls, but I recognized her instantly."

Nash's mind tumbled with a thousand questions. "What did she want? Did she speak?"

"The water parted and she came halfway out, exposed only to the top of her hips. And then she spoke, her voice as familiar and dear as always. She had heard my grief as I fished every night and she daily begged the Okwa Nahollo for a chance to console me until at last they granted her wish."

Incredible. Nash stood and paced the small porch, trying to wrap his mind around the strange tale. "But she died. Drowned in a boating accident." He stopped suddenly and whirled to face his grandfather. "Did the Okwa Nahollo kill her? Did they deliberately capsize her boat and drag her underneath to become one of them? My God, how you must hate them!"

"You misunderstand. They saved her life, took pity on the human whose lungs filled with water and could not breathe. They offered Nellie life, not death. And they accepted her as one of their own, just as they did with our ancestors who sought asylum rather than be forced on the Trail of Tears."

Nash propped a shoulder against a porch railing and

stared at Sam. His tears had dried and a gentle light lit his eyes and a slight smile played along his lips. "I don't get it," Nash said slowly. "I would think it would be hell knowing your wife lives only a fifteen-minute hike away, yet you can never be with her as man and wife are meant to be."

"I had many, many years with Nellie on land. And two unforgettable nights with Nellie under the sea—the woman I thought was lost to me forever. The spirits showed me great favor. I am grateful for the blessing."

If you stay with the Okwa Nahollo three days or longer, you can never return to land, his grandfather had once told him. "Maybe you should have stayed the third night," Nash said around the painful lump in his throat. "You could have been with Grandmother all this time."

"I was needed with my people here."

Nash shook his head. "It was too great a sacrifice."

"You must do what the spirits have called you to do. We all have our duties." Sam pinned him with a pointed stare. "Destiny denied leads to days filled with sorrow and regret."

Lily is your destiny, the seagull had proclaimed.

"Duty and destiny," Nash said heavily, the very words like shackles chaining his soul. "I've been told my destiny. Now I suppose you're about to tell me my duty." Of late, Sam had been hinting at it more frequently and directly.

"You have the gift to heal. It's a blessing, not a curse."

"Go on," Nash said between pinched lips. "Say it. You want me to stay in Bayou La Siryna and take your place."

Sam reached out to the porch railing for support and rose slowly, straightening his arthritic knees. Yet, as usual, he maintained a dignity accorded a wise man who had lived an honorable life.

Nash both respected and envied his grandfather's noble bearing. He could never, ever measure up to this man he admired. It wasn't fair that this was demanded of him.

"There is always a choice." Sam placed an aged hand on Nash's shoulder. The weight felt heavy, an anchor forcing him down. "Choose wisely."

Nash twisted out of his grasp. "Okay, now I *really* need to get out of here for some fresh air." He jerked open the porch door and walked down the steps.

"Take your time, Nashoba. I'll be waiting."

He turned around at the bottom of the wooden steps, suddenly remembering an unanswered question. "You said I missed the biggest clue that Lily was a mermaid. What was it?"

"Her siren's voice. Its effect on us is slight since our heritage is intertwined with the Okwa Nahollo. Your Lily is a beautiful woman, but the men in this town are unnaturally attracted to her charms."

For the first time, the thought of Lily's past relationships angered Nash and he chided himself for the useless jealousy. He had his own past of easily accepting the attentions of many women and then as easily letting them go. *Just like my father*, he thought with disgust. His dad's numerous affairs had been the root of his parents' divorce.

Sam cut through his thoughts, as if sensing their direction. "Haven't you ever wondered why women are so drawn to you? I suspect male siren blood has been passed in our family from generations of intermingling with our Okwa Nahollo neighbors."

It excused nothing. Behavior trumped biology and he was responsible for controlling his actions. It had taken the deaths of two women to drive that point home.

He walked, almost ran, to the woods and up the red dirt path littered with pinecones, instinctually seeking solitude and the peace of nature. The bracing scent of pine and the musky odor of oak moss clamored for notice above the pervading ocean smell.

Nash leaned against the tall column of an oak and let

his senses absorb it all. The whispering of the wind rattling through the trees like the sky's breath of life, the ground vibrating from small animals scurrying about their business, the soles of his feet tingling with earth energy from a tangle of tree roots expanding ever deeper in its thirst for life-sustaining water. The pores of his skin welcomed the sun's heat and his blood pounded in time to the breaking waves at sea.

Something broke the tranquil pattern. Something *not right* drew him to explore a dense thatch of scrub. A high-pitched chirping of distress beckoned Nash in a plea for help that could not be ignored.

A tiny bird ruffled its wings and Nash separated the shrub's branches for a closer look. Two marble-sized black eyes regarded him with both hope and terror. "I won't hurt you, little one," Nash promised. He disentangled the bird from where it was pinned beneath brambles. An agitated squawk from above told him momma bird was nearby. He guessed the little one had dropped from its nest and was too badly hurt to do more than roll about in the tangle of branches and vines. Gently, Nash freed the baby bird and held it in his cupped palms. A faint, erratic heartbeat fluttered against his fingers.

Now what?

He closed his eyes and willed that the bird be spared. Warmth and energy flared in his hands as if providing a miniature incubator. The bird ceased its struggle and its heartbeat slowed to an even pace, pulsing stronger. Nash opened his eyes and the bird hopped to its feet, tiny claws scratching into the flesh of his hands. He flattened his palms to provide a launching pad. The bird shifted from one foot to another, testing its balance. Then it flapped its delicate wings and was airborne in a flurry of fuzzy feathers. Nash watched as it flew upward to a nearby pine, where momma bird and the rest of her brood welcomed him with noisy tweeting.

Nash bent one knee up, propped an elbow on it and rested his forehead on the tips of his fingers. He felt drained, shaken and—profoundly humbled. *I have the gift. So where do I go from here?* He stood up and looked skyward, shaking his head. "Not so subtle, spirits," he called out.

A small brown feather stuck to one sweaty palm. He peeled it off and tucked it into the drawstring medicine bag belted at his waist. It would stay with him the rest of his days, a reminder of his first healing.

He slowly made his way out of the woods and returned to the cabin. His grandfather was halfway across the backyard, waving a cell phone. Nash frowned and quickened his pace. "Go sit down," Nash yelled. "I'm coming." Sam shouldn't be exerting himself like this; he should be resting. He hurried to Sam's side and took his arm, leading him to the porch. "Don't scare me like that," he chided. "Whoever called can wait."

Sam breathed heavily, as if he'd just completed a marathon. "It's—"

"Sit down and rest before you give me the message."

Nash settled him in his chair and waited as his grandfather collected his breath.

"Sheriff Angier called," he rasped. "Who is Opal Wallace?"

Nash's heart hammered. *Not another accident.* "My assistant. The woman who set up the island shoot."

Sam's eyebrows drew together and he affixed his sternest gaze on Nash. "You never mentioned her name."

"So?" What the hell was going on?

"Opa. *O-p-a*," Sam spelled out. "Choctaw for *owl*."

"Oh-kay," Nash drawled. "I'm in the dark here." Bewilderment flashed to unease. "Has something happened to her?"

"No, no." Sam fluttered a hand in front of his face as if clearing cobwebs. "But don't you remember all I've taught you about the animals? Owls are a sign of evil. Impending death."

The unease flared to an alarm that Nash tried to quell. "That's a superstition. Why did Angier call about Opal?"

"She's here."

"Huh. I wasn't expecting her back for another week."

"She's not *back*, Nashoba. Sheriff says this Opal never left Bayou La Siryna. She's been here all along."

The sweat on the back of his neck chilled and stung like ice chips. "But…why would she stay?" He felt as if he were moving in slow motion, half-buried in thick mud. His mind sludged through the implications. None of them good.

Sam gave a slow nod. "Now you know your enemy."

Chapter 17

Lily grinned at her friend's wild muddy-red hair blowing in the breeze like an out-of-control forest fire. The temporary purple streaks of color she'd put in were gone. "I thought you were in the Appalachian Mountains taking photos of wild herbs. We weren't expecting you back for another week."

"Nah, it turned out to be easier than I anticipated. Didn't have to tromp about the trails much searching for specimens. It's as if I was meant to be back on the island with—*oomph*." Opal's right foot twisted free from her sandal and she stumbled in the sand.

Lily put out a hand and steadied her.

"Drats." Opal bent over, slipped both feet out of her old but still serviceable Birkenstocks and carried them in her hands.

Lily noticed Opal's wide freckled feet were unpedicured. Her gaze traveled upward and took in the cut-off shorts with loose threads dangling haphazardly. She wore

an old faded T-shirt, a faded khaki cloth bag slung diag-
onally across her body and not a single piece of jewelry.
It was one of the things Lily liked best about her—Opal
didn't bother with artifice. Her warm, friendly smile said
take me or leave me, and it was her most endearing feature.

Opal wiggled her brows. "Do I pass or fail inspection?"

Lily cocked her head to one side, as if seriously considering the question. "Pass. You look great. Fresh-faced
and lively as usual."

"And you look amazing as ever." Opal gave a theatric
sigh. "It's so unfair. If you weren't my friend I'd hate that
about you."

Lily laughed. "I've missed you. Even tried to call you
a couple of times but couldn't get through. Figured you
were in the boonies with no signal."

They resumed their way to the lodge.

"I'd have called or at least texted you if I could have. So
what are you doing out here today?" Opal asked. "More
drawing? Or has Nash recruited you as his assistant in
my absence? Looks like I might have been squeezed out
of a job."

"Don't worry. I'd be the world's worst assistant. I talk
too much when he's trying to sneak up on the birds."

"Has Nash managed to get the mating shots of the rail
clappers?"

"Probably not. He's been…distracted lately."

Opal winked. "I can guess why."

"No, it's not *that*," Lily said ruefully, climbing the porch
steps. "Come inside, and I'll bring you up to speed on everything." She stopped suddenly and Opal slammed into
her back. "Sorry. Just wondered if you'd rather sit on the
porch."

Opal glanced backward, apparently watching the retreating backs of the elderly bird-watching couple as they

headed toward the woods. "Let's go inside," she said. "More privacy that way."

Lily snorted. "I think you've forgotten how remote this place is."

Opal made her way to the sofa and flopped down, propping her tanned legs on the coffee table and slinging the tote bag beside her.

"Make yourself at home," Lily said unnecessarily. "Want some iced tea?"

"Tea? Let's drink something a little more fortifying. How about a glass of wine?"

"I don't think we have any."

"Sure you do. There are bottles of sangria in the cupboard below the sink."

"There are? I hadn't noticed." Lily scurried to the kitchen.

"Pour it over some ice, will you, sweetie?" Opal called from the den. "I'm parched."

"No problem." Lily opened the cupboard and, sure enough, there were a couple of sangria bottles. She fixed a glass of ice and carried it to the living room along with the wine. "I'm glad these are the twist-off tops. I haven't noticed any corkscrew openers here."

Opal straightened and put her feet on the floor. "Nothing but the low-end stuff for my gourmet tastes," she joked. "Hey, aren't you going to join me?"

"It's a little early in the day."

"Oh, come on. Don't make me drink alone. What kind of hostess are you, anyway?"

Lily hesitated. Oh, what did it matter? It wasn't like she was going anywhere. "Okay. Be right back."

Opal smiled. "Take your time. We'll have some fun girl talk all afternoon. When do you expect Nash to return? I assume he's out taking shots."

"He's not here. His grandfather isn't doing well. Nash

is staying with him until Sam's friend arrives later in the afternoon."

"Oh, that's too bad. What happened?" Opal waved a hand. "Get your drink first and then you can tell me."

Lily returned to the kitchen and grabbed a glass. This would be fun. She'd never had a wine-and-girl-talk kind of day. Glass in hand, Lily went to the den, where Opal paced.

"There you are," Opal said brightly as Lily poured herself some sangria. She stood next to Lily and clinked their glasses together. "Cheers. Here's to a revealing afternoon."

"Revealing? Oh, you mean like sharing confidences, I suppose."

Opal took a sip. "Mmm. So good. Drink up."

Dutifully, she tasted the wine, her mouth exploding with the sweet tang of blackberries and citrus.

Opal returned to the sofa and patted the seat beside her. "Come tell me what happened to Nash's grandfather."

"Poor man had another heart attack and was in the hospital until they released him this morning." Lily sat down and kicked off her shoes, then tucked one leg beneath the other. "Sam has refused another bypass surgery and nothing Nash says can change his mind."

Opal shook her head. "Never underestimate the stubbornness of a man, huh? Nash taking it hard?"

"Yeah." Lily took another swallow of the sangria. "He's pretty crushed." Here she was having company all day and lazing about while he cared for Sam. "As a matter of fact, I should call and see how they're doing." She scanned the coffee table for her cell phone.

It wasn't there.

"Where's that damn phone?" she muttered. "I could have sworn I left it right there."

"Maybe you took it in the kitchen when you got the glasses," Opal suggested helpfully.

Lily stood and frowned. "I don't think so, but let me see. Be right back."

"You might want to check your bedroom and the porch while you're at it," Opal called from behind. "I'll call your number so you can hear it ring." Opal rummaged through her bag for her phone.

"Great. Thanks."

Back in the kitchen, she checked the countertops. Not there. With a sigh of exasperation, she went to the bedroom, checking nightstands and the dresser top. Still no phone. Lily peeked in the bathroom and then to the unused back bedroom. She must have left it on the porch earlier when she was talking to Shelly. Lily retraced her steps and passed back through the den.

Opal held up her phone. "It's ringing. Think you might have turned the ringer off?"

"I never do that. Don't hang up— I'm going on the porch to look."

Outside, her gaze swept the porch, but there was no sign of it and no ringing, either. Lily lifted chair cushions and searched the floor, thinking it might have dropped. Damn it, she'd lost another one. Lily jerked open the screen door and stalked back to the sofa.

"No luck?" Opal said with raised brows, turning off her phone.

"None." She flopped next to Opal and crossed her arms over her stomach. "I can't believe it. This is the third time in the past year."

Opal patted her arm. "Don't be upset. I'm sure it will turn up. Here—" She picked up Lily's glass and held it out. "Relax. You'll find it later. No sense getting all worked up."

"I guess," Lily said with a sigh. "Sure is frustrating, though." She sipped the wine, willing it to mellow her sour mood. A hint of bitterness mingled with the fruity taste.

Lily raised the glass to her nose and sniffed. "Can sangria go bad? This has a weird aftertaste."

Opal laughed. "Nah, you're probably used to the gourmet stuff and not this cheap shit I picked up at the gas station." She raised her glass. "The more you drink, the better this will taste."

Lily followed Opal's cue and downed another mouthful. A flavor of bitter almonds lingered, but it wasn't too bad.

"Anything else go on while I was away? Twyla give you any more trouble?"

"Yes and no. There's been trouble, but Twyla's not to blame. We're actually friends now—or at least not enemies."

"Tell me about it."

Lily recounted the break-in and hang-up calls, drinking more of the sangria. It was like she couldn't get enough liquid—her mouth was parched and her tongue wanted to stick to the roof of her mouth. Opal said something, but Lily couldn't focus enough on the words to catch their meaning. She stared into Opal's blue eyes until the color shifted, became alive and splashed like seawater spilled into a miniaquarium. And she was in that water, her mermaid fishtail swishing back and forth.

Back and forth.

Lily's stomach roiled with motion sickness.

"I feel funny," she said. "That sangria doesn't agree with me."

He had to get to Lily and warn her about Opal. Nash checked the time on his cell phone and cursed. "The noon ferry's already run. I should have insisted Lily stay with me today."

"I'm sure she's fine," Sam said. "You told me she promised to have a family member stay with her."

Nash barely listened to his grandfather's reassurances as he speed-dialed Lily's number. It rang and rang and rang. He punched in Tillman's number, who picked up on the first ring.

"Nash? We've got a problem. Landry and I've been reviewing the old case files the past few days. We decided to focus on Opal since she came to Bayou La Siryna with you. After a thorough background check, we now suspect Opal Wallace is the person who broke into Lily's house and may be responsible for the deaths of Rebecca Anders and Connie Enstep."

"Why?" he asked quickly. A small, still-rational part of his brain wanted something more concrete than Sam's association of her name as a sign of evil. He'd known her for years, had never once suspected his friend and assistant might be the cause of so much grief.

"Did you know she was once a person of interest in the murder of her foster brother, Thomas Drake? They apparently had a secret long-term affair and when he tried to break it off, Opal stalked him. A restraining order was issued and Drake died four months later. An autopsy revealed he'd been poisoned by white snakeroot. The case has never been solved."

"Shit." His skin crawled as if a hundred hairy tarantulas had been loosed on his body.

"There's more," Tillman continued. "Not long after Drake's death, Opal was committed to a state psychiatric hospital for an acute psychotic episode. Given her prior arrest, the background of mental health issues and the fact she's lied about her whereabouts, I'd say she's our prime suspect."

"What do you mean, Opal lied about her whereabouts?"

There was a pause and Nash tensed, anticipating more bad news.

"Opal never left Bayou La Siryna. She's been holed up in a motel right outside of town."

Hearing it from the sheriff instead of his grandfather seemed more damning and official. All doubt fled. Nash jumped to his feet as adrenaline flooded his system. "Then go take her in! What are you waiting for?"

"We can't. She's on Herb Island. She disembarked on the ferry as Shelly boarded."

"Damn it! Who's with Lily now?"

"No one except Opal. Lily thought she'd be safe with her."

Nash balled his left hand into a tight fist. Lily was alone with a psychotic killer. It was hard to imagine Opal as a killer, but the facts were too incriminating to think otherwise. "How soon can we get over there?" he growled.

"I've been trying to call Ned, but can't reach him. The next scheduled ferry is hours away. In the meantime, our office is contacting everyone we know with a boat large and sturdy enough to get out there. I know you're worried. I would be, too. Landry and I are doing everything possible—"

"Call me when you find someone," Nash said, cutting him off. "I'm going with you." He turned off the phone and faced his grandfather's worried eyes. "Lily's alone on the island with Opal and no one can get out there for hours. If something happens to her—" He couldn't go on, couldn't form the horrible words. "I never suspected Opal. Never. I thought she was my friend. And she never made a pass at me or indicated she had feelings for me. She told me once she was having a long-term affair with a married man. Like an idiot, I believed her story."

"Don't blame yourself." Sam placed a hand on his shoulder. "You aren't the first person to ever be deceived and betrayed by a false friend."

"It's all my fault." Nash's fingers curled into his palms. "I led Lily straight to a killer and there's nothing I can do to save her."

"There is a way to the island," Sam said. "But you may not like it."

* * *

"Poor baby." Opal stroked Lily's head. "Your hair's so pretty." She ran her fingers through the long locks. "And silky, too."

Lily closed her eyes and relaxed into the comforting touch of fingers stroking her scalp and the nape of her neck. The nausea subsided, replaced by a deep lethargy. She felt weighted down and longed to curl into a ball and sleep. For days.

"I wish I had your hair."

Lily yawned and roused herself. "There's nothing wrong with your red hair. It suits you."

"It's a curse," Opal said. The words came out loud, harsh. "I mean—" she gave a small laugh "—I wish I looked exactly like you. There's this guy… Well, he doesn't ever notice me *that* way. Know what I mean?"

Lily opened her mouth, but Opal cut in before she could speak.

"Of course you don't know what I mean. All men love the lovely Lily."

The singsong bitterness in Opal's voice made Lily's spine prickle with unease. Maybe Opal was like the other human women after all. And here she'd thought she'd found a true friend.

Opal laughed again, her face returning to its plain, open warmth. "Sorry. It's the alcohol talking." She poured them both another glass and raised hers in the air. "To friendship."

"I don't want any more." Her voice sounded weak and plaintive, as if she were a small child protesting something forced upon her.

"Fine. I believe you've had enough now," Opal said gently. "You look paler than usual. Feeling a bit strange, my dear?"

The room went fuzzy, the edges of everything blurred

like one of her impressionistic watercolors. Maybe she had landed inside one of the paintings. Maybe her own body would become wave-washed until all that remained of Lily Bosarge would be an indistinguishable smudge on a forgotten canvas. She tightened her hands, welcoming the sharp pain of her nails digging into her palms.

"I'm still here," she said, sounding like a lost, confused child even to her own ears.

Opal smiled, but there was no warmth or comfort in it. Something about her expression hardened, became cruel. She ran a finger down the faint scar on her right cheek. "You see this atrocity?"

"It's barely visible," Lily protested, overcome with the need to cajole the stranger beside her. Where was that damn cell phone? Lily swiped her hand across the coffee table as if the phone would magically materialize. She'd left it right there, she knew she had.

An explosion of glass on the hardwood floor echoed in her head, like shock waves from a dynamite detonation. Lily clasped her hands to her ears and watched a rivulet of sangria spill over the edge of the table. It slowed to droplets, like blood dripping from an IV. "I need my phone. I need to call Nash and—"

"Shut up!" Opal hissed. "You shut the fuck up."

All traces of friendship were wiped out. Opal's eyes deepened to a blue blackness of fury and her thin lips pursed. A wall of hate smacked Lily's body like a wet towel, sharpening her hazy senses. Understanding flashed. "You're the killer," she whispered. "It's been you all along. You hate me because you're in love with Nash. You put something in my drink…"

"Yeah, genius. I hate you." Opal threw her glass against the wall and it exploded. Tiny glass shards and sangria cascaded downward in slow motion, like a red waterfall. Lily couldn't stop staring at it, all the while willing her mind to concentrate on reality. "What did you put in my drink?"

"A little angel's trumpet, my dear."

The answer filtered through her drugged trance, though the sound was distant, as if it had come from the abyss of an underwater volcano.

Opal's voice had abruptly reverted to a calmer tone and pitch, but Lily scrambled to stay on guard. *Once a monster is out of the bag, it can't go back in.* A hysterical giggle bubbled out of her throat.

"That's right. Let the drug take hold. It will make everything so much easier." Opal thrust her face in front of Lily, studying her dispassionately. She was like a hawk zeroing in on some small, helpless prey, certain of victory.

"What's angel's trumpet?" Lily asked, struggling to understand what was happening to her mind and body.

"A poisonous flower, also known as hell's bells or the zombie cucumber." Opal took hold of Lily's right arm and jerked her to a standing position. "I boiled one of the leaves and made a special tonic." With her free hand, Opal opened the shoulder bag slung securely across her body and pulled out a glass vial half-filled with a sickly yellow liquid. "I've plenty more if I need it, so you better be a good girl."

She slipped the vial back into the bag and Lily saw it was filled with more vials and clear packets of dried herbs and flowers. A witch to-go kit. Lily giggled even as the horror mounted. She pointed at the bag, laughing. "It's like a poison sample pack, a murder-on-the-go kit, a witchy traveling broom tote or a— Ouch!"

Opal's fingers dug into Lily's upper arm, sharp as talons, forcing her to walk toward the back door on wobbly legs. All the while, she kept up a one-ended conversation, delivered in the patient tone of a teacher instructing a student.

"I selected it just for you," she droned on. "It has a hal-

lucinogenic effect and often makes one euphoric and sub-
missive. Came in handy with Nash's other lovers, too. It
was all so easy to set up the drug overdose for one and
then the car accident for the other. The best thing? It's not
a substance likely to ever be checked for in an autopsy."

How had she not seen the crazy beneath Opal's friendly
facade? Even through the drug haze, everything clicked
into place. Lily's heart kicked into high gear, as if it were
trying to hammer a hole out of her chest. No doubt another side effect of the angel's trumpet. The door opened
and Lily took heart at the sound of the ocean. If she could
only reach the water... But even if she changed to mermaid form, there was no way of gauging what affect the
drug would have on her mermaid metabolism.

She tripped going down the porch steps, but Opal's
grip tightened, preventing a fall, preventing escape. Lily
dragged her feet in passive resistance, but Opal was firm—
and relentless.

"Where are we going?" she asked. The dry mouth was
worse; her entire palate felt encased in sand, her tongue
swollen and useless.

Opal ignored the question. "There won't be any pain,
not much, anyway. The end will be quick, like it was for
Connie and Rebecca." Opal clucked her tongue, chiding
disapproval. "If you all had minded my warnings and
stayed away from Nash, you could have lived. I'm not
unreasonable."

Nash. Lily's heart pounded erratically. If she died, he'd
feel responsible and devastated. She had to try to save
herself.

"Opal, this makes no sense. He doesn't love you. Kill-
ing me won't change that."

"Third time's the charm," she quipped, unperturbed.
"He'll realize he loves me and that the rest of you sluts
never mattered."

Holy Triton, the woman's so delusional she can't fathom logic. The nonchalance rattled Lily. There was no reasoning with a person living in a fantasy world.

Their march continued onto a small trail in the woods. Lily stumbled along, weak and disoriented. It felt like this was happening to a different person and her body and brain were disconnected.

Opal began singing—a children's melody. The mirthful, familiar tune was warped into something eerie and sinister. She'd heard it recently but couldn't place where.

"Ring around the rosie
Pocket full of posies
Ashes, ashes
We all fall down."

A glow of candles and the sweet odor of incense... Yes, that young girl, Annie, had sung it at Tia Henrietta's. Annie had tried to warn her. Now Opal was the one singing, turning the light ballad into a funeral dirge as they slowly made their way through the woods.

"Ring around the rosie
Darkness befalls thee
Ashes, ashes
They all must drown."

Opal stopped the demented warbling and came to an abrupt halt. "We've arrived."

They'd reached the end of the trail. A few feet ahead a small two-person canoe was tethered to a tree by a thick rope.

Lily stared incredulously at the faded green canoe. "You're taking me out on *that*?" She tried to hide the relief but laughter tripped out of her belly, great gut-wrenching guffaws that left her clutching her stomach. "Y-you're taking me out t-to sea?" Lily gasped in between the laughter, swiping at the tears running down her face.

Opal gave a twisted smile as she untied the rope and

pointed for Lily to board. "That's a good girl. Enjoy the mind trip. Keep laughing right up until the end."

She clamped her talons on Lily's arms again and forced her onto the boat. Lily did her best to avoid getting her feet wet. *Can't shift to my fishtail yet. Best wait until we go in a little ways.* Opal gave a rough push and Lily's butt landed on the metal slab that served as seating. She gulped in air, trying to stop laughing, but she couldn't get her body to obey her mind's command. *Mustn't let the monster know she's playing right into my hands.*

Opal withdrew the oar beneath Lily's feet and gave the canoe a push-off from shore before scrambling in and seating herself directly opposite Lily. In the tiny space, her knees crammed painfully into Lily's.

A little farther out and I'm home free. She could feel the muscles in her face contort into a wide, foolish grin that Opal would attribute as a harmless effect of the drug. *But you don't know how that drug will affect shape-shifting.* Still, she liked her chances.

"Won't be so funny when you hit water," Opal said smugly. "We both know you can't swim. Oh, you might manage a doggie paddle for a bit, but you'll tire after a few minutes. And I'll be right here, sitting in the canoe, watching. Waiting."

The canoe headed out to sea as Opal paddled; the freckled skin of her face and chest disappeared as she reddened with exertion. Lily hung on tightly to the sides as it rocked in the waves, preparing for the right moment to jump overboard. *Soon.* A little deeper.

She barely listened as Opal began singing, gasping between the words. Same tune as before, different lyrics.

"Leaves of angel's trumpet…"

She exhaled, arms straining as the oar dipped into the water.

On an inhale, Opal drew the oar into the air and nodded her head at Lily.

"Soon I'm gonna dump it…"

The boat surged ahead and Opal dipped the oar on the other side of the canoe and pushed, still singing.

"Die, bitch. Die, bitch.

Lily must drown."

Chapter 18

"I'll do anything to save Lily," Nash said. "Anything. It's my fault she's in danger."

"It will require a huge sacrifice on your part," Sam warned. "And a giant leap of faith."

It took all Nash's patience not to snap at his grandfather. He inhaled deeply, trying to quell the hope that there might be a way. Knowing Sam, he might suggest a flaky scheme like astral travel or some such. "Just tell me your idea."

"There is an ancient ritual passed to me from the spirits. It will grant you power to access the island undersea. But in exchange for this ability, there's a price."

He must be crazy. Undersea access? The glimmer of hope that had lit Nash's spirit died. "That's not possible."

"After everything you've seen and heard, after proof of your healing gift—" At Nash's sharp inhale, Sam nodded. "Yes, a spirit revealed to me that you saved a bird not ten minutes ago. And after all this, you still can't keep an open mind? You disappoint me, Nashoba."

His grandfather's words stung like a poisoned arrow, filling him with bitter regret. "I'm sorry, I want to believe there's a way, but it's ludicrous. How can I possibly—"

Sam turned his back on Nash's explanation and walked away, his steps labored, shoulders drooped. Nash easily outpaced him and blocked his path.

"Grandfather, I've never told you this, but you were the man I always looked up to as a boy. I admire and respect your wisdom and dedication to our people. But I'm not like you. This is all new to me. It's a big adjustment. Please, if there's a way to save Lily, I want to try."

Sam's eyes, dark as crow feathers, assessed his grandson. "When you entered this earth, the spirit of the wolf howled in recognition. You were born to be a protector, a spiritual man with special gifts. In the old days, you would have been the tribe's greatest hunter and provider. The ability for stealth, tracking and connection to the natural world and its signs are skills you've adapted for today's world. It's aided you in your career of capturing wildlife on film. But only you can decide whether to now accept your heritage."

A strong breeze picked up and Nash's attention was drawn past his grandfather to the trees beyond them, where limbs and leaves tussled, an alive, canopied shelter for birds and beasts. The rustling increased, became an agitated whisper for his ears alone. *Stay.*

He'd never sought any of this. But how could he deny offering help to those who needed him to intercede with the spirit world? *I was born and selected for a reason.* Nash's resistance faded and he was filled with peace. "I accept and I believe."

The wind softly settled down like a sigh.

His grandfather's face lit with pride. "You've chosen wisely. But before we begin the ritual, you must know the price. In return for revealing and granting you a special power, the spirits demand that once the ritual is completed, you may never leave Bayou La Siryna."

"Never?" The sacrifice was harsh, a complete abandoning of his adventurous lifestyle and ambitions. The storied career he loved, had worked so hard to build, would be ruined. He'd be stuck in this hot, small Southern town the rest of his days. Surely, there must be a little leeway here. "Not even for a few weeks now and then?"

"Never." Sam's voice was solid as the earth's core and as inflexible. There was no compromise, no bending fate.

"So that's why you've never left this place," Nash said slowly. "It wasn't because you didn't want to visit me, but because you were bound to the bayou." *All these years, he loved me as I loved him.* A hurt Nash didn't realize he'd harbored in some dark recess of his soul came to the surface and melted like ice in the noonday sun.

"I've always loved you through the years, Nashoba."

Nash nodded but couldn't speak. He hugged his grandfather and held tight, knowing Sam would understand what was in his heart, as he'd done when Nash was a child. His grandfather's dignified posture softened slightly and he briefly returned the hug. Nash pulled away. "I've made my decision."

"You're going to try and rescue Lily," Sam stated. "No regrets?"

"None." He pictured her face and body as they made love, so giving and free. Life without Lily was unthinkable. Nash wasn't sure when that had happened, but he guessed it was the day she had walked to him, naked and open, after his morning sun ceremony. And she belonged to this bayou as surely as he. "Lily's my destiny," he said simply.

Sam nodded. "Wait for me at the same place we did the healing for Kevin. The circle is already set. I have to go inside first and get the talisman."

Nash walked across the yard to the circle laid out with

large stones and shells. His skin itched with impatience to begin. Every second that ticked by put Lily in more danger. He paced inside the sacred circle and tried to ground himself in preparation for whatever was to come.

The cell phone in his back pocket buzzed. Nash hastened to answer, hoping for news that Tillman had secured a boat. A message from Lily lit the screen.

"Gone boating. See you later."

His brow wrinkled as he concentrated on the brief message, feeling more alarmed than comforted. The only boat on the island was a two-person metal canoe tied to a rope at the back of the woods. As far as he knew, Lily didn't even know it was there. Besides, why the hell would a mermaid go boating? Made no sense.

Opal knows about that boat. A flash of conversation flickered in his brain. The three of them had been picnicking under a shade tree when Opal suggested they all go for a swim to cool off. *I can't swim*, Lily had said. Facts scrambled about his mind, seeking arrangement: Opal and Lily were together—Shelly had relayed that news. Opal thought Lily couldn't swim, so why get on the small craft with no life jackets? If Lily could send a text, why hadn't she responded to his earlier calls?

The logical conclusion left his palms sweaty. *Opal sent this.* And if she had, the crazy bitch was about to kill again, only this time it would be death by drowning. Nash tried to take heart, knowing that if such was Opal's plan, it had a major defect. Pushing Lily overboard would be tossing her to safety.

He speed-dialed her number but, as he expected, there was no response.

Sam emerged from the back porch.

"We need to hurry," Nash shouted, stuffing the phone back into his jeans. "I think I know how Opal intends to kill Lily."

"I'll be quick," Sam promised. "You will have time to save Lily."

Nash eyed his approach with impatience and curiosity. Sam clasped a ten-inch knife in one hand and a bag of cornmeal in the other. "What's the knife for? Animal sacrifice?" he asked, only half joking.

His grandfather didn't smile. "There will be some pain."

Holy crap. The knife is for cutting my flesh. Nash squared his shoulders, determined to show no sign of weakness.

As before, Sam walked the circle's inner boundary and tossed the cornmeal skyward, appealing to the spirits for their blessing and expressing gratitude for past blessings received. As instinctual as breathing, Nash silently prayed to all the brave Choctaw warriors who had walked this land before him and whose spirits lingered yet.

He stood rigid and proud in the middle of the circle as Sam set down the empty bag of cornmeal and faced him.

"Take off your shirt and unfasten your hair," he instructed.

Nash shed his T-shirt and took out the leather band that secured his long hair in a ponytail. His tribe had once been infamous for their many tattoos; maybe his grandfather was about to carve one on his chest as a symbol of his unity with them.

Sam raised the knife upward with both hands. "By the Spirits, I ask that the blood of the Okwa Nahollo that lives on in Nashoba Bowman be magnified a thousand times a thousand times. May he breathe underwater and navigate the seas as he does on land."

He paused, closing his eyes and tilting his head to one side, as if listening to an answer. Nash strained to catch what was being communicated, but an unnatural stillness settled. The breeze died, and he couldn't hear a single bird or sense any animal movement. Even the constant crash of the tides seemed far, far away. A dark cloud passed over the sun, darkening the sky enough that the moon's outline was visible.

Sam opened his eyes and lowered the knife. "Do you vow never to reveal this mystery to anyone except tribe members and only as the need arises?"

"Yes."

His grandfather positioned the blade so that it lay flat across his palms. It was more than just a knife; Nash recognized it at once. For as long as he could remember, the knife had been mounted above the fireplace, ensconced in the center of a grapevine wreath decorated with white shells and eagle feathers. He'd been warned never to touch it because it was a sacred, ancient relic passed down through generations. For those deemed worthy by their ancestor spirits, it held great power.

Let me be found worthy. I have to reach Lily.

"Place your right hand on the knife and swear by your honor."

Nash positioned his hand so that it rested atop most of the blade and the handle, a bone carving of a woman with long flowing hair. The steel was as warm and throbbing with life as the bird he'd cupped in his palm earlier, whereas the handle was as cool as a stream of flowing water.

"I swear never to break the code of silence."

"And you must swear that from this day forward, you will remain in Bayou La Siryna, never a day's travel away from your ancestral home."

If he was too late, if Lily died, he'd be imprisoned here to a lifetime of loneliness, much as his grandfather had lived in his later years. *I have to try. She's everything to me, in life and in death.* "I swear to stay forever."

Sam's eyes softened in sympathy.

He understands what this costs me. The knife trembled

in Nash's hands and he saw that his grandfather's was shaking. With great effort, Sam again raised the knife upward in both hands. Shoulders and biceps strained, as if it weighed a hundred times its weight.

He was growing weaker. Rituals drained his energy and Nash feared that his grandfather's heart was overtaxed. He gripped Sam's forearms, helping him keep the knife raised.

The dark cloud blew away, the moon's outline disappeared, and the woods resumed its usual animal chatter. Full sunlight reflected off the blade's metal in a blinding flash.

"It is time," Sam pronounced.

Nash withdrew his support and Sam placed the edge of the hot blade to one side of Nash's neck.

"The pain will be brief," he promised. "And there will be no blood."

Sharp heat slashed across a couple of inches of his flesh. Nash kept his eyes fixed on the ocean, visible past his grandfather's shoulder. He clamped his jaw tight, refusing to utter a sound. Twice more his grandfather carved the same vertical lines directly beneath the original cut.

His knees wanted to buckle at the burning wave of pain and Nash stiffened his spine to stay upright.

"And now the other side," Sam said. "Almost done."

Again? Nash braced for the new onslaught.

His grandfather made quick work of it. Three new cuts were carved on the opposite side, in the same location as the first set of markings. His gut cramped in agony and he staggered. A faint drumming sounded in his ears, gradually increasing in tempo and volume until it drowned all other sound. His body vibrated in time to the pounding cadence until it abruptly halted, leaving his ears ringing in the sudden silence.

The pain was gone, exiting his body the exact moment the drumming stopped. Nash tentatively pressed his fingertips against the set of cuts on his right side. He traced three small lines of raised skin that felt like scar tissue. He lowered his hand and stared, expecting blood. But as his grandfather had promised, there was none.

"It's done." Sam's voice was weak and he drooped in exhaustion. "The gill slits are in place."

Gill slits. He remembered the faint scars on Lily's neck, same placement as his own now. His eyes narrowed at the tattoos on Sam's neck. And he understood. "Those tattoos cover your markings. That's how you lived undersea two days with Grandmother."

Sam gave a slight nod.

"But who did the cutting?"

"I did. Nellie provided this knife and told me what must be done."

Nash marveled at his grandfather's courage. His own initiation had been much easier.

"Now you can breathe underwater and swim to Lily."

"But how will I find her? How quick can I get there?"

"Enter the sea and all will be revealed. The spirits say this is the fastest way to get to the island." Sam's voice was so soft it was almost a whisper. "Go."

Nash hesitated. "Will you be okay?"

"Raymond will arrive shortly."

Nash noticed that he'd deftly evaded the question. He was frantic to reach Lily, every cell in his body screamed *run*, but what if Sam had another heart attack before Raymond showed up? "Maybe I should wait with you."

Sam shook his head. "No. The outcome will be the same whether I'm alone or not."

"You mean—?"

His grandfather silenced him by placing an index finger to his lips. "The time is near. Go in peace, Nashoba. I am well pleased with you."

Nash read the truth in his grandfather's eyes. *I'll never see him again.*

A brief clasp of the forearm and pat on his shoulder and Sam made his goodbye. "My spirit will always be with you."

He watched as his grandfather walked away, his steps slow but back straight and head held high. Overwhelming sadness rooted him to the spot.

A blue jay flew within inches of his face, beating its wings. *Scraa, scraa. Save Lily*, it screeched. Adrenaline trumped the temporary paralysis and he ran for the sea. Nash entered the water wearing only his boxers. At waist-deep level, he dove under a wave and swam as he'd always done. Eyes closed, mouth shut, arms forward, legs kicking behind. Nothing was different. His legs were still legs, no morphing into a fishtail. At last, his lungs burned for oxygen and he rose to the surface and gulped in air.

Shit. What the hell kind of idiot was he to believe his grandfather's fanciful legends? Nash turned his head in all directions, searching for the help he'd been promised. Water surrounded him in all directions—not even a damn seagull in sight. Nash treaded water, debating his options.

He could return to land in hopes Tillman had secured a boat. But by the time they headed out, they were probably going to get there too late. Or, he could continue swimming, but even if by some miracle he was able to swim the distance, he'd arrive exhausted and weaponless and still too late.

All hope rested on the undersea route.

Nash sank in the water again and pushed forward, repeating the same, familiar motions. This time, he tried to ignore the screaming of his lungs. But it was no good. He broke surface and sucked oxygen long enough to break into a litany of cursing.

It took his last ounce of strength to push his head above

water once more. Salt stung his eyes and he coughed up water. He glanced back to the barely visible shoreline and realized he couldn't return now if he tried. All around, the ocean stretched to infinity and the sun shone as brightly as it had when he started. Time and distance tangled into a Möbius strip he couldn't unravel. He'd never been so disoriented with the earth.

Think. Grandfather has never lied to me. I've seen and spoken to the spirits, sensed my ancestors roaming the bayou and fallen for a mermaid. Anything is possible. Before the ritual, he'd sacrificed his career and future happiness by agreeing to never leave the bayou. Now, he would sacrifice his life.

Nash sank below the surface and opened his eyes, bracing for the sting of salt. Light green water danced with swirls of tiny black specks and bits of shell and there was no sting. First hurdle passed. His body instinctually wanted to rise for air, but he fought the impulse. *My eyes adjusted, so why not my lungs?* Yet he couldn't bring himself to try until the last reserve of oxygen withered.

The moment was upon him. Life and death suspended in the next breath. *Now!* Nash opened his mouth and inhaled. The sea rushed in—and bubbled out on an exhale. He took another breath, then a third.

It worked! Nash placed fingers on each side of his neck where Sam had cut through flesh. Tiny currents of air flowed in and out. The ritual had opened superficial skin that had blocked the gills from functioning. Unknown to him, the ability had always been there, hidden under a thin dermal layer, awaiting discovery. Nash glanced down, curious to see if he sported a fishtail. But his legs were still human.

He swam forward with speed. *Must find Lily.* But which direction was the island? He couldn't tell. On a clear night, he might have been able to swim close to the surface and use the stars as a compass. But only the sun lit the sky. His grandfather said the spirits would help in navigating, but he saw and sensed nothing. Nash swam on, alert for a sign he was on the right track.

Look below.

Nash quit paddling, uncertain if he'd heard a voice or if the message had come from within. He gazed down at the darkness.

Come deeper.

The command was a vibration that rumbled in his gut and he obeyed at once. Down, down, down into the black, blind as a baby in a womb. Gradually, his eyes became accustomed and he made out shapes, which became clearer still—groups of fish, bits of driftwood, rocks and shells littering the ocean floor.

Phosphorescent globs of light appeared suddenly like a colony of giant fireflies. But the long, slender columns of light didn't flicker and they were tall and thin like bioluminescent strings of stalactites. Several of the lighted forms neared, coalescing into a ghostly human form. They were white, with elongated bodies and slender legs almost twice the length of humans'. Their long, silver hair billowed like clouds; the solid black of their eyes emphasized the paleness of their skin.

The Okwa Nahollo had arrived.

Perhaps they had been here from the start, ready to assist once he'd fully surrendered to the sea. Wonder paralyzed him at the appearance of the gossamer beings. Their figures rippled in the current and one of them drifted closer, lifting a hand and circling her fingers, beckoning him to follow.

Nash gathered his wits and nodded to show he understood. The pale people of the sea surrounded his body, swimming alongside him like a protective battalion. Cocooned in their midst, he felt no fear. Although he moved as fast as possible, they drifted effortlessly around him and were probably capable of much greater speed.

A shorter, younger one approached, just out of arm's length. A male child, probably in his early teens. The boy grinned at him and pointed to his chest. Thin black lines were etched in some kind of pattern. It took Nash several moments to grasp the design through the rippling water, but with a start he recognized it depicted the seal of the Choctaw Nation—an unstrung bow, with three arrows and a smoking pipe at its center. The tattoo's color had faded but marked the boy as one who had once roamed on land. Nash wondered if he'd drowned long ago and was taken in by the Okwa Nahollo, or if he was an ancestor who'd chosen to live undersea to escape the once-wretched conditions of reservation life.

Hurry. Almost there.

The message came from a point directly ahead, and Nash refocused on his mission. *Don't let me be late. I have to save Lily.*

Abruptly, they shifted upward and he followed. By degrees, the darkness lightened until he saw sunlight flickering on top of the water. He estimated they were within twenty feet of the surface when the Okwa Nahollo halted.

We dare go no farther.

A woman drifted closer and pointed upward.

There.

Above him was a dark object, about eight feet long, wider at the middle and narrowed into a point at both ends. A paddle dipped down, stirring the water, guiding it farther from shore.

His canoe.

Chapter 19

The singing stopped and Opal staggered to her feet, the paddle held out to her side in the position of a baseball player at bat, ready to swing.

"Get out," she hissed.

Lily shielded her face with her hands. "Okay, okay. Please don't hit me." She stood, drugged legs clumsy and awkward as she stepped up onto the raised bench where she'd been sitting.

Now. Jump.

She took one last glimpse at Opal's red, sweaty face, eyes focused in deadly intent, the bird of prey swooping in for the kill. Lily couldn't resist a smile of satisfaction. "Joke's on you."

Opal flushed an even deeper shade of crimson and her mouth twisted in fury. The paddle swooshed toward her, so close Lily felt it stir the air.

She expertly dove into the sea, legs together, toes pointed and nary a splash left behind as she descended. *Take that,*

Opal. Elation and relief made her giddy. Or was it the drug? She giggled—and swallowed a mouthful of salty water. Lily coughed and tried to draw a breath, but more water immediately clogged her lungs. *What's happening?* Panicked, she looked down, dismayed to find useless human legs where her fishtail should have been. She kicked frantically while parting the water with her arms.

Air. She needed air. Without it, her head would explode. Her lungs were a furnace, burning a hole through her chest. Lily clamored near to surface level, where Opal's face wavered above the churning water, peering down, paddle clutched in both arms, ready to strike.

But she had no choice but to break through for air. Her head bobbed up and she coughed up a mouthful of liquid before sucking in oxygen, the painful rasp of her inhalation loud as a siren. Another desperate gulp and then a sickening thump connected against her right cheek. Pain blazed and she fought the blackness of passing out.

Lily moved beneath the boat's hull, out of striking range. She lifted her hands and clung to the hull, trying to rock the boat and force Opal overboard. But she was too weak. *I'm going to drown, after all.*

The irony of a drowned mermaid registered before the darkness obliterated all thought.

Nash watched Lily's dive overboard. *She's safe.* He swam toward her, eager to reunite. This ordeal was almost over.

He got within a few yards before he realized something was terribly wrong. She hadn't transformed. Lily's face contorted with agony and she shot back up. Opal was there waiting and delivered a vicious blow that felt like he'd been struck, as well. Blood oozed from the side of her face as he covered the distance between them. She grasped the bottom of the canoe for a moment and then her hands dropped to her sides. She was sinking. Graceful even while unconscious, alabaster skin alit with a subtle pink-and-silver sparkle, lovely formed limbs slowly swaying as directed by the ocean current, long blond hair cascading above her elegant face like a staged spotlight.

An underwater ballet of death.

Nash grabbed Lily by the waist and pulled her by the canoe's side. She was so, so heavy, a dead weight in his arms. They broke surface and he positioned her torso over his right shoulder, thumping firmly between her delicate shoulder blades. Lily heaved water and drew a short breath before vomiting once again.

The wretched sound filled him with joy. He dared hope that he'd arrived in time. His body almost sagged and lowered back down in the sea from overwhelming relief.

"Wh-what? How did you... Nash?"

He'd entirely forgotten Opal. She plastered her body on the opposite side of the wobbling canoe, gaping as if a sea monster had bobbed up from the ocean's depth. The oar fell harmlessly from her hands. He scanned the canoe's interior, searching for a gun or knife, but there were no weapons. Not surprising—that wasn't Opal's modus operandi anyway. He searched for the shoreline and saw they weren't more than fifteen yards out. The canoe was small and he'd have to contend with Opal's possible interference if he tried to board. Lily's chest rose and fell against him, her breathing shallow but steady.

Land it was.

It seemed he'd been swimming for hours. Despite the adrenaline rush that had pushed him on the long journey, his body had used up its last reserve of energy. The hormone crash was sudden and complete. His legs became useless appendages and he barely kept Lily's head above water.

From underneath, dozens of cold hands imprinted upon

his back and legs, guiding and pushing his and Lily's broken bodies. In short order his feet and knees crunched against rock and shell. Nash sat in the shallow water, catching his breath, Lily cradled in his lap. A crowd of Okwa Nahollo floated nearby, in such large numbers it appeared as if a cloud had fallen from the sky and lay suspended beneath the water.

The youngest boy broke away like a wandering wisp of smoke and waved goodbye.

"Thank you," Nash called out, unsure if they could hear. He touched a hand to his heart and patted it, a final gesture of gratitude. These were his people—his kin—and the allies and friends who had saved his ancestors. And now they had saved him and Lily, as well. Without their help, his life would have become unbearably lonely.

The columns of light departed in a brilliant ripple, leaving no trace of their presence.

"What was that?" Opal screamed. She'd seen them—or seen enough that she appeared shell-shocked. She stood on the canoe, staring at him as if he were a ghost. "How did you get here? I don't understand what's happening."

Nash ignored the questions and dismissed all thought of Opal. She wasn't going anywhere and he'd deal with her later.

He looked into Lily's wan face, fear forming a tight band across his chest. She was breathing but remained unconscious. He tenderly pushed away tendrils of hair plastered against her face. An open gash cut across her right cheek, marring the perfect beauty of her alabaster complexion. He lowered his lips and kissed her forehead, which felt cold and clammy. Nash desperately sought something he could do to help her. Perhaps her lungs still contained water—he'd heard of it happening before when people drowned hours later from accidents. They called it "dry drowning" from fluid buildup in their lungs.

It couldn't hurt to try to pump more water. Nash laid her in the sand on her stomach, head turned so that the undamaged side of her face didn't grind into sand. Straddling her back, he pressed his hands into her spine and several minutes later was rewarded with a trickle of brackish water that ran out of her mouth. He continued the ministrations until he was certain there was nothing more he could do.

Lily coughed and her eyes fluttered open, seeking to understand where she was, what had happened. Nash scrambled to lie beside her and she focused on him, smiling as if it cost her great effort. "You came for me." Her voice sounded bruised and gravelly, holding nothing of its usual siren's cadence.

"You're safe," he promised. "Help's on the way." Speaking of which—where the hell was Tillman? Nash had no idea how much time had passed.

He glanced back again at Opal, frowning when he saw she was paddling their way. He rose to his feet to intercept her before she got anywhere near Lily. For all he knew, the crazy woman might yet have a knife or gun stashed somewhere.

Nash waded up to his thighs in the water and raised his hand for her to stop. Opal stared at him with a wild, pleading look. She was a stranger to him, this woman he'd worked with for years, had considered a friend.

"Please don't be angry with me. We went for a little ride and she fell overboard. I tried to save her."

"Liar," he spat out. "I saw you hit her with the paddle. You were trying to kill her."

Opal stretched out a hand, beseeching. "No, I was trying to help Lily, get her to grab on to the oar so I could pull her in."

"Game's over, Opal. I know who and what you are now. So do the cops."

Her eyes flickered nervously past his shoulder, and at her sharp inhalation, Nash glanced behind.

Lily had pulled up onto her knees and rocked back and forth on all fours like a crawling child attempting its first tentative steps.

The sight enraged him. "What did you do to her?"

"Nothing. I—"

"Stop lying. I know what you've done. You killed Rebecca and Connie." Nash tried to control the fury long enough to find out what she'd done to Lily. It had to be something more than throwing her in the water. If that was all, Lily would have shape-shifted and swam away. "I'm asking you for the last time. What did you do? Slip her some kind of poison or drug?"

Opal jumped out of the canoe and waded forward. "Please. Nash, forget her. She's nothing." Tears ran down her face and she sobbed, her whole body shaking. "I did it all for you. Can't you understand? I love you."

Horror and revulsion hit him with the frigid shock of an ice bath. Its chill numbed and then burned along his nerve endings.

"You love me, too," she insisted, stumbling and almost falling into the water. She righted herself and surged forward. "You come to me every night in my dreams and tell me so."

Before he could realize her intention, Opal lunged forward and flung herself at him, wrapping her arms about his waist and sobbing into his bare chest. He smelled the sweat of her desperation.

Nash stepped backward and grabbed her forearms, peeling her off his body. She was surprisingly strong, clinging like a leech sucking blood.

She stared at him, imploring. "Make love to me like you do when you come to me in dreams. This was supposed to be *our* time. None of the others ever loved you the way I do. Can't you see that?"

All he could see was what a fool he'd been. The face of his friendly, slightly homely, competent assistant and friend was erased forever. It was as if in the past he'd viewed Opal through a diffused camera filter that had cast a haze on the truth. Now that the filter was removed he could read the sharp longing in her eyes and the clear gleam of delusion that twisted her lips and face.

It was diametrically opposed to the revelation of the real Lily. Lily's true nature made her appear even more beautiful, more vulnerable, more sweet. The crows had recognized her dual human/mermaid nature and communicated that Lily was his true destiny. Too bad the birds couldn't detect evil in humans.

"You're delusional," he told Opal curtly. "The cops are on the way. You'll spend the rest of your life in prison or locked up in another psychiatric hospital. Until they arrive, all I want to hear from you is what you gave Lily."

Her eyes flashed in an instant, igniting to fury. "Lily, Lily, Lily!" she screamed, writhing, breaking one hand free from his grasp. "What about *me*, Nash?"

Opal beat her chest so hard he wouldn't be surprised if a rib cracked. He released her other arm and stepped back.

"You're supposed to love me. *Me!* Everything I did, I did for you." She gouged her face and neck with her fingernails, leaving a track of blood as savage as if she'd been mauled by a bobcat.

After all the years he'd thought of Opal as a friend, a competent assistant and talented photographer in her own right, after all that time—he'd never really known her. Never suspected the torment and savagery hidden underneath the sunny, calm exterior.

She twisted her face to one side and lifted her chin. "It's because of this, isn't it?" She jabbed an index finger into the slight scar that ran from ear to mouth. "You think I'm hideous. Not worthy."

Nash gritted his teeth, impatient with Opal's ranting. He lunged toward her and snatched her right arm above the elbow. "Tell me the drug you gave Lily or, so help me, I'll beat it out of you."

She threw her head back, bursting into maniacal laughter. "Go ahead. Do it. I'd rather be hit than ignored."

Nash pushed her away in disgust. The woman was hopeless.

A reed-thin voice spoke from behind. "Angel's trumpet," Lily said. She stood, swaying slightly. "A hallucinogenic she slipped in my drink."

Nash rushed to Lily's side and put an arm around her waist to prevent a fall. Lily leaned into him. "I'm better," she whispered. "It's starting to wear off."

He held on to her tightly, grateful she was in his arms again and appeared stronger. Another minute and he would have been too late. He shuddered and Lily weakly ran her hands down his back, reversing their roles and acting as comforter, strengthening his mind and spirit.

A scream pierced the air and they broke apart.

Opal's hands were clasped against her ears, eyes and mouth widened in pain. "No, no, no!" she shrieked, as if the sight of he and Lily together was driving her crazy.

She stumbled back to the canoe, which had drifted a few yards out, and awkwardly heaved herself on board.

"Surely she doesn't think she can escape to sea on that thing," he muttered as the sound of a large motorboat approached in the far distance. About time. Lily needed medical attention.

Opal jerked her head in the direction of the sound and then stood unsteadily on the canoe, facing him from a good fifteen yards out. She continued staring at him as her hands reached into the shoulder bag slung across her body and scrambled through it.

A gun? Nash moved in front of Lily, shielding her from danger.

Opal extracted two thin glass vials. She quickly unstopped the lids and swallowed the contents in two gulps.

"What the hell are you doing?" Nash yelled, instinctively moving toward her.

"Drinking the last of the angel's trumpet and poisonous juice from white baneberry. That should do the trick." Her voice was flat and her eyes vacant.

"For God's sake, Opal." He couldn't help feeling sorrow for her—for the friend he'd thought she'd been.

"My life is nothing without you," she continued in the same matter-of-fact monotone. "I'd rather die than see you—" Opal bent over, clutching her chest "—with another woman."

Nash ran until the water hit midthigh, and then he started to swim.

Opal turned her back on him and dove under.

He glanced over his shoulder at Lily, who motioned him to go on. "I'm fine," she called. "Get her."

Undersea again, Nash's eyes adjusted. The Okwa Nahollo were gone, but he had no trouble spotting Opal's pale, thrashing legs and arms, her mass of red hair swirling in the current like spilled blood. He made his way over and grabbed an arm, pulling her toward the surface.

She fought him. Resisted with a panicked fury that might not understand he was trying to save her life. Nash placed his face within a foot of Opal's—hoping she would recognize him and cease struggling.

Her eyes were wide-open, bulging and bloodshot. Nash pointed up, gesturing he wanted to pull her to air.

Opal flailed her arms and legs, still fighting him off.

To hell with trying to communicate. Nash grabbed underneath her arms and swam up, Opal twisting like a snake in his grasp. When he reached the canoe, Nash flung himself inside, one hand still firmly gripping Opal's ankle. Her body went limp and he pulled her into the boat, muscles heaving with the dead weight. She lay facedown and he turned her over. Opal's eyes stared unblinking into the sun overhead.

Dead.

Nash attempted to save her as he had Lily, but whatever concoction had been in those vials Opal had swallowed had swiftly done its work.

His enemy had been found and silenced, but Nash took no pleasure in it. So many people had been hurt over the years. If only he'd realized sooner what was happening right beneath his nose. He never once suspected Opal was mentally ill and that he was the focus of her obsession. She'd befriended his past girlfriends and claimed to have a secret lover, a married man. And all this time he and the police had looked for suspects among women he had dated and rejected. What a tortured, miserable life she must have secretly lived.

The roar of the motorboat was upon them.

He stared at the stranger who'd claimed to love him. Opal's top had wedged under her armpits, exposing her freckled chest and plain, white bra with a safety pin attaching a broken strap on one side. Nash pulled down the T-shirt to cover her. "I hope you are finally at peace," he whispered before standing.

He waved his arms, shouting in the wind, "Over here."

Chills racked her body in waves and the sound of the men grew fainter as they shouted commands and lifted Opal's limp body onto their boat. The roaring in her head drowned out everything and her peripheral vision narrowed. *Must sit down.* Lily sank onto the sand and shivered. The sun held no warmth and its light faded, leaving nothing but pinpoints of light and dark specks. Where was Nash? She needed him to hold her, to share his body heat and reassurances everything was all right.

But it wasn't.

It was as if her body had roused itself only long enough to see that Nash had survived and Opal had been captured. Now it was spent and she was so cold, so tired. Her body was betraying her again, as it had done undersea when it was unable to shape-shift. She closed her eyes against the spinning landscape that made her stomach rumble with nausea.

Blessed heat bore down on her shoulders. Someone had placed a blanket on her. She huddled into it and opened her eyes to a blur of people—brown uniforms with silver star-shaped badges and men dressed all in blue with stethoscopes dangling from their necks.

"Lily, can you hear me?"

Nash squatted in front of her. His face was so intent and drawn it made her want to cry.

"I'm here,' she said, realizing as she spoke that her throat was still parched and burning.

A man in blue crowded him to the side and put a blood-pressure cuff on her sleeve. He listened intently to her heart rate and nodded. "Steady, but weak. Let's get her to the hospital."

No! "No hospital," she rasped.

Tillman dropped to a knee and waved the medic away. "Lily, you have to go."

"You know I can't."

"It's okay. Nash told us about the angel's trumpet. They'll do a chest X-ray to make sure there's no fluid remaining, and then pump your stomach in case any of the drug remains. I promise I won't let them draw blood or run other tests."

A strong hand engulfed hers and squeezed. She knew it was Nash without even looking.

"I'll be with you every minute," Nash vowed.

Lily nodded and closed her eyes again as he scooped her into his arms and lifted her. His warm breath whispered in her ear.

"Chi hollo li."

She had no idea what the words meant, but it washed her soul in immediate solace.

Chapter 20

Sunbeams lit every shadow in the bayou and sparkled atop the calm Gulf waters, inviting folks in Bayou La Siryna to luxuriate in the fine summer afternoon.

Weather not at all fitting for a funeral. Lily closed her eyes against the sun's determined brightness as she stood by the cottage window. It was the second funeral in as many days, although the first should more properly be called a burial instead, because no one had come to mourn Opal Wallace. A plain wooden casket and a tiny stone marker in the county pauper's cemetery were all that marked her life's end.

But Samuel Chula Bowman's service had filled the funeral home. All morning, lines had formed around the building with people coming to pay their respects. Lily had never suspected that the quiet man who'd lived so far in the backwoods was this universally well-known and loved.

A sudden tingling crept up the nape of her neck. Someone was watching her. Lily turned from the window and caught Nash staring at her from across the room, brows drawn in concern.

He shouldn't have to worry about her when this day was so difficult for him. Lily forced a smile and circulated among the few guests that remained at Sam's cottage, picking up empty paper plates and refreshing drinks as needed. It seemed like it should be late evening instead of late afternoon, and she was weary. The fatigue from the angel's trumpet had eased but hadn't entirely gone away, even after a week had passed.

She'd been pronounced fit at the hospital after getting her stomach pumped and spending a few hours hooked to an IV that replenished her body with fluids and vitamins to treat dehydration. Nash had been busy arranging his grandfather's burial, so she'd returned to her own home every night. Mom had at once moved back in with her to play nurse. The attention had been nice—for the first few days.

But lately her mom's nervous gaze and hovering left Lily feeling smothered. Jet and Shelly weren't much better. They visited daily and the three women huddled together often, speaking in hushed tones. If she ventured too close, they stopped talking and studied her quizzically.

Finally, the remaining guests took their leave.

Lily gathered up the last of the dishes and took them to the kitchen sink. As she rinsed and placed them in the dishwasher, she kept glancing out the window, eyes drawn to the small patch of blue on the horizon. A deep sigh escaped. Although she had twice ventured into the sea this past week with her family, her mermaid fishtail hadn't emerged.

Lily feared it never would.

"You've been working too hard," Nash scolded, nuzzling his lips by her ears. His arms wrapped around her waist from behind, and she leaned into his warm strength. "Why don't you lie down for a nap and I'll finish up here?"

Lily sighed again. She was so sick of being sick. Sick of taking naps, sick of worrying. But even worse, now that the funeral was over, how much longer would Nash continue to stay in Bayou La Siryna? They hadn't addressed anything in the past week. The little strength she'd had, Lily had spent giving police statements or helping Nash with funeral arrangements.

"Hey, you." Nash guided her body around so that she faced him. "Why the long sighs?"

"Sorry. Don't pay attention to me. You're the one having a tough day. I know how much you loved Sam."

"I miss him, but he lived a long time and was prepared for death. At least, as much as anyone can be." Nash's voice was grave but controlled.

"I never knew his middle name was *Chula*. Is it a Choctaw name?"

He nodded. "It means *fox*. Fit my grandfather perfectly. He was wise, shrewd and concerned with family."

"Just as *Nashoba* fits you. Like the wolf, you're my protector. If you hadn't come when you did…" Lily shuddered.

His face tightened. "I can't stand to think about what might have been. If I had been a second later—"

"About that," Lily cut in. "How did you appear out of nowhere? I know the story you gave Tillman and Landry about a friend loaning you a large commercial vessel. Must have been a ghost ship, because no one saw it."

"Lucky for me, the local sheriff's department is run by your BILs," he joked. "So convenient."

She didn't smile. "I may not be on my game lately, but I've noticed you won't give me a straight answer whenever I ask you questions about that day."

A guarded expression darkened his green eyes. "What do you remember?"

"Lots of my memory is hazy. The doctors say that's not an unusual side effect from a hallucinogenic drug. I clearly remember losing my cell phone and pouring sangria for me and Opal. After that—" She paused, struggling to bring events into focus. "I only remember a few details, like stumbling through the woods and hearing a children's song. I remember being frightened and Opal's face above me when I was underwater. Then there was pain, and when I woke up I was lying in the sand and you were with me."

"Anything else?"

Lily rubbed her temples, trying to grasp wisps of broken details. But it was like trying to remember a dream after awakening. A snatch of memory floated through her mind like a cloud being swept away by the wind, yet a tiny trace remained... "Wait. There is something else. I was being pulled through the water and you were holding me. But—oh, this will sound crazy—"

"Don't say that. You're not crazy. Go on," he urged.

She wished she'd kept her mouth shut. "Okay, here goes. I thought I saw white shapes all around us, like undersea ghosts. Only I wasn't scared, their presence felt comforting. I sensed...they were helping us."

Lily waited for him to laugh, to tell her the ghosts were merely part of a drug-induced fugue. But his face was set, eyes hard as agate. "Nash?" She touched his chest. "What is it?"

He looked past her and stared out the window. He didn't want to tell her what had happened on the island. But why? It made no sense. "What are you hiding? Tell me."

"I can't." His voice was clipped, and he avoided her eyes.

Hurt burned at the back of her throat. "You can trust me," she said quietly.

Nash stuffed his hands in his dress slacks and faced her. "Damn it, Lily. It's not a matter of trusting you. I took an oath of silence and I won't break my word. Don't ask it of me."

"An oath to whom?" She frowned and shook her head. "I don't get it."

He stood immobile and unyielding and silent.

The divide between them was sudden and absolute. For the first time, Lily truly understood how keeping secrets had the potential to destroy faith and love between a man and woman. Nash must have felt this way when she wouldn't tell him her true nature. Yet he hadn't abandoned her even when he'd come face-to-face with her lies the night she'd shape-shifted from land to sea, unaware he waited for her.

Lily slowly stretched out a hand over the gaping chasm between them. "Okay," she whispered.

His eyes softened with hope and the tight muscles in his shoulders relaxed. "Okay? You can live with my silence on the matter?"

"Without you, I would have no life."

He crossed the distance between them in a heartbeat and she was in his arms. His fierce strength was more precious to her than ever before. He kissed her and she melted into his fire, giving and taking and yet needing more, needing all of him, heart and soul and body. Nash groaned into her mouth and she pressed her hips into his arousal.

"My sweet Lily," he murmured, running hot kisses down her neck and the hollow of her throat.

His hands cupped her breasts and she moaned. It seemed like forever since they'd made love. "I've missed you," she said breathlessly. "Missed this."

Nash leaned down and rested his forehead on hers, his breath hot and sweet against her face. His heart thumped wildly beneath the hand she rested on his broad chest.

"God, I've missed you, too." His voice was husky and raw. "But are you sure you're up for this? You've been so sick—"

Lily kissed his lips, stopping his protests. "Not that sick," she laughed shakily.

The desire in his eyes reflected her own passion. That age-old look of understanding and intimacy that passed between man and woman flashed silently in the charged stillness. Nash held out his hand and she accepted it, following her lover to the bedroom.

Much, much later, when the August Alabama sun began dipping beneath the treetops, Lily lazily rested her head on Nash's lap as they rocked on the back porch glider. She wore nothing but one of his oversize T-shirts and panties. He'd changed from his earlier formal wear to an old T-shirt and gym shorts, and in Lily's eyes he looked as sexy in the casual outfit as he had in the suit.

She closed her eyes, enjoying the soft stroke of his fingers running through her tumbled hair. The breeze was cool and ocean waves tumbled in the distance like a lullaby. She drifted toward slumber, her mind blank and peaceful, body sated from lovemaking.

"Did you try to go in the water today?"

Nash's voice jolted her back to reality.

"Yesterday. It was a no-go. Mom keeps assuring me that I'll be able to shape-shift again in time." She yawned and stretched her feet and arms like a cat awakening from a nap. She'd probably been sleeping as much as any cat for days now.

"If my grandfather were still alive, I bet he could heal whatever's wrong."

Lily sat up and settled in his lap, hope flaring her to attention. "How?"

"He said all illness was caused when someone's soul was injured. For healing, he connected to caring spirits, power animals and plant life. Sam believed health was the result of restoring a person's spiritual power."

"And you think my soul was injured by the attack?"

"I think it's possible."

She remembered Sam involving Nash in the ceremony for Twyla's son. "And he was grooming you to take over for him one day, wasn't he?"

"Yes. But I couldn't ever live up to his work. He'd been healing for years. It was something he felt called to do ever since he was a young man."

Lily cupped his face with her hands, fevered with excitement. "I believe in you, Nash. Heal me."

"Don't get your hopes up," he cautioned. "I'm not sure I can."

"Try. Please. You have a connection with the spirits—I've seen it in you."

"I'm willing, but—" He stopped. His muscles tensed beneath her, his gaze locked on something beyond the porch. Nash raised a hand over his brows, shading his eyes from the sun.

Lily scrambled off his lap and followed the direction of his stare. "What is it?"

"There," he said, whispering as if afraid of disturbing something. He pointed to the far right side of the tree line in the backyard.

"I don't see anything."

"Right there, under the cypress where Sam used to chop wood in the shade. His old wheelbarrow is still leaning against the magnolia."

She squinted into the dark greenery. "There's nothing there. Wait. Is that…a fox?"

"It is." His voice was hushed, deep with excitement. "Unusual to spot one this early in the evening. They're nocturnal hunters. Stay here."

She waited as he went to the porch and pushed open the screen door. His movements were slow and silent, cautious not to startle the fox.

The animal didn't move other than twitching its long black bushy tail tipped in white. It regarded Nash intently with its pointed face and intelligent eyes. His fur was a reddish color with a white underbelly and paws dipped in black.

Lily's skin tingled. *Chula.* Did Nash really think this could be Sam?

Nash came within a few feet of the fox and stopped as if hitting an invisible wall. He slowly hunched down until almost eye level with the fox.

Lily rubbed the goose bumps on her arms, watching them stare at one another in some sort of silent communication. At last Nash stood and raised one arm, elbow bent, a gesture that could mean goodbye or "message received." Or both. The fox turned and trotted off into the woods, tail held high.

She could wait no longer. Lily ran out the door, down the steps and across the yard. "Well? Was it Sam? What did he say?"

"Seems you got your wish. I'll contact the spirits for a healing. Your body needs to be made whole so you can be fully at one with land and sea again." A rueful smile played on his lips. "Don't get your hopes too high, Lily. This is all new to me, but I'll do my best."

She wanted to jump up and down and fist-pump the air. This would work; she knew it deep in her soul. But for Nash's sake she restrained her enthusiasm and tried to match his somber mood. After all, this was serious business and sacred territory. "I understand. When do we start?"

"Now."

Lily headed to the circle of stones where Twyla's son had had his healing. She was moving at a dignified pace, but she wanted to skip with joy.

"Not here," Nash said. "For this, we must go to shore." He turned and walked in the opposite direction and she followed.

He moved with a slow but steady gait and she stepped into place beside him, glancing from time to time at his preoccupied, silent profile. She didn't attempt conversation, sensing that Nash was mentally preparing for the healing. Twilight deepened the shadows but he walked sure-footedly, eyes focused on the distance. They scrambled down a clump of brush, arriving at a small patch of sandy soil where the sea gently lapped at the shore.

Wordlessly, Nash stripped out of his clothes and she followed his lead. Still silent, he waded into the water up to his knees.

Lily hesitated, not sure if he needed to be alone. Nash turned and held up an index finger. "Wait here."

He dove under, disappearing in the green depths. She ached to join but dared not risk ruining the process. This might be her only chance to become a mermaid again. She'd never imagined losing her ability to shape-shift. It felt as if part of her soul were amputated. Niggling doubts crept in. What if this didn't work after all?

She studied the water where Nash had submerged. It seemed too long since he'd dove under. She waited and waited, growing more anxious with every second that passed. Nash needed air. No human could hold their breath this long. Was he in danger? Lily shifted from one leg to the next and then paced, eyes constantly scanning the empty surface of the sea. *Where are you? Come back to me.*

She couldn't stand it any longer. Lily stepped forward, intent on saving Nash. But she halted at the sight of a mass of white floating in the distance. It looked as if someone had dumped piles of white sheets into the sea.

Just like before, when Nash had pulled her to land. Wonder enveloped her senses.

The underwater ghosts had returned.

A human form glided under the water's surface. Nash

arose and stood before her, his long black hair plastered against his olive skin. His eyes bore into hers. With a start, she realized the color of his eyes wasn't leaf-green as she'd imagined. They were the exact hue of this bayou water.

He came to her and clasped his wet hands in hers, holding tight. "The Okwa Nahollo have agreed to help. Don't be afraid. They've been the Choctaw's friends and neighbors for generations. They are similar to you, but not the same. They don't have fishtails or shape-shift, and their bodies are light as air."

"They helped us before. Out there on the island."

"Yes. It's what I couldn't speak of this morning until I asked their permission to reveal everything to you. You can never, ever tell anyone about their existence." His voice grew sharper. "Including your family."

"I won't," she promised.

Nash withdrew his hands and touched fingertips along either side of his neck. "We now bear the same markings. I breathe underwater, same as you." He dropped his hands and continued. "I have a distant heritage with the Okwa Nahollo, something I was unaware of until recently. The opening of these gills was my grandfather's final blessing, granted to save your life."

Lily reached up and traced his neck markings with wonder. "So that's how you did it," she breathed. "You changed your very nature for me." Her vision blurred with tears. "It must have hurt like hell. Are you happy with the change? Do you regret it?"

Calloused hands gently swiped the tears from her cheeks. "I am at peace. This is my home now. Forever."

Her mind tumbled with questions. Joy and hope and sadness mingled in a cauldron of confusion. She wanted him to stay so desperately, but not like this. Never against his own will. The sacrifice was too great and he might come to despise her over the years. "Is that the price you had to pay for changing? You're forced to stay in Bayou La Siryna the rest of your life?"

"It was my decision. With my grandfather's death, our people need a new healer and the spirits chose me."

"But it seems so unfair. What about your career? You love to travel and—"

Nash brushed his lips over the top of her scalp. "Hush. That isn't the only reason I stayed. I've traveled enough. It's time to explore new territory." He faced her again, placing his hands on the sides of her hips, grounding the two of them together on this spot of land where land and sea joined. *"Chi hollo li."*

His deep, serious voice rolled the unfamiliar words like a caress, wrapping her soul in joy. She had heard them once before but couldn't remember when or why, only that Nash had said them. *"Chi hollo li,"* she repeated slowly. "What does it mean?"

"It's Choctaw for *I love you.*"

"Oh, Nash!" Lily buried her face in his damp, broad chest. "I do believe I've loved you since I was a child and you found me when I was lost in the woods. I was so scared, but I knew that you would find me."

"And so I always will." He pulled her from his body and stepped back. "The Okwa Nahollo await us. You will be a mermaid once again, fishtail and all." He held out his hand. "Come."

Lily took his hand and they ran, laughing and splashing into the water. At waist level, they faced one another and embraced, sinking into the sea as one.

Together.

Epilogue

Three months later...

"Surprise!"

Lily blinked, confused by the bright light from the gargantuan chandelier above and the attention of the large crowd of well-dressed citizens packed inside the grand opening of Jet's new downtown shop. Her Pirate's Chest antiques store had done so well she'd purchased the vacant space next door for expansion. For weeks, a construction crew had been hard at work under a veil of secrecy.

The intent scrutiny of the crowd was puzzling. She stiffened her back, grateful to feel Nash's reassuring squeeze at her elbow. Her eyes sought out and found her family, grinning at her in some secret delight. Jet and Landry, Tillman and Shelly, and Mom cuddling her first grandchild, six-week-old Adrian Fields.

Jet raised a hand and dramatically swept it toward the

left wall, as if she were Vanna White displaying a grand prize on *Wheel of Fortune*.

Lily's breath caught as she spotted the paintings. *Her* paintings. Dozens of them ornately framed and individually spotlighted by brass sconces. The walls were painted in the palest shade of sea-foam green, which subtly suggested an ocean backdrop for her watercolor seascapes.

It was beautiful—perhaps perfect—yet she felt exposed and vulnerable at the sight of her intimate work on public display. Her right hand picked at the hem of her little black dress that skimmed mid-thigh. Automatically, she reverted to the Mona Lisa smile she hid behind to conceal her emotions.

A dreadful silence hung as she fidgeted with the hem of her dress. What if they all hated her work? Mocked her efforts as blatantly amateurish? She'd be an embarrassment to Nash and her family. It would even top all the years of ostracism and ridicule she'd endured from the Bayou La Siryna townsfolk.

Twyla swept forward, confident and elegant, holding a glass of wine in one hand. She flashed Lily a dazzling smile and flanked her side. "Welcome, Lily," she said, her voice carrying over the room. "We hope y'all enjoy our little surprise tonight. So many people have worked hard to make it possible. Your fiancé, Nash, your family and all your friends and new admirers. We're surprised and honored to have such a talent right here in Bayou La Siryna."

Applause erupted and everyone crowded around, talking at once.

"Remarkable."

"Who could have guessed?"

"I want to buy one."

Twyla held up a hand for silence. "There's more. Come back to the gallery next month for an amazing display of underwater photography taken by Nashoba Bowman. Best of all, the photos were taken right here in Bayou La Siryna's slice of the sea."

Lily turned to Nash, who smiled broadly and winked. He bent down and whispered in her ear. "See? Told you your paintings are exceptional. We make a good team."

The Mona Lisa mask melted and she bid it adieu. Happiness bubbled inside and she uncorked it like a bottle of vintage champagne. A genuine smile lit Lily's face as she nudged Twyla and pointed to her wineglass. "How about finding me a glass, as well? I could sure use it."

Twyla snapped her fingers and nodded toward the back of the room. At the signal, three men dressed in navy blue tuxedos moved forward, carrying silver trays of drinks, and passed them out to the crowd. A waiter approached her and Nash and they each accepted one. Before she could raise it to her lips, Nash held his glass in the air and silenced the crowd.

"Here's to Lily Bosarge," he said, the pride evident in his voice. "A fantastic artist and the woman I am proud to call my future wife."

More applause rang out and she scanned the beaming faces of everyone she held dear. Her circle of friends had widened exponentially over the past few weeks, due in large measure to Twyla's influence. Trusting another human female after Opal's betrayal hadn't been easy, but Twyla had won her over with many acts of kindness. Lily turned to her and clinked their glasses together. "To my first and truest friend."

She sipped the wine, knowing that *this* time there would be no ugly hidden surprise lying in wait.

Nash rubbed her neck and gave a playful squeeze. "Hey, I thought *I* was your truest and dearest friend."

"You're that and so much more." Unmindful of the audience, Lily rose up on her toes and kissed him square on the mouth.

And that drew the biggest applause of the night, among much laughter and teasing. Lily cast a quick glance at her mother. Adriana slowly nodded, a silent gesture of acceptance of her daughter's decision to seek her own happiness in her own way. There would be no more talk of returning to sea and living with the merfolk.

Lily had to acknowledge her sister's clever stroke of genius in naming her son Adrian in honor of their mother. Adriana had been present at the home birthing and had fallen instantly and totally gaga over the tow-headed baby boy. Lily stifled a grin, recalling Landry's grumbling that his mother-in-law seemed in no hurry to ever leave the bayou. But he was so besotted with Jet, he'd suffer anything to make her happy.

Just as Nash was equally determined to lavish her with love and affection.

All of them had followed their hearts. And all of them had fought and won against great odds. And if sometimes Shelly was haunted by dreams of an escaped one-eyed killer on the loose, or if Jet remembered an ex-lover launching a spear at her undersea—the reward of love was worth the trials.

As for herself, the image of Opal's determined face as she raised an oar, poised to strike, would sometimes return with a clarity that set her heart pounding erratically. But the horror of that day was fading as she and Nash planned their future and lived each day grateful for the opportunity to be together. Tillman and Landry were solid and serious and had the power of the law on their side.

With Nashoba she'd found a protector, a healer and a forever love.

Amid the gallery exhibition's noisy camaraderie and cheer, Nash pulled her aside and gazed down with his intense green eyes, searching her heart. "Are you truly happy, Lily?"

More than I ever dared dream. "With you—always. *Chi hollo li.*"

* * * * *

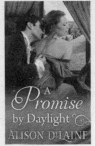

MILLS & BOON®

The Thirty List

At thirty, Rachel has slid down every ladder she has ever climbed. Jobless, broke and ditched by her husband, she has to move in with grumpy Patrick and his four-year-old son.

Patrick is also getting divorced, so to cheer them-selves up the two decide to draw up bucket lists. Soon they are learning to tango, abseiling, trying stand-up comedy and more. But, as she gets closer to Patrick, Rachel wonders if their relationship is too good to be true…

**Order yours today at
www.millsandboon.co.uk/Thethirtylist**

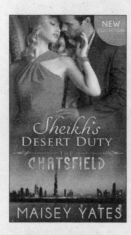

MILLS & BOON®

Why not subscribe?
Never miss a title and save money too!

Here's what's available to you if you join the
exclusive **Mills & Boon Book Club** today:

✦ *Titles up to a month ahead of the shops*
✦ *Amazing discounts*
✦ *Free P&P*
✦ *Earn Bonus Book points that can be redeemed
   against other titles and gifts*
✦ *Choose from monthly or pre-paid plans*

Still want more?
Well, if you join today we'll even give you
50% OFF your first parcel!

So visit **www.millsandboon.co.uk/subs**
or call **Customer Relations** on **020 8288 2888**
to be a part of this exclusive Book Club!

S_2014

MILLS & BOON®

nocturne™

AN EXHILARATING UNDERWORLD OF DARK DESIRES

A sneak peek at next month's titles...

In stores from 19th June 2015:

- **Goddess of Fate** – Alexandra Sokoloff
- **Possessed by the Fallen** – Sharon Ashwood

Available at WHSmith, Tesco, Asda, Eason, Amazon and Apple

Just can't wait?
Buy our books online a month before they hit the shops!
visit www.millsandboon.co.uk

These books are also available in eBook format!